I0640263

# SPELL OF THE EYE

## ELLIS KROSS

# E / K

. . .

First Edition, September 2017
Written by Ellis Kross
Edited by Sidonie Lailler

ISBN: 978-0-9976453-4-7
Kross, Ellis, 1983—
Spell of the Eye
I. Title. Fiction. Mystery/Horror

**ISBN: 978-0-9976453-4-7 pbk.**

Story by Ellis Kross
Book Design by Izzy
Interior Photograph by Collage_Best (istockphoto.com)
Back Cover Artwork by SavaSylan (istockphoto.com)

This is a work of fiction.
Names, characters, places, and incidents
are the products of the author's imagination.
Any resemblance to actual persons, living
or dead, is entirely coincidental.

Printed in the United States of America

. . .

# SPELL OF THE EYE

## 1. 25 /ps

*Every night, I see myself dying.*
*I often wonder what it would feel like if I actually*
*died in my dreams, if I stayed in long enough to*
*commit my soul to the void. If I died in my dreams,*
*would I die in real life?*

HOGAN imagined violence—and he laughed.

The quiet eleven-year-old pulled his thoughts away from the fiery horror and focused on the white screen before him as if he was waiting for a celestial light from above to bring the blank canvas to life. The anticipation grew with each breath until it nearly smothered Hogan. He, like many others before him, reached deep within himself and found a way to carry on.

He found a way to save them.

Even though only a couple of measly seconds elapsed, to Hogan time felt as if it had ceased to exist; in fact, time felt as if it could no longer be measured nor predicted, yet time was simply that, gone.

Once more, a wake of an overwhelming sense of malaise washed over Hogan, leaving behind nothing more than an empty theatre consumed by a haze of gray. He, like many others before him, did only what came natural to him. He rebelled; and he did so in a manner that would suggest an act of pure evil. What a feeling it was, though, to resist!

Hogan readjusted his eyes, caressed away the blackness, and found himself visually breaking through high soundproof ceilings and tracking his head upward in a stupefied gaze at a monstrous swell of ominous clouds with the veiled flickers of lightning passing through a brilliant night sky like glowing varicose veins. The appearance of the clouds alone displayed the potential of an approaching storm—a bad one, Hogan knew. However, he wasn't quite certain of what was coming or what had already come and was now thriving in a kind of ingenious disguise among the land of the living. Something *was* going to happen, Hogan thought. In the deepest, most cavernous corners of his mind where ideas dwelled, Hogan knew there was a possibility that at any moment the clouds could perhaps break open for good, flood the theatre until water was brimming over, and sweep away not only himself, but also everything the rain touched into an endless stream of wickedness.

The boy could only wonder what that day looked like.

The Flood.

The Fall.

And then, it happened, *not* the flood nor the fall, but a changeover.

Thoughts turned into images, then images into something as tangible as the hand before his eyes.

The transition happened so smoothly from one frame to the next that even Hogan himself was caught in a state of downright confusion.

With his bloodshot eyes pinned open, he glanced around the vacant theatre, first mapping out an exit in case things went terribly wrong, then second, mentally piecing together the recent chain of events that occurred before the changeover began. Hogan's eyes snapped back to the screen, which played the movie, *Total Recall.*

The flicker of the film projector brought forth moviegoers alike, only heads without faces Hogan could see for they were facing the screen. Noises came in ripples: the *crunch* of popcorn or the *rustle* of candy wrappers.

Only minutes into the action movie, the story was thrust into high suspense:

Douglas Quaid, who was being played by actor, Arnold Schwarzenegger, cringed in the most horrific and believable expression only Hollywood could buy. The depleted oxygen of the red planet caused Quaid's eyes to bulge in an over-the-top, cartoon-like fashion while memorable grunts twisted the entire theatre.

The tension building among moviegoers appeared as if the air had been sucked out of the theatre, and Hogan knew he was in for an experience like no other.

Seated beside Hogan a curly-haired woman sporting a jeans jacket balled herself into the shoulder of her handsome date and grabbed hold of his hand, her other hand covering her mouth in both staged disgust and intense pleasure. Hogan acknowledged the young woman's award-winning reaction and the way she clung to her date like a child did to a blanket. Excitement flared between the two.

For a moment, just as Hogan longed for the light, Hogan longed to have what they had—whatever it was that the two had, he so desperately wanted it like nothing ever before.

For a moment, Hogan leaped through the wakes of time and witnessed his very own death.

A sudden hot flash of panic dropped like a weight on his chest, forcing him to dive deep for a breath.

He pulled his gritty hand from the tub of buttery pop-corn; and with a momentary blip of awe, Hogan stared at each finger glistening in the flicker of awesomeness.

Before the boy could wrap his head around the immediate transition, the thought of what occurred just minutes ago seemed like a distant speck of light lost in a dark horizon.

Hogan's last thought: Apolline.

*Did she really call me?*

And like that, the thought vanished before it could turn into words hanging on his lips.

Another light entered the theatre, a brighter and yellow light, tempting Hogan to turn his eyes from his hand.

He gave in and peeked over his shoulder; then he mindlessly turned back around, then gave the strange man a second peek. . . TROUBLE!

Once a peek, now a sturdy gaze, he carefully watched the silhouette of a ticket holder waving the flashlight along the tops of the adult moviegoers.  And Hogan, only eleven, clearly stuck out like a weed on a putting green.

Hogan slid farther down in his seat but it was already too late.  He had been spotted!

The ticket holder called out, "Hey!  You there!"

Hogan dropped the tub of popcorn and made a run for it and the ticker holder chased after him.  He hurdled over the two smoochers next.  The young woman yelled out, "Watch it, kid!"

Then, he shot directly toward the exit sign, raced down a narrow aisle with the ticket holder right on his tail, reaching after him.

Hogan slingshot around the first row and darted through the exit door.

The door swung open, not from his charge, but from the blustery wind catching the door at the right moment.

The door slammed shut behind Hogan!

Once outside in the alleyway surrounding the Pavilion, Hogan continued his escape.  Halfway down the alley, he heard the exit door opening up for what sounded like inches behind him.  He never broke stride as he glanced over his shoulder.  Yet, he kept running and never slowed down.

The ticket holder didn't bother chasing after the boy.  Yet, he waited at the doorway, not running, not doing much of anything really but just standing there, watching Hogan in pure amusement.  He let out a sound that only a stubborn horse would make and waved his hand at Hogan in defeat.  Then, he mouthed something to Hogan but Hogan was too far away to make out words; however, Hogan had a pretty good idea what was being said about him, and surely it was not too complimentary.  Wouldn't be the first.

Hogan ignored the ticket holder and slowed down his

pace.  He hooked a left around the Pavilion and ventured down a much darker alley laced with distant meows and stirrings of accumulated filth.  Hogan hesitated but continued forward through the alley even though the immediate thought of danger lingered at the forefront of his mind.  The *thuds* of a hollow metal box drummed throughout the alley, causing Hogan to stay at high alert.  Even the most innocent shadows appeared like lions stalking in the dark.

Hogan rounded a corner and a monstrous shadow was revealed in a halo of light cast from a dim floodlight.

Only a couple of feet away from Hogan stood a finicky orange tabby picking at what appeared to be roadkill.  Hogan didn't realize what the cat was eating until he got a closer look.

*But it couldn't be*, Hogan wondered.  But it could.  And it was.

The sight of a dead white cat caused Hogan to take a more cautious step backward.

Somehow, the cat sensed Hogan's presence and belted its head toward Hogan.  Blood was caked around its mouth and whiskers.  Its eyes went cold and black for a moment but only a moment before the cat let out a low pitch growl, then a hiss.

"Easy girl," Hogan whispered.

The cat suddenly flinched; and then it darted past two more figures which came to light: one a tall man standing behind a dumpster; then another, a crouched figure bobbing back and forth like a junkie in urgent need of a fix.

More curious than before, Hogan stepped to the side for a better angle at the two scalawags dancing in the dark and realized that the bobber was no junkie, far from one.

Hogan pointed out the details: the glimmering jewelry, looped earrings and baggy necklaces; the rubbing of silver clinking and clanking; the suction of flesh.

He focused on the man with his hands rested over his hips, his head lifelessly cocked back as if he was staring at the stars or something celestial.

Suddenly, the man's head jerked toward Hogan's direction, his eyes like iridescent pearls in the blackness.

Next to come forth was a clown-faced woman crouched below. She rose from a kneeled position, grabbed the lumbar region of her back with one hand while, with the other, wiping the smear of lipstick from the bottom of her chin.

"Enjoying the show, kid?" the man said loosely.

Hogan didn't reply to man's remark—in fact, he didn't make a sound. Too shocked.

"Buzz off!" the man cried out as he flung a beer bottle at Hogan. The glass shattered around Hogan's feet, a couple of shards catching Hogan's new Jordan's.

Hogan suddenly made a run for it! Nobody chased after Hogan—not even a wisp or whimper—but still, Hogan ran.

He made it to an unusually desolate Main Street splicing through the heart of downtown. Hogan wondered why the streets were so dead, and he thought maybe the increase in wind might've played a key factor in people's Saturday night plans; nonetheless, he stayed close to the streetlights above the sidewalk as he passed each alley.

A cult of shadows swayed in the firelight of a drumfire down one alley.

Down another, a lanky shadow appeared as massive as a god along the side of a building.

As Hogan made a right onto 5th Street, he heard a growl of a creature lurking closer.

Behind him the shadows started to come together, each one once trapped behind the safety of the streetlights, now interlacing like a piece of twine. Two beams of headlights splashed against the side of the wall, bringing out the twig-like shadows, which thickened at first, then evolved into a more human form. A pair of eyes, like the eyes of that cat earlier, revealed themselves in the night human darkness.

Hogan quickened his pace and as soon as he turned back around, the blood rushed through his veins. His body jolted and he found himself on his back.

"Hoagie!" a child shouted out.

A wave of relief washed over Hogan once he saw the face of a friend, first the freckled face of Elisa, then Freddie with his regal white teeth and bright hazel eyes, then, last but not least, doughy-face Chi.

Freddie extended his hand and helped Hogan to his feet.

"What happened?" Elisa asked. "We were looking everywhere for you—"

"—So, did you get in?" asked Freddie.

"Yeah," Hogan said. "But barely. Didn't matter anyway. About five minutes into the movie, I got caught."

"No way!"

"Caught? By who?"

"I don't know," said Hogan. "The guy who was taking tickets? I don't know. Maybe."

"Must've been that tool, Ryan Hightower. The guy's a total buzz kill. Did you know his little brother, Kyle, tried to join the Four Horsemen last year—"

"—Yeah," Hogan said, walking alongside Elisa.

"What a major tool," Elisa said sourly. "He got all mad at me just because I was a girl." She said from the corner of her mouth, "You know, like I had any choice."

"I wish I was a girl," Chi said to himself.

The others looked at Chi strangely.

"I mean, like for a day."

Elisa cut through the awkwardness, "Kyle told me only a 'man' should be a part of the horsemen and—you know what—I replied by telling Kyle that boys weren't allowed."

"Nice one, Elisa," Freddie said. "It's not called horseboys. It's horsemen."

"You got that right."

"And who names their kid *Kyle* anyway? It rhymes with bile!"

"—So," Chi blurted out, "how was it, Hoagie?"

"You mean, how was the five minutes of *Total Recall*?"

"Details! I *need* details!"

"It looked pretty sweet from what I saw."

"Just sweet? Not amazing?"

"Yeah, Chi," Hogan said and rolled his eyes. "It looked pretty amazing. So, how was the rest of *Gremlins 2*?"

"Hey," Freddie said, crossing his arms. "It was either *Gremlins 2* or *Back to the Future 3*—"

"—Trust me, Hoagie." Chi put his arm around Hogan. "You didn't miss anything."

"Seriously, what was up with the bat gremlin?"

"I know, right?"

"So, what now?" Elisa asked. "Anybody hungry?"

—

Elisa spent the last five minutes stealing tortilla chips from Chi's nachos from behind his back and doing her own little experiment by holding the flame of her Zippo lighter underneath the chips until each chip was burnt to a crisp—it wasn't until Chi noticed how much his nachos had shrunk that he retaliated against Elisa.

"Hey, cut it out, firebug!" Chi yelled. "Buy your own nachos!"

He snatched the Zippo from Elisa's hand and flung the lighter across the restaurant.

"Don't be such a spaz!"

"Me? A spaz? I'm not the one wasting food—"

"—I'm totally doing you a favor, Chi," Elisa said, as the burnt tortilla chip crumbled in his hand.

"How are you doing me a favor? I'm hungry—"

"—You're always hungry."

"I know, right," Freddie impersonated Chi, as he used his most common expression of saying "*I know*" to everything.

The comment provoked a couple of laughs around the table.

"I can't help it that I have a super high metabolism."

"Maybe it's your Mexinese heritage or something."

"I prefer the term Chinican myself."

"My cousin was the same way," Freddie said. "He went to the doctor and he found out that he had a tapeworm."

"Oh shut your black ass up!" Chi shouted out. "I don't have a tapeworm!"

Both Elisa and Freddie looked at one another almost in a state of shock.

"Oh come on! Really?" Chi rallied. "You can make fun of my heritage all day and I can't say the word *black*?"

Freddie waved off Chi's comment while Chi turned his attention toward Hogan, who hadn't taken a bite of food since the gang arrived at the fast food restaurant, Mr. Machos Famous Tacos and Burritos. Most of Hogan's Famous Mr. Macho's Nachos had been pushed around a gummy pool of melted cheese.

"You sick, Hoag?" Chi asked and sipped from the double-extra large lime green soda.

"Nah," Hogan said quietly as Elisa stood up from her seat and fetched the Zippo from someone's basket of food. "Not hungry."

"You're not going to die on us, Hogan. Are you?"

"Funny."

"He's still thinking about Polly."

"Whatever, Freddie," Hogan said, louder now.

The name alone, Polly, made his stomach turn. An image came to Hogan's mind, more or less, a reflection of an image.

Before the image could take shape and fill with color, the image faded away into a gray haze; however, the little bit of image that Hogan had received stayed with him like an ink-blot on his mind. In his mind's eye, Hogan could see Polly standing directly behind him in *Arcadia*, the reflection of her face in the glass of an arcade game. She had so much hate, he remembered, and sadness. She was staring at Hogan, although not making a peep or any facial gestures, just staring at him with this scowl on her face. The more he thought about the expression, the more it had slackened into a blank—almost dead—expression.

"Just saying," Freddie chirped, pulling Hogan from the momentary daze. "You haven't talked much ever since you bumped into her at Arcadia."

"She's not my type."

"Oh yeah? And who is your type, Hoagie?"

"Hoagie likes them 'chubby' girls."

"Yeah," Freddie joked just as Elisa sat back down at the table. "A chubby girl to put on his Hoagie roll."

"Yuck!" she cried out. "You're sick, Freddie!"

Chi laughed—and imagined Elisa in a more intimate setting.

"More cushion for the pushing," Freddie said, grinning.

The rest of the gang burst out laughing, including Hogan.

"There it is!" he teased, pointing at the smile on Hogan's face.

Suddenly a pale man came rushing through the door, his shirt covered in strings of blood. He was delicately holding his arm close to his body. Hogan was first to turn toward the commotion, then the others followed suit.

The arm, Hogan noticed, appeared mangled, nearly beyond recognition; the entire sleeve on the arm was torn to shreds. He found the nearest person who happened to be one of the cashiers. He tried to warn her, telling her that she and everybody in here—as in the fast food joint, Mr. Macho's—was doomed. The cashier kept pressing, trying to calm down the man, who was out of breath. Yet, he wasn't listening to her. He was adamant about their fate.

The gang had trouble making out what he was saying for the words came out like water from a kink in a hose.

Freddie could only make out a couple of words; in fact, the only word that grabbed his attention: *Monster.*

"Did he say *monster?*" Freddie echoed, his face slackening.

"I know!" Chi chimed in. "That's what I heard too!"

Hogan stood from the booth and made his way toward the frantic man.

Freddie suddenly grabbed Hogan by the arm.

"Are you serious, Hoagie?" said Freddie, his eyes widened with fear. "That man could have like AIDS or something."

Hogan said casually, "Really?"

"Do I look like I'm joking? Seriously, Hogan! Don't do it!"

Hogan slipped his arm from Freddie's grip; and as Hogan made an attempt to help the frightened man, a sudden explosion let out a deafening *boom* throughout the parking lot and caused one of the restaurant's windows to shatter!

Several kids shouted out with cheers of triumph while the other late night stragglers quickly scrambled to safety underneath tables.

Hogan, along with the rest of the gang, hurried outside Mr. Macho's where a purple Mustang erupted in a ball of flames in the parking lot.

Freddie headed back to the entrance.

"Is that your car, mister. . . "

Before Freddie could finish his sentence, the man was nowhere in sight.

The same woman—the cashier—who had kindly helped the man was now lying motionless on the floor.

While the others stood on the sidewalk and admired the flames at a safe distance, Hogan shouldered past Freddie and crept back inside Mr. Macho's.

On the floor was a long streak of blood slithering in a serpentine-pattern toward the bathrooms.

Hogan checked on the woman's condition. She had a cut on the top of her forehead, but it didn't look life threatening to Hogan.

He called out to the man but received no response.

"Hogan!" Freddie yelled from the doorway. "What you doing?"

"Look," Hogan said, pointing at the blood trail.

As the gang hung back, Hogan followed the blood trail to the girls' restroom.

Freddie was livid: "Are you crazy?" he said to Hogan. "What are you doing? Have you lost your mind?"

Finally, Freddie's concerns reached a boiling point.

"Hogan," Freddie said out of desperation, "what part of

the word *monster* don't you understand?"

Despite his half-ass attempt at convincing his friends to band together, Hogan never wandered from his wayward path. Yet, he stayed close to the blood trail like any hard-boiled sleuth sniffing out a cold-blooded murderer. Instead of a gun, all Hogan had was a spork to defend himself. And if it came straight down to close quarter combat, he knew a thing or two about wrestling—professional wrestling that is. He had a mean chop slap. And if the topic should enter a conversation filled with the many doubts of an eleven-year-old versus a monster—and not to mention, a kid who only weighed in around a buck ten—he would simply say, "Ask Chi."

Resilient and determined, Hogan balled his fist tight and inched his way into the ladies restroom. The blood trail led through a basement-sized window next to the last stall. No body, Hogan noticed. No monster. Even the window frame itself was too small for any average adult. So, immediately, the inevitable question came to Hogan like the acid climbing up his throat: *What kind of monster could do that to a grown man and still fit through that window?*

As Hogan was about to exit the restroom, his eyes came across a blood puddle underneath the piping of the sink. He tracked the dripping blood to the sink where a severed hand rested in the center of the bowl.

Hogan flinched from the sight of the hand; then, once he realized that it was, in fact, a human hand, he crept closer and closer as if the hand was a spider or some kind of pissed-off insect that didn't mind sinking its fangs or pincers into human flesh. What really caught his attention was the wristwatch next to the hand. He inspected the wristwatch. Except for several droplets of blood, the wristwatch appeared undamaged; however, the minute hand was stuck on the number twelve. The ticker was not ticking at all, which made him wonder why anyone would wear a broken watch.

Either way, Hogan was intrigued by the wristwatch—so intrigued that he decided to grab it from the sink with a wad of balled-up toilet paper.

He stuck the thing—blood and all—inside his pocket.

Suddenly, the door to the last stall shot opened!

Hogan jumped like a cat.

Then, Freddie entered the restroom.

Freddie jumped too!

"Jesus!" Freddie cried out. "You scared the shit out of me!"

Hogan turned back to the girl poking her head from the last stall.

"What was that?" she asked, her voice trembling.

Her face said it all, a story untold, the paleness, the billowed eyes, the jaw as slack as a knapsack, the trembling of her lips, the hunched dweller-like posture.

"I don't know," said Hogan.

Freddie tapped Hogan on the shoulder.

"Is that what I think it is?" asked Freddie.

"Yep," Hogan said seriously. "It's a hand."

—

After Hogan and the rest of the gang gave their statements to the cops, Freddie invited everybody back to his house—and since everybody was shaken up from the whole ordeal, they agreed to spend the night at Freddie's, except for Elisa, whose parents had completely forbidden their eleven-year-old daughter from sleeping over with three boys. That was the number one rule. She could hang out with them, go to the movies or arcade, ride their bikes through the woods. She and the boys could pretty much roll around all day in the mud, but when it came to sleeping in a roomful of boys who were up to no good, it was like mortal sin. By the time Elisa's parents picked up their daughter, the red-eyed boys were levels deep into *Ninja Gaiden*. Instead of monster hunting, they figured what better way to lower the excitement but with a joystick.

The boys didn't catch a wink of sleep. They were too

amped, too curious, too uncertain of the future, and simply too engulfed in the massive ripple effect of their own wild imaginations—what kind of creature could do such a thing? Regardless, what a way to kick off the summer!

For the remainder of the sleepover, they exhausted the late hours of night by going through three bags of cheese doodles and a six pack of grape soda while trying to make some kind of sense of what type of monster out there in the monsterverse could cleanly cut off the hand of a person.

When asked about the creature, Hogan mentioned that it most definitely had to have claws that were not only long enough but also sharp enough to cut through bone as if it was made of butter.

Not once did Hogan ever mention the wristwatch in his pocket.

Not even a peep from Hogan.

## 2. The Case of the Severed Hand

*I'm not one to believe in monsters—I always knew
that they only existed in the stories we told ourselves.
But what if there really are monsters in the real
world, hiding underneath our noses? If so, I sure
hope they don't wear socks.*

THE next day, Detective Steve Billups and his brand
new, fresh-out-of-the-Academy partner, Detective
Gabriella Augustine—or Gabby, as Billups called
her—greeted Hogan at the front door as soon as he was leaving Freddie's house.

The scar-faced detective, Billups, reached for his billfold
in his inner coat pocket and displayed the badge for Hogan,
as if it was an involuntary reaction, like a sneeze of authority.

Hogan leaned closer and studied the detective's badge;
even went so far as to grab the billfold from the detective's
hand to read the name, Stephen Billups. Badge number:
1211867.

"Take a picture," the detective said haughtily, "and it'll
last longer."

A smirk was growing somewhere behind Augustine's
smooth, milky face, but the smirk never quite spread into a
full-on smile. Her face hardened as soon as Hogan drew his
attention toward her.

Billups informed Hogan that he and his partner had several questions for him—and his friend, Freddie—but mostly
Hogan since he was the one who discovered the lone hand in

the ladies restroom inside Mr. Macho's. Billups, an abnormally tall individual standing at six feet eight inches, looked like a giant standing next to Hogan; and when the detective kneeled downward and arched his broad shoulders which were shaped like the top of a telephone pole to tie the shoelaces on his right shoe, he did so with a slight grimace on his face.

The four, including the detectives as well as Hogan and Freddie, moseyed toward the edge of the sidewalk. Freddie had this thing about cops. He didn't want them anywhere near his house. At times, he'd even get upset whenever he saw a cruiser driving through the neighborhood. It wasn't that he didn't like cops. He just didn't trust them. So, naturally, the least Freddie could do was to pretend that he was leaving with Hogan—going to the arcade, wherever—even though he was just saying so long to his friend.

Freddie followed Hogan halfway down the driveway as if the two were leading the two detectives back to their car. And Billups was somewhat curious as to why the boys were obviously leading them away from the house—he figured it possibly had something to do with Freddie's parents—but he was *more* curious as to why Hogan decided to follow the trail of blood. Why? Why not just leave it alone?

He voiced his curiosity to Hogan in a short and concise sentence.

The initial reflex of any eleven-year-old would be to call the police, the detective suspected, even his parents.

He gave Billups a shrug and said mindlessly, "I don't know. He needed help. So, I helped—tried to, at least."

Not the response the detective wanted, but, more or less, nothing that he didn't expect.

The detectives wanted to know if Hogan or Freddie saw anything out of the ordinary, anything that they didn't give in their statements last night; and when the question was asked, Hogan already knew what the detective had found— or better yet, hadn't found.

*The watch*, Hogan thought. *He knows.*

"He was scared," said Hogan. "That, I know."

The two detectives believed this 'guy' to be an ex-con named Killian Blanc, the type who didn't get 'scared' too easily, but that was Hogan's story and he was committed to sticking to it.

"So, what gave you the impression that he was scared?" asked Augustine, following her partner's lead.

"I could see it in his eyes," Hogan replied and turned to Freddie, who was bobbing his head at a seizure-like pace, which, in Freddie's case, was his way of agreeing with everything Hogan was telling the detectives. "He looked like he was telling the truth—"

"—The truth being that he was being chased by a monster?"

"Yes," Hogan said sharply. "You're a cop. You should know that monsters come in all shapes and sizes, right?"

"That's right!" Freddie said overzealously. He realized how much zeal he was using in front of the detectives and he toned down his voice and then said in a more serious manner, "Monsters can even look like you or me."

While Augustine already made her way toward the car, Billups handed Hogan and Freddie a card holding contact information and said to the both of them, "If anything else comes to mind—anything—please let us know. All right?"

The boys nodded.

As the detective walked away, he stopped at the curb of the driveway and said over his shoulder, "And lay off the scary movies for the next couple of days."

—

Hogan killed about an hour at Arcadia while his father was shopping for a new string trimmer in the neighboring hardware store. While Hogan was bouncing from one game to another, mainly staying close to side-scrolling beat 'em up games such as *Teenage Mutant Ninja Turtles*, *Ghouls 'n Ghosts*, *Double Dragon*, and then last but not least, spending most of his money and time on the mega-popular game, *Rampage*, he found himself getting distracted and periodically looking over his shoulder. His eyes would drift from the action in the game to the many ghostly reflections in the glass, the murky faces behind him. Strangely, Hogan found himself searching for one face in particular. He knew she was there; however, he couldn't see her, couldn't find her, couldn't hear her. Instead, what he found was the face of a man with gray eyes and a heart as black as tar.

Hogan kept it casual and carefully drew his focus back to the game. Those gray eyes kept pulling Hogan back. It wasn't in his nature to be paranoid—insecure maybe—but Hogan started to become extremely paranoid from the sight of the strange man standing several arcade games away. He held his eyes on the man and studied his features. He was a bearded man in his mid to late thirties who carried an added ten years to his face; and to Hogan, he appeared as if he was on the threshold that separated a man from an old man.

The bearded man held Hogan in his gaze; then once he realized Hogan's interest, he, like Hogan, pretended to play an arcade game.

Hogan clearly knew he wasn't a gamer—even the way he played the game seemed off. He was randomly tapping buttons as if he was swatting at a fly. And he was looking around at other kids and mimicking their moves.

After Hogan caught the bearded man looking directly his way for a fifth time—this time in a slow and more dubious way—he eased away from the arcade game and moved closer to a crowd of people, hoping to lose the stranger. He spotted him again in the corner of his eye as he moved to yet another arcade game; occasionally, he was shooting his eyes toward Hogan's way. Hogan decided to do the one thing his father taught him *not* to do, which was to confront a suspicious stranger, especially one with possibly immoral intent. Hogan's father taught him to seek out an adult whom he trusted, like a friend's parent or someone he knew from church, or even stay together with other kids and blend in.

Hogan disobeyed everything his father had taught him and made a move toward the bearded man. He snuck around the pinball machines when the bearded man was caught off guard by the constant hiccup of startling noises throughout Arcadia.

Hogan kept low to the ground, not a crawl, but more like a squatted gait. He used the game machines around him for needed cover. He finally made his way to the arcade game the bearded man was 'supposedly' playing.

Fists curled, Hogan leaped in front of the game, *Bubble Bobble*, and shouted out to the empty space, "Gotcha!"

The bearded man was nowhere around.

Hogan frantically searched for him but he couldn't find him anywhere. His paranoia reached the highest level and he started to get lightheaded.

People around him started to freeze in his mind; certain expressions remained like a still frame in his mind. Hogan realized it was happening again and soon his breakfast was going to make an immediate climb.

He left Arcadia before he passed out and tried to ignore the people around him.

As Hogan made his way toward the grand exit sign, the bearded man stood before Hogan, blocking his path.

"Why are you following me?" Hogan said, voice trembling. He backed away and took a couple of steps from the bearded man.

"You have something that doesn't belong to you, kid," he said resonantly as he looked around the arcade.

"What are you talking about?"

"It's not safe here." The bearded man faced Hogan and Hogan could see the conviction on his face. Hogan never felt the least threatened by the man. He felt as if he was a friendly, but he wasn't ready to trust him. Not just yet.

"What do you mean?" asked Hogan.

"They're watching you right now."

"Who's watching me?"

"I can't explain right now. Your life's in danger, kid."

Hogan tried to locate an adult close by but couldn't find any.

"I'm not here to hurt you."

A distant buzz of the arcade distracted the man's attention long enough for Hogan to make a run for it.

Again, it was off to the races.

Hogan darted from the exit, zipping around booths and greeting machines.  He made his way to the food court and took a moment to catch his breath by an ice cream cart.  He spotted Polly sitting at a table by herself.  She was staring at Hogan.  Hogan felt the urge to talk to her, but she appeared as if she was prime for confrontation.

Not too far away from Polly stood the bearded man; he was frantically searching for Hogan.

Then, Hogan's off to the race again.  He ran into a department store and sought cover inside a clothing rack.  The bearded man walked right by Hogan and didn't even know it.

—

When Hogan met back up with his father by the entrance of the mall, Hogan didn't mention a word of the bearded man to his father.  Not like they talked much anyway—in fact, it was a task in itself to squeeze a couple of words from Hogan.  His father found a folded piece of paper wedged underneath the windshield wipers of the station wagon.  He snatched the note from the window before his father could grab it.  Hogan read the note to himself:

*Meet me behind the Darwin Drive-Inn in one hour.*
*Come alone.*

—

As soon as Hogan got back from the Four Corners Mall, he immediately rode his bike to Freddie's, which was only a six houses down from his house.

By the time he reached Freddie's, Freddie was hanging out at the creek behind his house, gathering various insects like beetles and stink bugs for Larry, his pet iguana.

Hogan broke the news about everything that happened at Arcadia and did so in one single breath.

He informed Freddie about the bearded man, the mysterious people watching him, the note, and then, after a seesaw of doubts, which came in the form of a long and heavy sigh, he told Freddie about Polly.

"What?" Freddie broadcasted. "She's totally stalking you!"

"I don't think so," said Hogan. "I think there's more to it."

"Like what?"

"I don't know. There's something about her that isn't right."

"Yeah," Freddie said as he kneeled down to scoop a beetle from underneath a rock. "You're right, Hoagie. Something isn't right. She isn't with you. My cousin once told me if you don't ask out a girl you like then it could really mess you up in the head. Like, I'm talking long-term side effects."

"And where are all these 'cousins' you're always talking about?"

Freddie brushed aside Hogan's comment.

"Seriously, Hoagie," said Freddie, "are you going to ask her out or what? She's like totally obsessed with you."

"I just have a feeling about her."

"A feeling?" Freddie said amusingly. Then he suddenly hissed and snapped back his shaky hand. "That little, that little. . . shit bit me."

"I'm serious, Freddie," Hogan said, his voice rose to a near shout.

"What? I hear you!"

Hogan paused.

"I think she's like sad."

"I thought you liked sad girls."

"No," Hogan said. "Not like that kind of sad. I think she might hurt herself."

"No way," Freddie joked and stomped on the beetle. He smacked Hogan on the shoulder, nodded toward the house, and said, "She's just trying to get your attention. That's all. Clearly, it's working."

—

Once the word got out that Hogan's life might've been in danger, Chi and Elisa showed up at Freddie's in minutes. Everybody was aware that Hogan was heading directly into a trap. Elisa suggested that this guy could've been a perv. Chi had his mind set that he was a serial killer and Hogan was going to be his next stuffed puppet. Freddie, being an avid paintball gun collector, was casually prepared. Among other things, Freddie was also a knife enthusiast—Freddie alone owned about as many knives as Hogan carried in his kitchen, from pocketknives to switchblades (even last year when he'd carve his name into everything he could find, the fifth graders in his class branded Freddie the nickname The Kid with Knives, which later spawned the inevitable name, Freddie Kruger; and after that, the nicknames only evolved from Shaq—the name Shaq taken from Freddie's middle name Sha-quan Demarious—to Dee to Nefarious Demarious).

Freddie sorted through his many tote bags of weapons until he came across one item in particular inside an orange cooler. He busted out what he had been saving for special occasions: a bag of paintballs from the freezer.

Chi exclaimed, "Frozen paintballs!"

A grin cut across Freddie's face.

"Better believe it," said Freddie, pulling out one of the paintballs from the icy bag.

"It's hard as a rock!"

"You're telling me," Freddie said. "One shot with one of these babies and he'll be wishing he never messed with the Four Horsemen."

The gang huddled together and stacked each one of their hands on top of one another.

It was nothing more than a ritual they did before a big game. A rite of unity.

—

While Freddie took his sniper position on the second floor of The Links, an abandoned apartment complex behind an overgrown golf course that had been shut down many years ago due to financial reasons, Chi and Elisa, both armed with paintball guns carrying regular paintballs, anxiously waited for Hogan's signal. They kept waiting. Nothing.

Just as Hogan and the gang were about to call it quits, the bearded man finally showed up. He was alone.

"I didn't think you show—"

"—I'm not alone," Hogan said before the bearded man could utter another word.

"Whatever," the bearded man said nonchalantly. "You made quite a scene at the mall today. I told you, 'I'm on your side.'"

"How can I trust you?"

"You can't. All I need is your ears."

"My ears? What do you want with my ears?"

The man sighed and shook his head in aggravation. "I need you to listen to me, kid. You've gotten yourself into a heap of trouble. Do you understand?"

"Trouble?" Hogan said. "What kind of trouble?"

"Major trouble," he said and stepped closer to Hogan. "You have something that belongs to The Eye. Now, he desperately wants it back."

"I don't know what you're talking about," Hogan said, backing away.

The bearded man pulled out a rolled-up manila folder from his coat pocket, revealing the shoulder holster carrying a Smith and Wesson revolver.

From above, Freddie screamed, "Gun!"

Suddenly, a yellow paintball struck the bearded man in the right thigh and the paint was so hard that it didn't even splatter. Yet, it shattered into pieces on impact.

"Ouch!" he cried out. "What the hell was. . . "

Following the first shot two more paintballs splattered over his side and chest. Blues and pinks. More shots. By the time the bearded man tried to shield himself, he looked like a Jackson Pollock painting.

—

Before he could make any sense as to what was happening, the bearded man with his arms and legs tied in ropes was being hoisted in the back of Elisa's older brother's rust-colored Volkswagen van. Freddie stuck the paintball gun to the man's temple and seethed, "Tell us want you want from us, monster, or else I'll make you wish you never messed with the Four Horsemen!"

Chi butted in, "Hey, maybe this slimeball had something with Tommy Winters' disappearance."

"Tommy Winters?"

"You know," Chi said, "the seventh grader who went missing in King Town."

"If that kid went missing in King Town, then it'd be all over the news."

"This pervert doesn't look like he's from King Town."

Freddie jammed the barrel of the paintball gun underneath the bearded man's chin.

"Why don't you ask him?" Chi asked, which, in return, forced Freddie in a moment of deep thought.

"You from King Town?" Freddie finally asked.

The man didn't answer.

"My cousin told me about you people," Freddie seethed. "What were you jesters going to do with Hogan? Hold 'em ransom like you do with innocent people? Tell me!"

"Chill, you two," Hogan said while he patiently flipped through the black and white photos inside the manila folder.

"I think he's really trying to help."

Chi peeked over Hogan's shoulder. Glanced at the photos. "So," Chi said, "are these your victims, monster?"

"Damn you, kids," the man said, his aggravation reaching a new level of red on his face. "My name is Mike Morrow. I'm a former detective with Orson Valley Police Department. Last year, my sister was killed by the same *monster* that killed Killian Blanc last light."

Chi grabbed one of the photos from Hogan's hand.

"Freddie," Chi said quietly, looking over the photo, "I think he may be right."

Chi showed Freddie a photo of the so-called monster; however, the shadowy monster was hard to make out. The monster appeared nothing more than a blurry werewolf-like figure creeping around an alley at night.

Mike made his best attempt at trying to wipe the paint from his face, as well as his beard. He pointed at the photo, flinging several drops of paint onto Freddie's clothes.

"I took that photo last week," Mike said. "This thing or 'monster,' whatever you call it, only comes out at night—"

"—What does it want?" Elisa asked Mike.

Hogan wished Elisa hadn't asked the question.

"I don't know," he said, turning to Hogan. He narrowed his eyes as if he and Hogan had a sort of unspoken agreement. "Whatever or whoever gets in its path—let's just say if you ever try to get in its way," Mike directed his attention directly at Freddie, "then it's not going to be pleasant for you."

"How come you haven't killed it?"

"Yeah," Freddie said, now much louder. "You're a cop, right? Don't you have like cop powers? You got all kinds of weapons to kill it. Seems like the other thing you people are good at are killing things."

Mike hung his head and said quietly, "I wish it were that simple, kid. I'm afraid this thing is the least of your worries."

"What does that even mean?"

"It's the monster's boss that you have to worry about."

"Monsters don't have bosses," Chi said, laughing.

"This one does," Mike replied.

"Enough, Pea Brain," Freddie said angrily. "Start making sense."

Mike's eyes sharpened on Freddie, the upper part of his cheeks washed over with cherry red and he carried a look that indicated that he was about an insult or two away from wringing Freddie's neck.

"All I know is that they call him 'The Eye.'"

"The Eye?" Freddie said sarcastically. "That's original!"

"I know!" At the same time, Chi smirked and nodded at Freddie as if he was trying to seek Freddie's approval. In return, Freddie ignored Chi and acknowledged the look on Mike's face, the darkness behind it, and he backed off. The smirk melted from Chi's face from the sight of Freddie's candid reaction to Mike's look.

"Believe what you will, kid," Mike said. "The Eye is real and he has the power to turn a child like yourself into an old man."

"So, what? This Eye dude is like a witch or something?"

"I don't know who or what he is, but he's the real deal. I've seen with my own eyes what he can do to people."

Freddie laughed as well and hit Hogan on the shoulder.

"Come on, Hoagie," he said boldly. "Let's get out of here. This guy is nuts."

"If you don't believe me," Mike said to Freddie, "then come see for yourself."

## 3. Irreparable Damage

*It's really happening. I can feel it in the air, the tension. Can you?*

HOGAN, or any of the boys and girl for that matter, weren't allowed to ride in a car with a complete stranger. Not only was it their parents' orders, but it was also a rule—more or less—a slogan that was recited during the first week back from summer break: *If you don't know them, then you can't ride with them.* The same went with accepting candy from strangers. In some but not all cases, strangers equaled danger—rightfully so, that was what teachers and school faculty enforced. Even if Hogan and the gang decided to disobey their orders, they, especially Freddie, weren't entirely comfortable about riding in a car with a grown man who claimed to be a former police officer who claimed he was chasing after a super villain who supposedly called himself The Eye. They rode their bikes to the edge of town and met Mike at a retirement home called The Villas.

Mike was already there, waiting at the doorway.

Freddie was last to join the others. Hogan noticed that they were missing a horseman. He turned around, noticed Freddie not moving an inch from the bike rake, and waited for Freddie to follow. "I don't trust this dingbat," he said to Hogan.

"I don't know either, Freddie, but I think we have to hear him out. I mean, what if he's telling the truth—"

"—That would be insane, Hoagie! Listen how ridiculous it sounds: some bonehead called The Eye, who turns kids into people like my Pappa Johnny, running loose in Orson Valley?"

"I know it sounds ridiculous, but *what if*—"

"—Hogan's right, Freddie, you know," Chi said ecstatically. "I mean, this is something straight out of a Carpenter movie!"

"Don't be such a dork, Chi!" Freddie's voice softened and he said despairingly, "It sounds cool in a movie, but not in reality." Freddie remained glued to his bike while the others locked their bikes in a bike rack and made their way to the retirement home. Chi hesitantly turned around, waiting for Hogan, who was still patiently waiting for Freddie to join. Freddie tightened his grip over the handlebars of his bike and watched a crow flying through the sky. Hogan didn't budge one inch after he secured his bike. He finally said to Freddie, "You coming or what?"

"Go on without me," Freddie said emotionlessly and sat down on a curb and crossed his arms over his legs. "I'm cool out here," he said, his voice becoming more distant.

Persistent, Hogan made his way back to Freddie.

"Don't be like this," he said. "A horseman never abandons another horseman, remember?" Hogan hesitated, but then reached out his hand to Freddie. "Even though you don't agree with him, Freddie, it doesn't mean you have to ignore him. Hear him out. Try to understand him. It's the least we can do."

"We don't have to do anything!"

Freddie didn't waver; yet, he remained distant.

"Remember that one time I went with you to see Cool Con and The Jimmies?"

Freddie could barely bring himself to look at Hogan.

"So?" Freddie snapped.

"Really?" Hogan planted his hands over the sides of his

hips. "Do I really look like someone who would listen to Cool Con and The Jimmies?" He answered his own question before Freddie could answer. "No," he said briskly. "I did it because you didn't have anyone to go with." Hogan paused; and standing defensively, he waited for Freddie to make a move at him, but Freddie appeared as if he was sinking farther into the curb. Hogan blurted out, "I hate Cool Con! He's completely full of himself! But I went anyway because I knew how much you liked him."

Freddie looked at Hogan as if Hogan had just committed a crime.

Hogan shrugged and said out of the corner of his mouth, "It actually wasn't that bad of a concert, to be honest."

Freddie attempted to come back at Hogan, but he really didn't have much to say to Hogan. So, he said it under his voice.

"All four of us have an obligation to one another," said Hogan. "That's what friends are for. We have each other's back. No matter what, remember?"

Freddie smacked his gums and stood from the curb.

"A'ight, Hoagie," he said, grinning. "You win. *But* if this guy starts some shit then he's gonna feel the wrath of the Four Horsemen."

"If he starts anything," Hogan said, "then I'll sic Pluto on him."

—

Hogan and Freddie joined Chi and Elisa and followed Mike into The Villas where Mike instructed all four of them to write their names on a sign-in sheet at the front desk.

Once everybody had signed their names, one of the caretakers greeted Mike and she escorted Mike and the gang to a recreational room where a saggy shoulder man sat in a wheelchair next to a table with the game Checkers.

According to Mike, the old man wasn't much of an old man at all but the withered shell of what used to be a kid no older than Hogan himself. His name was Raymond Hefty, Mike informed them. His friends used to call him Rammy. The gang remained speechless from the sight of Mr. Hefty in the wheelchair. His eyes were still and vacant, so much that it was hard to distinguish if there was any life behind them. And even when one of the boys attempted to wave at Mr. Hefty, he didn't even adjust his eyes toward the sudden movements.

"What's wrong with him?" asked Hogan.

"You're looking at the work of The Eye," said Mike.

"The Eye did this to this old man?"

"*Not* an old man," Mike repeated. "Like I said, a kid no older than you."

"Of course, the old man used to be a kid," Chi said flippantly. "Everybody who's old used to be a kid at one time."

"Well, duh!"

"Mr. Hefty was once athletic like you kids, once had a drive," Mike said and stood next to Mr. Hefty. "His friends said he was good at baseball, then one day, he got caught in The Eye's gaze—"

"—How?" asked Elisa. "I mean, why?"

"He strayed away from his friends and family at a birthday party," Mike said as he kneeled down to Mr. Hefty's level. "Later that night, when he never returned, they sent out a search party. The very next morning, they found him in the woods; however, he wasn't the same person. They found him just like this."

"Wait a second!" Freddie blurted out and like Chi earlier, looked around at the others as if he was getting approval for his disruption. "Are you telling me this is Raymond Hefty, the fifth grader?"

"Raymond Hefty?" Hogan said in confusion.

"You know, Raymond Hefty, the kid who dropped out of school two months ago—"

"—Why would any person want to do this to him?" Elisa asked, more concerned by the sight of the old man. "I mean why did this Eye person do this to him?"

"It's not a question of why, darling. It's a question of *when*."

"Okay," Freddie said carefully. "So, *when* did The Eye turn Rammy into—you know—an old dude." He turned to the old man in the wheelchair and held out both hands to guard himself. "No offense, dude," he said innocently.

"It would be easy for any elderly man to be offended by your comments, but I'm afraid what you see is what you get. You're looking at a ten-year-old boy in the body of an ninety-plus year old man."

The rest of the gang appeared mortified from the recent news.

Hogan pounced on the empty spot of silence and asked Mike, "When did this happen to him?"

"Two months ago," Mike answered as soon as the questioned was asked, "like your friend here said, about two lunar cycles ago."

"You mean, two months ago he was just a kid like us?"

"That's what I'm saying, kid." Hogan took a step back from Mr. Hefty, the sudden whispers ping-ponging throughout the recreational room, which caused Hogan to lose focus. He ignored the whisperings and squared himself to Mike, focused on each word dripping from his lips. "Recently, there's been a spike in elderly people popping up around town, especially after every lunar cycle," Mike said. "Children gone missing. Retirement homes filling up by the numbers. Homeless shelters. The truth: it's the work of The Eye and his appetite is growing exponentially. Whatever he's planning for the next lunar cycle, it's going to change the world. And with your help, we can stop him."

"I don't believe you," Hogan said nauseously, shaking his head.

Mike pulled out a photo of the young ten-year-old Raymond Hefty. He pointed at the rare Texas-shaped birthmark on the side of his neck. Compared it with the same birthmark on the old man's neck.

"Believe me now?" Mike said to a yet again speechless

Hogan. "Believe what you will, kid. *The Eye is real.* I sure as hell hope you don't have to find out the hard way. Otherwise," Mike turned to the old man in the wheelchair, "you seem like a smart kid. You know."

—

Overwhelmed, mystified, and downright petrified by the latest discovery, Hogan parted ways with the rest of the gang and paid a visit to Clayton's Watches and Repair located on the south end of Main Street.

Clay, a slender man who always wore clothes that were two sizes way too big, welcomed Hogan with an exuberant howdy. Hogan brushed Clay's rather corky nature aside, skipped through the small talk, and slammed on the countertop the wristwatch that he stole from Mr. Macho's.

"What is this thing?" asked Hogan.

Clay's eyes flicked downward at the wristwatch, gave Hogan a once over, and said foolishly, "It's called a watch, son."

"I know it's a goddamn watch, but what makes it so special?"

Clay's wide eyes displayed displeasure for Hogan's language. He chose to let Hogan's frustration simmer while he grabbed the microscopic lens on a necklace around his neck and placed it to his eye. He examined the watch.

"Well," he chirped, "it's not like your everyday watch. It uses a new technology powered by the sun called Eco-Drive."

"Whatever that means," Hogan said over Clay. "Why doesn't it work?"

"Well," he said, slapping his tongue against the roof of his mouth, "if I had to guess, the watch doesn't work because it's been kept in some kind of dark storage for over six months— maybe longer. But don't you worry about a thing. It's a simple fix. Just hold the watch under the sunlight for ten minutes or so and it should be working as good as new."

"That's it?"

"That's it," Clay says kindly. "Pretty amazing, huh?"

"So, I hold the watch in the sunlight for ten minutes and it'll work?"

Clay walked around the counter and walked Hogan outside the store.

"Let's find out," he said, patting Hogan on the back.

They stepped outside onto the sidewalk and Hogan held the wristwatch underneath the glaring sunlight.

After ten minutes expired—Hogan spending every second of the time intensely waiting for the minute hand to twitch with life—the watch still didn't work. Hogan and Clay continued to wait in an eager state of both confusion and dismay.

"That's weird," the watchmaker said drunkenly. "Well, come back inside and I'll take a closer look at it."

Hogan and Clay headed back inside the store where Clay took the watch behind a curtain. Clay sat Hogan down at his workshop table and opened up the wristwatch with a special tool. The whisperings were happening again. Even Clay's voice itself sounded like a distant whisper. Hogan pinpointed the source of the whispers and they were guiding his attention toward a painting on the wall while Clay precisely rummaged through the internal guts of the wristwatch. The painting was blurry. From what Hogan could make out, it was a painting of a green hill with four children flying a kite. For some odd reason, Hogan found himself getting lost in the painting.

Clay grabbed Hogan's attention with a clearer and much more raised voice.

"Son?"

Still no response from Hogan.

"Son?" the watchmaker said, nearly shouting.

Hogan snapped from his trance.

"Yeah," he said with a flinch. "What?"

Clay let out a sigh of frustration and held up a tiny object with a pair of tweezers.

"Found what was obstructing the power source."

Hogan leaned in for a closer look at the object underneath the lamp and realized it was a black tinted contact lens.

"Who'd you say this watch belonged to?" said Clay, more worried.

"It's mine," Hogan said, as if he had just been insulted. "Why?"

"Don't lie to me," Clay said fatherly. "Where did you find this watch?"

With his eyes squinting, Hogan said with a kind of raw anger climbing in his voice, "I told you, 'It's my watch.'"

"Is that so?"

"It was a birthday present.'"

"Okay, okay. Sorry for asking."

Clay carefully placed the contact lens in a small mason jar. Closed the wristwatch. What did you know?

The minute hand on the watch started ticking away.

He handed the wristwatch back to Hogan while, at the same time, he secretly pushed aside the mason jar.

"Are you forgetting something?" asked Hogan.

Clay hesitated; then he started acting aloof.

"Mr. Clayton," Hogan said louder, "the contact lens."

"Right," he said bashfully as he handed Hogan the mason jar. "Are you sure?"

"I'm sure," he said as he shared a long gaze with Clay as if they both had an unspoken understanding of the repercussions of the object that he held in his hands.

Clay finally let go of the jar and sent Hogan on his way.

—

*Who are you?*

For the longest time, Hogan stared at the photo of the shadowy figure—Hogan showing no regard for the integrity of the photo, which had been folded in half leaving a jagged white crease down the middle of the photo. Hogan flipped over the photo and found a phone number, which happened to be the number of the hotel, Days Pass. He called the number and Mike answered after the second ring.

They decided to meet at the closest Pancake Village.

—

When Hogan arrived at the restaurant, which was known for serving breakfast all day to retirees and the late night partiers, Mike had already reserved a booth next to the front window.

Hogan took a seat across from Mike.

"Where are your friends?" asked Mike.

"I dunno," Hogan replied grumpily. "Does it look like I have a leash on them?"

"Whatever," Mike said and sipped from a cup of green tea. "So, you hungry, kid?"

"For your information, my name's Hogan, *not* kid."

Mike's left brow lowered slightly. He softly shrugged his shoulders and slid a menu across the table. Hogan took a glance at the menu as if it smelled to high heaven, then turned his repulsion toward Mike.

"Get some food in you," Mike demanded. "You look like you can use a little protein in ya."

"I'm *not* hungry."

"Eat."

"Are you deaf?" said Hogan. "I'm not hungry."

"I'm not going to tell you again."

Hogan didn't respond to Mike. Yet, he looked into his eyes and realized that the guy meant business. Finally, he picked up the menu and gave it once over before pulling out the mason jar from his pocket. He slid the jar across the table. Mike looked over the jar, the contact lens inside.

"Where'd you get this?"

Next, Hogan pulled out the wristwatch.

"I found this watch at the crime scene," Hogan said. "I think it belonged to that man who you mentioned, Blanc, or whatever his name was. It wasn't working—the watch—so I took it to a watchmaker and he said it needed sunlight to power. I held it under the sun. It didn't work. So, I gave it back to the watchmaker. He opened the watch." Hogan pointed at the mason jar. "He found that inside."

"This?" Mike said, pointing at the black contact lens.

"Yep. *That.*"

Mike carefully placed a napkin over the mason jar and stuck it in his coat pocket.

"What are you doing?" asked Hogan.

All of a sudden, his personality changed from cool and even-tempered to more fidgety. He looked over his shoulder a couple of times, then scanned the entire restaurant.

"What's wrong?" Hogan asked Mike.

The waitress stopped by and asked Hogan if he'd like something to eat as she poured him a glass of lemon water from a pitcher.

"Give us a moment, will you?" Mike said snappishly.

Turned off by Mike's unexpected rudeness, the waitress trotted away.

Mike leaned in closer to Hogan and asked, "Were you followed?"

Hogan took a moment to think.

"No," he said. "I—I don't think so."

"Were you followed, Hogan? Yes or no?"

"Ah no. I wasn't followed. What is that thing?"

"I wanted to mention it earlier but I didn't want to freak you kids out and make a scene at The Villas." Mike looked around the restaurant yet again, then leaned over the table. "According to the people who knew Killian Blanc, he used to be an apprentice for The Eye. He wanted to learn the art of *black magic,* but he saw that The Eye was planning a spree of murders on the first night of the Crow's Moon in which The Eye calls the 'Night of the Mortals.'"

"The Night of the Mortals?"

"I don't care much for the name either," Mike said and took a sip of tea. He placed the mug aside, played with the handle a bit, then regained his composure. "You see, Hogan, the whole idea is to draw his power from the moon and anyone who gazes upon the light of the moon will be stripped of eternal youth—"

"—Like Mr. Hefty?"

"*Just* like Mr. Hefty," Mike followed. "The Eye's spell will literally turn the moon into his own weapon."

"You're serious?"

Mike took another sip, nodded his head while swallowing.

"My sources indicate that Blanc wanted no part in The Eye's masquerade," Mike said, "so he recently stole something extremely valuable from The Eye when that bastard wasn't paying attention. The Eye found out about Killian Blanc and how he had betrayed him; and in retaliation, he unleashed the monster on him. That's when Blanc stumbled onto you and your friends."

Hogan pointed at the mason jar.

"So, what is that thing in the mason jar?"

"It's The Eye's Lens."

"Lens?"

"That's right."

"And I'm guessing he needs it for this Night of the Mortals."

"You got it, Hogan. Now, you know what's at stake."

*It all makes sense*, Hogan thought. The other night, he had the most vivid dream—or better yet, a nightmare—and even till this day, scenes of the nightmare remained as clear as day. There was one scene, Hogan remembered, where he was scaling a needle-thin tower that was in the shape of a giant minute hand; and below, an alien-like creature was chasing after him. Hogan had to be at least thirty stories in the air. At least. Below, on the ground, were hordes of people, all of them were distinguishably ancient-old, zombie-like in the way they groaned and staggered back and forth in the slowest waltz ever; however, they were *not* zombies. They were old. Just old. In Hogan's nightmare, every human on earth was as old as shoelaces.

Hogan pulled himself from creepy thought and nodded at Mike.

"I'm in," he said confidently. "So, what do we do?"

"*You* do absolutely nothing, Hogan," Mike said. "Go home. Forget all of this happen. Hell! Write a story about it. I, on the other hand, will make sure The Eye doesn't get his hands on the Lens."

"Won't The Eye be after you?"

Mike placed his tea aside and drifted in reflection.

Over the restaurant ambience, Mike said in deep reflection, "My sister was leaving nursing school when she was murdered. It wasn't until after weeks of investigation that I realized the thing that killed my sister was neither man or animal but somewhere in between."

"This thing," Hogan said, "why did it go after her?"

"It was getting late in the night. The only explanation I could come up with was that she got caught in the wrong place at the wrong time." Mike faced Hogan and stared at him directly in the eyes. "This thing," he said, "you see, it doesn't care if you have a brother or sister or someone who loves you. It's driven by hunger and it will destroy anything that gets in its way. It doesn't have feelings like you and me, Hogan. It's a killing machine. Plain and simple."

Another wave of silence set in over the conversation. Hogan broke through the thick, gooey silence with a question that caused Mike's eyes to gloss over with tears: "What was your sister's name?"

"Her name was Melissa."

"Sorry for you loss."

"Me too," Mike said under his breath.

## 4. Four-Legged

*What is the one thing all monsters have in common?*

HOGAN spent the earlier part of dusk contemplating his next move. It wasn't at all common for an eleven-year-old to have so much on his mind. He could've very well stayed there in the house, not make any move that would put not only his own life in jeopardy but also his friends, not make a big fuss in the matter, not do much of anything but just go back to his everyday life. He didn't exactly know how to explain it, the pull. Hogan was indeed left at a crossroads. One side was pulling him one way while another side was pulling him in a total opposite way.

After Hogan made up his mind, he left without telling his father and rode his bike to Freddie's where Freddie and his family, including his mother, father, and two older sisters, were eating supper. Meatloaf it was.

While Freddie was picking through his vegetables, Hogan anxiously waited outside the kitchen window and tried to wave down Freddie whenever Freddie's parents weren't paying attention.

Finally, after several minutes of ducking and dodging in Japanese holly bushes, Hogan was successful.

Freddie asked his mother if he could be excused from the table, but his mother demanded that he finish his brussels sprouts.

In two bites, Freddie scooped the brussels sprouts into his mouth, didn't even bother chewing. Yet, he stood from the seat with both of his cheeks puffed outward like a puffer fish and murmured to his mother something along the lines, "Are you happy?" The words came out all jumbled up as if he was speaking tongues through a dog muzzle.

Freddie's mother shooed away Freddie while, in return, Freddie rushed outside and spat out the mouthful of brussels sprouts over the deck. With the sleeve of his shirt, he cleared the leftover food from his mouth and searched for Hogan in the backyard, but he couldn't find him anywhere. His eyes moved toward the lit tree house. The light always remained off, but this time it was on. Inside, a tiny shadow was moving back and forth inside. Freddie climbed up the tree house via the sturdy 2 x 4's that his father had nailed into the oak tree and saw Hogan biting his nails while pacing back and forth, as if he had a world of information on his mind. Freddie wasn't the least prepared for what Hogan was holding, the intel on Mike and what Mike told him at the Pancake Village, Killian Blanc, The Eye and his diabolical plans to turn the entire world into the Night of the Living Dead, then The Eye's mutated lapdog, which, as of now, Freddie was calling the monster—Hogan preferred the "Thing," but both he and Freddie were up for new and more creative nicknames.

Once Freddie was filled in on The Eye's master plans, he immediately contacted Chi and Elisa via walkie-talkie.

Both Hogan and Freddie hopped on their bikes and met up with the rest of the gang on the cul-de-sac on Freddie's street where they made an A-effort attempt at conceiving their own plan of action.

"We track down this Mike dude," Chi first suggested in a round robin-like fashion. "Without him, everything else is a bust—"

"—Mike has the Lens, right?"

"Yeah," said Hogan.

"That means this Horus cat will be after him."

"Mike said it'd kill anything in its path. He said it was a killing machine. His words—"

"—Horus? Who's Horus?"

"The monster," Freddie told Chi. "Pay attention!"

"Horus? I mean, really?"

"Yeah. You don't like it?" He turned to Elisa. "Izzy?"

Both Elisa and Chi looked at one another but didn't say a word.

"What about the Thing?"

"The Thing is out."

"Hoagie was the one who named it," Freddie said. "I'm open for any other suggestions?"

Chi asked, "How about '*The Shadow Stalker?*'"

"No," Hogan blurted out. "Not Shadow Stalker. We're sticking with Horus."

"Whatever—"

"—We need weapons to defeat Horus," Freddie chimed in. "Lots and lots of weapons. I'm talking Schwarzenegger-type firepower.'

"Oh yeah!" Hogan said. "And how are we going to do that, Freddie? We can't just use knives and paintball guns to defeat Horus. We need to think outside the box!"

"My old man has a rifle," Elisa said lackadaisically.

"We're not using guns," Hogan said over Freddie before he could utter another word.

"How else are we going to stop Horus?"

Hogan pointed to his temple.

"Why are you pointing at your head?"

"We outsmart it, you genius," Hogan said sarcastically. "I mean, how smart can this thing be? Mike said it was sort of like an animal. So, how do you catch an animal?"

"We lure it."

"That's right. We lure it into a trap."

"A trap? And how exactly are we going to make a trap

large enough to hold Horus?"

"The old Smitten's building off Orkin Street."

"You mean the abandoned steel factory?"

"Yes, Freddie," Hogan said. "The abandoned steel factory."

"Don't be a dick."

Hogan rolled his eyes, ignored Freddie.

Not missing a beat, he said, "Me and Chi were snooping
around there a couple of weeks ago. There's this one room
with solid walls and a sliding door made out of metal. It's
secure. So, we place the lure inside the room, slide the door
shut behind it."

"Then what?"

"What do you mean?"

"What exactly are we going to do with Horus once we
catch it, Hogan?"

"We'll be with Mike, right? *He* has a gun."

"I thought you said we weren't going to use guns."

"We're not, Freddie. We have Mike."

"So, the whole plan is depending on some douche we
hardly even know? I don't like it. Not one bit."

"It's the only way, Izzy."

Chi looked around at the others and asked the most obvious question: "So, what are we going to lure it with?"

———

The gang made a pitstop at the grocery store, Earth Supply,
where they ended up filling two shopping carts full of pack-
ages of every part of a cow: T-bones, filet mignons, sirloin,
ground up hamburger, ribs. Hogan wondered if it would be
enough meat to satisfy Horus. He decided to fill up another
shopping cart with meat. Just in case. The question, once
they reached the checkout lane, was "Who's paying for all of
this?"

—

Carrying three to four bags of raw red meat at a time, the gang headed to the same hotel where Mike was currently staying.

When they arrived at Mike's room—eager to tell Mike all about their plan to catch the notoriously elusive Horus—the door was partially cracked opened, just far enough for Hogan to witness the narrow frame of horror inside.  Part of the doorway had been clawed as well as chewed through by at least ten-inch long incisors.

Hogan stepped forward and eased open the door, only to find the entire hotel room trashed to pieces.  The room appeared as if a bomb had recently gone off inside.  Everything was everywhere.  An overturned lamp, which was still flickering with light, had a bloody imprint of a hand on its side whereas another one remained smashed to pieces.  The mirror above a TV, also knocked over, had been shattered.  Several droplets of blood were scattered over the shards of broken glass.

Suddenly, a piece of glass fell from the wall!

The sudden noise caused Chi to jump and let out a shrill cry.

"Jesus Chi!" Freddie whispered sharply.

"Sorry," he said softly.

"Did you pee your pants?"

"No," Chi drawled.  "Shut up. . . "

Hogan did some more inspecting.  One of the two beds, he saw, had been flipped over.  Projectile consisting of long streaks of blood splattered in a slashing pattern along the wall.  On the broken dresser was a puddle of blood.

Freddie accidentally touched the blood on the dresser, leaving his entire palm covered in dark blood.

Horrified, he wiped his palm over his pant leg, unaware of the potential danger that he had now placed onto his own person.

"It was just here," Hogan droned, as he kneeled down

and touched a warm mug on the floor, black coffee spilled out all over the carpet.

Suddenly, a resonant voice from outside the hotel room: "A'ight, you fools! There better be a good explanation for the damn racket you've been making! I got guests bugging me to. . . "

The sound of the scruffy man's voice caused the entire gang to jump!

Behind the gang stood a landlord with his hands planted on his hips, clueless about the horror.

Once Chi took a step away from the landlord, the chaos was revealed to the landlord. The landlord's mouth opened in a gaping yawn from the sight of the room.

". . . What in Sam Hill!" groaned the landlord.

Hogan stepped outside the room and followed a couple of droplets of blood leaving the room.

Right now, he didn't know whose blood it belonged to. Either way, he managed to convince the others to follow the blood despite the landlord's desperate attempt to stop the gang.

They pushed aside the landlord and followed the blood down the stairs, droplets of blood getting closer and closer together. They ended up tracking the blood trail to a parking spot on the side of the hotel.

Hogan noticed the two sets of black skid marks on the asphalt. He was no detective—far from one—but it didn't take an individual of great intellect to figure out that whoever was hurt had left the scene in a hurry.

—

Panic spread from one horseman to the next.

"Now what do we do?" Freddie said while riding alongside Hogan. His fear level was at an all-time high. "Without Mike," he stuttered, "our, our entire plan is ruined—"

"—I know," Chi said.

"Forget the plan, you guys," Elisa said over Chi. "What

if he's injured?"

"Just a minute ago you were calling him a douche."

"Yeah, but still, he might be messed up."

"He'll be fine."

"How do you know?"

"I just do," Hogan said, peddling faster. "There's another way. What about the car compactor at Jimmy's Junkyard? We place the meat inside the compactor. Horus goes into the compactor. We turn on the compactor while Horus is inside. Squashed like a bug! No more Horus."

"That's one way of solving our monster problem."

"Have you actually seen how *slow* those things work? Once Horus realizes the compactor has been turned on, it'll clearly escape. It can't be that stupid, can it?"

"It's not a bad idea, but it's too risky, Hogan."

"We need to find Mike. If he's injured, he might be at the hospital, right?"

"Guys," Chi said from behind as he pulled the grocery bags of raw meat inside a small cargo trailer, "what are we going to do with all this hamburger?"

"Don't even think about taking it home with you, Chi," Elisa said bossily. "That stuff needed to be refrigerated like an hour ago. You could get sick."

"Yeah, but if I take it home and put it directly into the refrigerator, I should be okay, right?"

"Always thinking of yourself," Elisa mumbled, shaking her head in annoyance.

"No, Chi," Freddie said from the front. "It's for Horus. Not you!"

"I'm just saying," Chi said naively. "If Horus doesn't want to eat all this meat, then it's all going to go to waste."

"No, Chi!" Elisa and Freddie said simultaneously.

"*But* think of all those starving kids in those poor countries. Think how many kids all this meat would feed. It'd feed like an entire village—"

"—You're not taking the meat, Chi! End of story!"

"A'ight. Geez."

Chi pouted and looked over his shoulder at all the meat. The sight alone made him lick his chomps. *So much meat*, he thought, *so little time*.

—

The gang decided to head back to Freddie's to regroup and come up with a better plan of attack.

At around the halfway mark to their neighborhood, they stopped outside Finn-Berry Park and gave Chi a minute to catch his breath. Hogan wasn't too keen on stopping, considering what was lurking out there in the night—and somehow, even though Hogan had a feeling that something was going to happen, not once did he ever warn Chi about the looming danger or even make a better attempt at trying to encourage him to keep up the pace.

"Just give me a sec, will you?" Chi said, out of breath.

"Why don't we trade," Hogan said unsteadily. "I'll pull the trailer. You can take my bike."

"Thanks," Chi said as he got off his bike.

"Hey—hey guys," Freddie stuttered.

Hogan acknowledged Freddie's tone, the unsettled nature of it. He turned to Freddie, who was staring at a lanky shadow cast from the amber-colored floodlights positioned above the blacktops.

"What is it, Freddie?"

"Can we hurry it up please?"

As Hogan and Chi traded bikes, Hogan heard the sound of a cackle behind a playground.

"Did you guys hear that?"

"What was that?"

"It sounded like ah—like ah a baby."

Hogan set Chi's bike onto the ground and checked out the strange noise.

"Hoagie," Freddie whispered, "we have to get back. . ."

Pushing aside his friend's most evident concerns, Hogan inched his way into the dimly lit park. He tracked down the source of the noise, which was coming from a hunched over figure dressed in a glossy navy blue rain jacket. It was no longer raining; yet, the atmosphere was filled with a light drizzly mist—almost soupy in its dampness—and when the amber light hit the wet spots along the jacket, it cast a reflection of light.

Beside the strange figure was a rat-sized dog on a leash; however, the doll-like dog wasn't moving.

With its back turned to Hogan, the person rattled on like a toddler, his or her voice—he couldn't quite identify the sex—bouncing in and out of pitch. He made his best guess.

"Ma'am," Hogan said as he cautiously approached what he assumed was a loosely hinged elderly lady walking her dog despite the rainy conditions. Hogan couldn't make out what she was saying.

The words were gibberish, alien.

"Is. . . everything. . . okay?"

Hogan eased down his pace to a kind of wobbly amble as soon as he concluded that the lifeless dog—a white Pomeranian—wasn't even standing or sitting alongside the lady. Yet, the little furball was being dragged.

The lady snapped her head to the left, then to the right, then once more a game of back and forth; then she statically rotated her head over her shoulder as if she had a crick in her neck. Hogan still couldn't make out the lady's face for it still remained awfully disguised in the reticent shadows of the night; however, one thing was certain: Hogan could see her nose quickly bobbing up and down in short bursts, dog-like in the way it sniffed the air. He listened closely to the airy sounds being vacuumed into that black space of her nostrils. He soon came the conclusion that she wasn't sniffing the air. She was sniffing Hogan, tasting his scent with her nose, as if she could no longer see or hear; and instead, she relied upon her incredible sense of smell. Her nose was her eye, her mouth. She fully rotated around, Hogan remaining just several feet away. All Hogan could make out now were her eyes or her lack of eyes. All that remained of them were two black holes where two eyes used to be underneath the hood of her rain jacket. Her fingers violently popped out of joint, her knuckles swelling, then cracking in a cringing delight. The skin of her face sluggishly fell from her skull, revealing a set of *new* eyes, reptilian-like, piercing through the darkest of night.

Next to pop out of joint were the lady's knees. The skin of her legs split apart like loose seams, revealing two scalier, darker legs. The legs unfolded and stretched outward and once the legs were fully extended, the lady's flesh slid from her entire body like an evening dress.

A dark figure bloomed from the remaining fold of flesh. The last thing to tear apart was the rain jacket, but it didn't matter by then. Hogan was already convinced.

Several other similar, darker figures moved through the trees above, swinging from one limb to another.

Hogan counted three more of them.

Altogether, there were five creatures, one growing before him, three moving through the tops of trees, and then the last one, creeping from a manhole to the left of Hogan.

"Hogan. . . " Freddie said, his voice like a rattle, ". . . I think we should get back to the house!"

"That—" the wind had been completely knocked out of Hogan, "—that sounds like a good idea."

As the monster stepped from the shadows to reveal itself—slouching at least eight feet in height, with an added foot after standing upright, gnarly hands as long as Hogan's arm and claws about the size of sabers—Hogan's eyes were drawn to its left hand. It appeared as if it was missing; severed from its wrist. Two things immediately came to mind: Killian Blanc was the first; then werewolves. Even though these creatures didn't look anything like werewolves, Hogan wondered if their bite had the same effect as a werewolf. Bitten or cut by one could cause any man or woman to turn into one. Could, he wondered.

Whatever the case might've been, he didn't have time to think anymore about Killian Blanc. Hogan needed to do exactly what Freddie cried out. And that was. . . run!

Hogan ran away, the monster chasing after him as soon as Hogan made his first stride. Leaves and branches fell all around Hogan, the limbs above shaking.

Suddenly, the monster chasing after Hogan was pelted on the side of its elongated face with a T-Bone steak!

The monster was quick to bounce on the meat as soon as it hit the ground. It ripped into the T-Bone with its fangs and swallowed it in two bites.

Chi unhooked the trailer of meat while Hogan made a dash toward his bike. The distraction alone gave Hogan enough time to make it to the bike. He hopped on his bike while the rest of the gang peddled away. The other monsters revealed themselves, all five of them, the fifth one still mopping up the juice from its lips from the appetizer. Hogan peeked over his shoulder for a moment and witnessed something unexplainable. . .

One monster, a much slender one, walked into another one, its flesh adhered to the other monster's flesh like two pellets of water coming together.

The three other monsters joined themselves to the now one monster.

Hogan took yet another look.

The five monsters had now become one!

Hogan peddled faster and finally caught up with the rest of the gang. Hogan took yet another peek over his shoulder, but the monster was nowhere to be found.

—

Out of breath, exhausted, and straight up scared out of his wits, Hogan insisted on stopping to regroup but the other three horsemen were too scared to change course. Peddling meant surviving. The faster, the better.

Once the gang reached Main Street, Freddie broke away from the rest of the gang and peddled as if his feet were on fire.

With his chest burning, Hogan slowed down his bike as he called out to Chi, who, in return, slowed down and called out to Elisa, who, in return, called out to Freddie, who, in return, finally turned his shoulder.

"What are you doing?" said Freddie. He slowed down his bike and made a U-turn. "You blew it!"

"Relax, Freddie. It's gone," Hogan said to Freddie. "It took the bait."

Freddie shouted back, "We were supposed to catch it, you idiot! All you did was feed it! And not just an *it*! But more than one! You fed them!"

"It *was* one!"

"Were you not seeing the same thing I was looking at? I counted at least four."

"Five actually," Hogan corrected.

"Okay," Freddie said angrily. "Then what are you saying, Hogan?"

"I'm saying they all came together, like, somehow all five of these things morphed into one."

"How is that even possible?"

"I know what I saw. You have to believe me—"

"—Forget this," Freddie waved off Hogan. "I'm outta here!"

Hogan as well as the other two horsemen remained utterly speechless, their faces pale and slack from the sight of Horus looming behind Freddie in the shadow of the sandwich shop. Freddie was completely unaware of the massive beast ready to take a chomp out of him.

"You guys can continue to act like you don't have a freaking clue as to what's going on!" Freddie shouted, still mindless of the upcoming bloodbath. "Me, I'm done with this shit! I'm done with hunting down monsters! I'm going back home, back to my bed, back to my comic books where everything makes sense!" Freddie heard Horus growling behind him. He started to shake. With his jaw dropping, he slowly turned his shoulder. *I'm completely*: those were the only two words Freddie could muster before his entire body locked up with fear.

"Watch out, kid!" a man screamed from behind.

The thunderous gun blast of a shotgun crackled through the desolate streets, the shot hitting Horus in the arm!

Horus stumbled backward from the gunshot.

The gang located the mysterious shooter standing at the corner of the intersection.

"Mike!" Hogan hollered out. "He's alive!"

"Get outta here!" Mike yelled out as he unloaded one shell after another at Horus.

A mechanic named Just Julio—nobody really knew his last name, so he got stuck with Just Julio—who was good pals with Chi's father, stepped out of the garage to see what all of the commotion was about and ended up paying a severe price.

Horus took a bite out of Just Julio's arm, held him in its mouth, and the force of the bite lifted the mechanic—who weighed over two hundred pounds—off the ground. Horus thrashed from side to side like a crocodile, Just Julio swinging back and forth as if he weighed as much as a plush toy. Another gunshot caught Horus in the side, causing Horus to release the mechanic from its jaws. The mechanic flopped to the ground, his forearm missing from the bite.

The mechanic ended up passing out from the extensive loss of blood.

Horus turned his furious appetite toward the gang and made a charge toward them. The first one to catch the blunt force impact of Horus's wrath was Elisa. Horus knocked her to the ground and as the lanky creature was about to sink its teeth into Elisa, Hogan shielded her body.

The creature threw a curling right hook at Hogan, the tip of its claw somehow got caught inside the band of Hogan's wristwatch; and as it pulled its arthritic hand away, the tip of its claw released the band, snapping the clasp in half.

The links rained over the wet asphalt and to Hogan, it sounded like the white noise of a staticky television.

Horus stepped forward, crushing the wristwatch beyond

obliteration.

Hogan's eyes fell onto the wristwatch—or what was left of the watch, which wasn't much at all but pancaked metal and shattered glass.

Horus suddenly made yet another swipe at Hogan!

In mid-swipe, another gunshot *rang* out!

The shot hit Horus square in the shoulder, forcing it to seek cover.

The rest of the gang rushed to Elisa while Horus scampered down an alley.

Hogan checked for any injuries on his body and thankfully, found none; then he checked on Elisa. She said that she was fine, but she ended up with a fairly significant injury above the left side of her hip during the fall. She shook off the momentary daze and sprang to her feet as if nothing even happened.

While the rest of the gang gathered themselves underneath the streetlight, Mike limped after Horus.

Once more, he told the kids to get out of there but Hogan was not going to leave Mike alone to fight Horus.

The rest of the gang peddled away, except for one of them.

Hogan was struck by the sudden thought of home, going back there to everyday life, to the norm, the clichéd, the redundancy, the emptiness. He stopped in mid-peddle and dropped his bike to the ground and picked up a wrench, which must've belonged to Just Julio, and followed Mike, causing the rest of the gang to follow as well, including Freddie. They caught up with Mike, who nearly came close to blowing Hogan's head clean off.

"You don't listen," Mike seethed. "Do you, kid?"

"You can't fight Horus alone."

"Horus?" he said, confused. "Who the hell is Horus?"

"That's what Hoag's calling the monster," Chi said before Hogan could answer the question. "Personally, I think Shadow Stalker is much better. But now that I've actually seen it with my own eyes, I think '*Maneater*' sounds much cooler. I mean, Chi-Ching!" Chi made the sound of a cash register, "that's a million dollar idea—"

"Wow," Freddie said flatly, "the Chinican here just used his name in third person."

"So!"

"Not only that, he used his own name as a sound effect." Freddie turned to Chi, his face long and humorless. "You seriously hit a new level of narcissism."

"Narcissism?" Chi replied. "Shut up! You don't even know what that word means!"

"It means you're totally obsessed with yourself—"

"—Are you two through?"

Chi rolled his eyes.

"Fine," he said carelessly. "It's Horus."

"You kids shouldn't be here," Mike said with urgency. "Go home. Lock your doors. Go to sleep. Go back to your lives. Pretend all of this never happened. . . "

"*Never* happened? No way!"

"How are we supposed to do that?"

"You just do, all right," Mike said, grimacing.

He grabbed his side and pulled away a handful of blood.

"You're hurt?"

"I'll live," he said quietly. "I cut myself on some broken glass."

"Are you sure it was glass?" Hogan said suspiciously.

"Yeah, kid," he said, his voice trailing off. "I'm sure."

Mike moved his eyes toward the end of the alley where a sickly-looking man dressed in a windswept black duster proudly stood. Everything about him was black, including his persona. Except for the strange glossy right eye, he was decked out in black—a black gat hat, gloves, boots, a scarf wrapped around his neck and the lower part of his chin.

"Is that. . . "

"Yeah," Mike said as he held out his hand the same way a parent would do while protecting their own child. "Get behind me. Now!"

The gang backpedaled behind Mike.

From his sheath, The Eye brandished his sword, which was called the "Devil's Toothpick," an instrument of death known to dice continents in pieces and slice an entire world in two; and when the rare steel was released from its cryptic sheath and touched earth's air, the sword ignited in an inextinguishable blue flame.

"There used to be an amazing Cantonese restaurant on this street," The Eye said in his seductive yet ever so villainous accent. He arched his head upward and smelled the muggy night air. "I can still smell it now. We used to love living in the city. Every night we'd visit a different country. Now, she is gone. And all that remains is the constant yearning for flesh. The temptation insufferable. How weak I've become! The flesh: so desirable and yet so perishable. Like food left to rot over time. I must take what I cannot have. And you, boy, will not get in my way—"

Hogan leaned in closer to Mike and whispered, "What in the hell is talking about?"

"You have something that belongs to me," The Eye said to Hogan as he approached the gang.

"Come any closer," Mike said and pulled out the mason jar carrying the Lens, "and I'll destroy your little toy here."

Mike whispered through the corner of his mouth for Hogan to grab the lighter from his pocket.

Hogan did as Mike demanded and grabbed the lighter.

"Now," he whispered, "crumble up some paper—wood, whatever you can find—from the scrap pile, toss it in the oil drum, and set it on fire."

"Playtime is over, Mr. Morrow. Make it easy on yourself and just hand it over. It's *that* simple."

"Nothing's ever simple."

Hogan rushed toward the scrap pile behind the building and grabbed armfuls of wood from several broken pallets and sheets of damp cardboard and tossed them into the oil drum. It took a while for Hogan to get a fire going; but once he did, the entire oil drum filled with flames.

Mike held the mason jar over the fire.

"So be it," The Eye said.

He suddenly stabbed the sword into the street! The impact of the sword caused the concrete to fissure!

A long and jagged crack in the street opened up, revealing the sewers below, then shot like a lightning bolt toward Mike and forced the ground the shake. Mike loosened his grip on the mason jar. He couldn't hold onto it any longer. The jar slipped from his hand. . .

Before Mike could pick up the cracked jar, The Eye was already on top of him with the black tip of his blade inches away from his face.

"Now, now, now, don't be a showoff in front of your new friends, Mr. Morrow, or they will perish too. Surely, you wouldn't want more bloodshed on your hands. Now, would you?"

The Eye cracked open the mason jar with the strength of his grip, delicately sorted through broken glass, and finally picked up the contact lens; and as The Eye placed it in his left pale eye, Hogan pounced with the wrench in his hand. His attempt to strike The Eye failed miserably as The Eye, with only a couple of fingers, grabbed hold of Hogan with the same arm holding the sword.

"You are quite a brave individual, Mr. Hill," he said as Hogan squirmed around in his grip. Hogan's attempt was rather fruitless for The Eye carried the strength of a dozen men combined.

Elisa suddenly cried out, "Let him go!"

Mike reached for the pistol tucked underneath the belt behind his back and just as he aimed the pistol at The Eye, The Eye flung Hogan at Mike with a flick of one hand.

In that little amount of time, when Hogan was flailing through the air, something as rudimentary as a thought was few and far between. Mike didn't have time to think. The only option Mike relied on was action, *not* thought. He was only given a cracked window of opportunity to take out the great warlock and prevent the Night of Mortals. His chest remained free and exposed for a bullet; however, that meant

Mike would have to shoot the boy at point blank range and hope maybe the bullet would not hit any major organs or bounce around his ribcage like a pinball; yet, the bullet had to pass through Hogan like the tip of a led pencil piercing a sheet of paper, and hit The Eye.

Mike pressed his finger along the trigger, but he did not squeeze.

Instead, he braced himself for impact.

Hogan slammed into Mike; Hogan's head spearing into Mike's gut, causing Mike to fall backward.

The wind was momentarily knocked out of Mike and the violent collision had given The Eye just enough time to escape.

As The Eye dashed away, Freddie leaped at The Eye at the very last second. As Freddie was about to snatch the sword from The Eye's grip, The Eye caught Freddie in his deadly gaze.

Freddie grabbed his stomach in agony, stumbled backward, knees buckling. He fell to the ground. He stared at his hand, the palm, and then the front. Each one of his fingers started to bend and curl, the joints along his knuckles swelled, then the tips of his fingers contorted in the most crooked and painful positions.

Even his posture, a lanky boy who was tall for his age, reaching the threshold of five feet, well above the average height of an eleven-year-old, started to hunch over.

His shrinking bones made the sounds of cracked leather tightening; and by the time his transformation took hold, he stood nearly six inches under his normal height. He ran his arthritic hands through his now gray hair and soon realized he didn't have any hair.

Freddie pulled his hands away in shock.

Below him, he held two palms full of gray hair. He caught a glimpse of himself in the reflection of a puddle in a pothole.

The horror on his face becoming more wrinkled by the second nearly stole the breath away from his lungs.

Freddie turned to Hogan, then to the rest of the gang. They could hardly recognize their friend. "What's happening to me?" Freddie whimpered, both of his crippled hands shaking.

Hogan gasped, "Freddie. . . "

Mike didn't bother chasing after The Eye once he witnessed the boy's transformation. The sight alone of watching an eleven-year-old rapidly withering and deteriorating with age sent a blood-fueled shiver of rage through Mike's bones.

Before he could take aim at The Eye, The Eye vanished into the night like a cape crusader. Mike knew, however, he was nothing like any cape crusader. He was far worse.

And soon-to-be a dead man.

## 5. Searching for a Cure

*I've met the devil and he goes by the name, The Eye.*

CAUGHT in a temporary state of shock, the gang—including Mike Morrow, who wasn't officially a horseman but, more or less, a loyal ally—snuck Freddie into the bottom floor of Hogan's parents' basement.

When Mike stepped foot into the basement, he suddenly became withdrawn from the gang. His face was somewhat pale and bloodless and he was glancing in a sort of child-like fascination at the 1980 movie posters decorated on the walls: *Near Dark*, *Dead Ringers*, and other '80's movie classics. He was jolted from his daze from a stinging blow to his left arm. The blood ran wild into the upper corners of Mike's face. Chi's face was red, too; however, he failed to observe Mike's frustration. He, too, was just as frustrated as Mike, and he had every reason to be.

Chi threw up his hands and asked if Mike was going to help or what—the *what?* part of the question leaving Mike even more dumbfounded from the boy's candid behavior.

At one point, while all three horsemen were scrambling around and grabbing blankets, pillows, and bags of ice, and trying to make Freddie as comfortable as possible, for every inch of him hurt like holy hell, Hogan's mother, a motionless, rather expressionless woman who remained entirely cloaked in darkness, surprisingly opened the basement door and from the dimly lit doorway asked in the most monotone voice if Hogan was okay.

Hogan stopped digging through a closet full of pillow-cases and suddenly froze. He robotically rotated his head toward the silhouette of his mother standing at the landing of the staircase. He told her in a subdued voice that every-thing was okay—even though it was far from okay. She didn't respond, didn't even utter a word. Instead, she shut the door behind her and walked back to the master bedroom while Hogan continued to nurse his friend, who was getting worse by the minute. By the time Freddie's transformation was fully complete, Freddie appeared as if he was a ninety-year-old man!

Freddie was groaning, "What—What are these. . . these marks on my arms?"

"They're liver spots, kid," Mike said in a serious tone, and yet his answer came off more like a cruel joke.

"Liver spots!" Freddie exclaimed.

"It's what old people get," Chi said. "Go ask my Nana Blanca. She's got them all over her body."

Freddie cupped his aching hands into his face and started crying.

"We need to do something quick—"

"Like what?"

"How do we reverse the spell?" Hogan asked Mike.

Silence built between the two.

Mike hung his head and struggled to look Hogan in the eye.

"My first option," Mike said over a sigh, "you're not go-ing to like, but I say we make it easy on your friend here."

Elisa asked, "What do you mean *easy?*"

"You know exactly what I mean," he said and pointed at Freddie, who had curled himself into a ball. "Look at him. He's suffering."

"Go fork yourself!"

"Elisa," Hogan said patiently, "please. . ."

He tried to calm down his friend, but she wasn't having it. She was huffing and pacing around the basement with her arms buried into her chest. The frustration was driving her like a steering wheel.

Meanwhile, Chi switched on the TV and started flipping through channels: a habit that he often resorted to whenever he was feeling tense and hungry or a little bit of both. Also, Chi usually ate whenever he was nervous, but Hogan didn't have any food lying around, except for a few candy wrappers, which were filled with old crumbs. Chi came across a TV commercial of the famous film director and producer, Curtis Saeman. The camera panned away from a fireplace mantle covered in black and white photographs of Curtis doing outdoor activities such as fishing or hunting. Curtis entered the frame. He was sitting with his legs crossed in a cherry red leather chair, as old as the Constitution, by a fireplace made of mahogany and natural stone. While the low burning fire crackled behind him, he sipped on a tumbler of brandy. The camera did a tasteful CLOSE-UP of Curtis's sultry blue eyes, then his lips speaking the words: *Welcome to the Eleventh Hour.*

"What a 'tard," Chi murmured while continuing to flip channels.

He landed on a news channel.

The footage was old and taken earlier in the night. Cops had roped off the front of Clayton's Watches and Repairs. On the TV screen, coroners were wheeling a gurney carrying a body in a black bag to the back of an unmarked van.

"Guys!" Chi shouted out. "Check this out!"

Chi turned up the volume.

The reporter informed the people that Clayton Daniels was found strangled to death in his repair shop earlier today and if anyone had any information to please come forward immediately.

Chi said to Hogan, "Weren't you just there today?"

"It must've happened after I left."

"You think The Eye had something to do with Mr. Daniels' death?"

"Who else would it be?"

"Why would The Eye kill Mr. Daniels?" asked Chi.

Nobody had an answer to the question. So, they immediately directed their attention toward Mike.

"How the hell do I know?" Mike grumbled. "The Eye has exactly what he wants now and he'll use it tomorrow night underneath the Crow's Moon—"

"—How do we stop him?" Hogan said over Mike.

"We don't, kid," he said. "We can't. The only cure lies within The Eye's Lens."

"If we don't get the Lens back, then Freddie will die!"

"I'm sorry, kid."

Chi whispered closely to Hogan, "He can hear you. . . "

"I know he can hear me. Freddie *knows* what's happening. It sounds like you're the only one who doesn't have a clue as to what's going on!"

Chi pushed Hogan from behind hard enough to cause Hogan to lose his footing.

"You know, if you hadn't stolen that watch, then none of this would've happened!"

"How would I know that the watch belonged to the apprentice of a evil sorcerer who wants to destroy the entire world?"

"You big mouth!"

Hogan pushed Chi back.

Mike stepped in between the two as if they were two dogs fighting.

"Cut it out, you two," he said.

Chi uttered behind Hogan's back: "One of these days someone's going to sew your mouth shut."

"Is that right, Chi? Why don't you do it yourself?"

Mike held his finger in front of Hogan, held it there as if it was a weapon, and said, "Don't."

"He started it—"

"—There's another way—an alternative—one that you

may not like."

"Yeah!" Hogan followed. "What?"

"Before Missy died, she spoke of a mysterious woman who practiced holistic methods in order to cure the most incurable illnesses. Missy was convinced that she held the cure to cancer. I don't know the woman's name, but people call her The Curer. Like The Eye, she delves into the art of black magic. I think she may be able to help your friend but there may be a price to pay, especially when you open the door to the other side."

"The other side? What do you mean 'the other side'?"

"I'm talking about the worst place imaginable, kid. The place that can crush a man's soul like it was soda can."

"You're talking about hell, aren't you?"

"Worse."

"No," Hogan backed off. "No way. I'm not doing that to Freddie."

"How about walking up to The Eye and politely asking him if he can help you out? I doubt he will, but you can try yourself. Get back with me and tell me what he says—"

"—How do we find this Curer lady?" asked Elisa.

"Rumor has it she resides underneath the Rose Garden of Vancouver Manor." Mike paused. "I've never checked out the place myself. I figured if I ever got caught in The Eye's gaze, then I'd make it easy and just kill myself. It's the logical way for me but I see you guys are close to one another, so I'd say we give it a try since option number one is clearly not on the table."

"Vancouver Manor?" Chi said, thinking. "I thought that place was like some kind of haunted mansion. I've heard about ghost hunters going there late at night with these infrared cameras to film the supernatural."

"And what did they find?"

Nobody answered Mike's question. So, Mike answered his own question: "That's what I thought."

"We're wasting our time."

"Taking your friend to The Curer is your only option."

Elisa asked eagerly, "How long does Freddie have?"

"Not long," he said. "Few days. Maybe a week. Every-day his body will grow weaker and weaker."

Hogan said, "Let's hold up here for the remainder of the night. Get some rest. Then, at dusk we'll make our decision as a group."

"And what about the Crow's Moon tomorrow night?" Chi asked. "We must stop The Eye before he casts his spell onto the world."

"That's the world's problem," Hogan said and turned to a shivering Freddie. "Right now, we have more important issues."

—

Hogan abruptly woke to the sounds of thunder rumbling overhead.

Flickers of blue light danced around the basement in nightclub fashion. Each time the lightning flashed through-out the basement, the thunder sounded closer together and much more louder, too.

Hogan sat upright and wiped the sweat from his fore-head. Normally, the basement was as cold as an igloo, but tonight the air was warm and sticky. Hogan figured it was from all of the body heat in the room. He fanned his cotton tee shirt, which was damp around the armpits. The fanning helped cool him down a bit. He also peeled the sleeping bag from the lower half of his body and let his legs breathe, which helped tremendously. He turned to his right and no-ticed Chi was sleeping soundlessly. Hogan thought his friend might've been playing possum, which he was known to do from time to time.

Next to Chi, Freddie lay on his back, his arms crossed over his chest like a dead man lying in a coffin.

Hogan stared at Freddie for the longest time, wondering whether or not Freddie was breathing. He concentrated on his chest.

Another flash of lightning brought out Freddie's chest inflating from a deep breath.

Hogan found relief in knowing he was okay—for now, at least.  He turned to his left where Mike was slumped over in a chair, his head flopped to the side, shotgun gripped in hand.

Suddenly, another rumble of thunder caused the foundation of the house to vibrate.

Hogan aimed his eyes on the still shadowy figure standing just below the basement window.

Another flash of lightning brought out the callous and cryptic face of The Eye!  He stood seductively in the shadows of the darkest corner of the basement, his mad eyes locked onto Hogan's eyes; however, his eyes appeared to have no effect on Hogan.

Another flash of lightning told yet another story: in the same spot stood another figure, *not* The Eye, but a figure much smaller in stature.  Hogan peered closer.  A pale boy, Hogan witnessed, no older than Hogan's age, slouched in the corner of the basement.

Then, another lightning flash showcased the stark nothingness inside the basement, only the haunting aftermath of a young boy's imagination.

Who would've thought?

A coat hanger.

—

After spending several hours rolling around and not finding any sleep whatsoever, Hogan decided enough was enough.  He wormed his way from the sleeping bag and stormed up the stairs to his parents' bedroom.  They were both sleeping.  The TV was still running as it always did throughout the night.  Hogan's father, who was lying on his side of the bed, had fallen asleep watching highlights from Sportcentral, while Hogan's mother remained in the recliner tucked in the corner of the room.  Hogan stood hunched over at the doorway rubbing his sleepy eyes, telling his mother that he couldn't sleep. He couldn't see his mother, only her silhouette, for she remained outside the cool glow of the TV. She stirred in the recliner and with her legs spread out, told him to take a pill. Hogan nodded. He waddled to the bathroom; and in the dark, he grabbed a magic pill from the medicine cabinet. He gave the bottle a maraca-like until the pill fell into the palm of his hand; and to make sure he was about to wash down the magic sleeping pill with a sip of faucet water, he switched on a light. He looked down at his palm and suddenly flinched. His hand appeared much different than before. His hand was arthritic, like Freddie's hand. It was also covered in liver spots and bruises just like Freddie's.

Hogan moved his eyes toward the mirror and flinched once more. His mouth dropped open in awe.

Horrified from the sight of his wrinkly face, he stumbled from the bathroom and didn't even bother mentioning his deteriorated state to his mother.

On the way to the basement, Hogan headed through the living room. He couldn't believe what was happening—or better yet, what had happened to him. How come he hadn't felt the side effects earlier? He wondered if not looking directly into The Eye's gaze but rather through the corner of his eye had something to do with his *late* transformation. Freddie was only a few feet away from The Eye when The Eye turned him into a geezer.

*How could this be?*

The telephone suddenly *rang*, the sound startled Hogan! He contemplated whether or not to answer the call. What if it was him, the devil? *Calling to rub it in*, Hogan thought.

He listened closely after the first ring, the throb of the blood pounding through his ears making it somewhat harder to hear. Despite his own body noise, he didn't hear anything from his parents, not a grunt or groan or the most obvious question as to who would be calling at this hour of the night. Hogan heard nothing except himself. So, after the second ring, he picked up the telephone before it could ring a third time and softly spoke into the mouthpiece: "Hello."

The delicate voice on the other end said, "Am I speaking to Hogan?"

Hogan couldn't make out the voice, although it sounded feminine.

"Yes," Hogan finally said, his voice shaking.

"This is Elisa's mother. Sorry to call so late, but I was wondering if you've seen my daughter."

"She's here."

"She is?"

"Yes."

"Thank God," she said, relieved. "She had me worried sick all night long. We were about to call the police."

"I'm sorry—"

"—Would you please tell her to call me as soon as she wakes up?"

Hogan's fingers started to tingle, the sensation similar, if not the same, as the sensation he got when he slept on his hand for an extended amount of time—which was also what the sexually depraved individuals at his school called a Saturday Night Wrist. Tiny pinpricks would flare up over his entire hand and then his arm until the entire limb became completely numb as if the arm itself didn't belong to him.

"Can you give her that message, Hogan? Can you, my dear?"

The sensation intensified and Hogan had trouble breathing.

"Hogan," the voice on the telephone said with a clearer tone, "you must forget about her. Do you hear me, Hogan? You *must* move on."

He pulled the telephone away from his ear and somehow the telephone melted into his hand, now beige and porcelain, the same color and smooth texture as the telephone. Hogan tried to squeeze his once aged hand, but now it was completely frozen.

Hogan woke—and suddenly panicked. His hipbone was cutting off the circulation to his right wrist, which felt as if it had been swallowed by his waist. He removed his wrist from out of his side and spent a couple of minutes wagging his wrist with his other hand. His wrist looked like a sheet of lasagna cooked al dente. When that didn't get the blood flowing, he started beating his wrist against his thigh—even the floor—until he could finally make a fist with his hand.

Once the minor panic attack passed, the storm, Hogan noticed, had already passed as well, giving way to a pinkish horizon. The light from dawn crept into the basement. Hogan noticed Chi and Freddie were sleeping, like before, not stirring or snoring, both their bodies in temporary sleep mode and their screensaver was primed for wrecking—if it was any other morning, that would certainly be the case, shaving cream, magic markers, and handfuls of flour, but Hogan was in no mood to be messing with his friends. The notion of spraying shaving cream into Chi's palm and then tickling his face had crossed his mind. But that was all it was, just a notion. He turned the other direction and found Elisa wide-awake and staring directly at Hogan. Her eyes were red and tired.

She said to him, "Can't sleep?"

"I just had a bad dream."

"I think I only got a couple of hours of sleep. Did you hear that storm last night?"

"Yeah. It woke me up."

Elisa wiped the morning crust from her eyes and took in a deep-morning breath.

"My parents are going to kill me," she moaned.

"She called last night," Hogan said. "Your mother. She said to call her."

Elisa cringed her face in bafflement. "She did?"

"Yeah. I think."

"Well, did she call or not?"

"She did," Hogan said after a short pause.

Elisa asked, "Are you okay, Hogan?"

Hogan didn't respond to the question. Yet, he remained deep in thought.

"Do you think Horus is like a werewolf or something?"

Elisa cleared her throat.

"It—it didn't really look like a werewolf to me. Why do you ask?"

"One of them was missing a hand."

"So what?"

"So, Killian Blanc had his hand severed. What are the odds? I mean, what if there's a connection?"

"You really think that thing is the same guy who came into Mr. Macho's?"

Hogan hung his head, depressed.

"I don't know what I'm saying."

"But there was more than one, right?"

"I swear I counted at least five of them. What if they're really all the same?"

"I don't know, Hogan, but anything is possible."

"*What if* Killian Blanc was one of those things before we saw him in Mr. Macho's."

"You mean like a shapeshifter—"

"—Yeah. Exactly!"

"What are you guys talking about?" Chi asked, starting to wake.

Hogan quieted and said shortly, "Nothing."

"Hogan thinks Killian Blanc might be a shapeshifter."

"No, I don't!"

"You just said. . . "

"Just forget about it." Hogan got up and checked on Freddie. He asked Chi, "How's he doing?"

Freddie attempted to wake from Hogan's presence by cracking open his wrinkly eyes. They were more wrinkled than they were last night. Hogan wondered if it had something to do with the dark.

"Hey, Freddie," he said.

Freddie vacantly stared at Hogan and for a moment, he looked as if he didn't know who Hogan was.

"Freddie?" Hogan said again, "how you doing?"

"Leave me alone," Freddie groaned.

"Sorry," Hogan backed away.

Last to wake was Mike. He rolled out of the chair and checked on the others.

"How's he doing?" Mike asked Hogan.

"Would everybody just leave me alone. . . "

"Give him space, guys."

Mike and the rest of the gang stepped outside the house.

"I better get going," Mike said to the gang but mainly to Hogan. "So, what are you kids going to do for the rest of the day?"

"We'll keep an eye on Freddie," Hogan said.

"Please do. He might not act like it, but he needs you guys."

Elisa says, "I have to get back home."

"I know," Chi said tired as he kept a distance from Hogan. "Me too."

"So, what about Freddie's parents?" asked Elisa. "You know they're going to want to know where their son is."

"They can't know what happen. Not yet."

"Why not?"

"They just can't."

"So, what do we tell them if they ask?"

"If they ask any of you, just say that you haven't seen him—"

"—But he's sick, Hogan. He *needs* a doctor."

"The only person who can save him now is The Curer," Mike said.

"Then, we take him to see her," Hogan said over some thought.

"You're in charge."

"Then, it's done. We take Freddie to the Curer." He looked around at the others. "Agreed?"

Elisa cleared her throat.

"Okay."

Lastly, Hogan nodded at Chi.

"Whatever," said Chi.

"We'll take him at dusk," Mike said. "In the meantime,

you kids keep your head down."

"Where you going?" Hogan asked Mike as Mike started to walk away.

Mike said to Hogan, "I need more weapons."

## 6. The Seeds We Sow

*Tonight is the night. Tonight, we come alive.*

L ATER that morning while Hogan was spending most of his time scoping out his street in the neighborhood through the cracked blinds—his eyes constantly moving like an oscillating head of a sprinkler—a familiar car pulled up to the side of the curb across the street and parked. Hogan rested his eyes upon the two same detectives from before sitting inside the car. He wasn't aware of the vehicle right away because it blended in with the ancient willow oak trees which lined his entire street. What really drew Hogan's attention was the *squeaking* of what might've been wet brakes.

"What is it, Hoagie?" Freddie said from the creaky futon.

"You remember those two detectives who came by your house and asked us all those questions about Killian Blanc?"

Freddie thought long and hard about the past events, but he came up short for The Eye's spell was at the early stages of incinerating each memory in his head. Once the spell ran its course, nothing was going to be left of his brain but a big waste of space.

"No," Freddie drawled, his glossy eyes moving around in sheer bewilderment. "I don't think so."

Perturbed from Freddie's deteriorating state, Hogan said to himself, "Of course." He turned toward Freddie, walked closer to the futon, and said as if he was thinking aloud, "I wonder if they know anything about last night."

Hogan started to pace around the basement, most of his focus directed at the floor, each thought turning through his mind like a gear.

Freddie said over the heavy silence, "Last night?"

"Yes," Hogan said louder. "Remember? The Eye?"

"The Eye?" Freddie drifted for a moment and it was like he was caught in a state of constant bewilderment and each *word* or phrase or idea was like a new discovery for him. His eyes lit with wonder. "We," he stuttered. "We have to stop him!"

Hogan stopped pacing, studied poor Freddie and that childish wonder etched across his face, and he found himself delving straight into a state of depression.

"We will," he said optimistically, "but first," he rallied, "we're going to stop by Vancouver Manor and find a cure for you."

The temporary excitement fled Freddie as quickly as it passed him and a gnawing pain had taken its place. Freddie gripped his hand, which looked much worse than it did last night. Even Freddie's index finger was like a warped sausage link that had been stuffed too tightly into a casing; the tip was bent to a near ninety-degree angle. Both his pinkie and ring fingers had already started to badly curl into a letter c position. Hogan thought Freddie's pinkie finger was broken for sure.

"Whatever you do, please hurry," pleaded Freddie.

Hogan grabbed a glass of lukewarm water from the table and handed it to his friend. The poor boy could hardly hold the glass in his two hands.

Hogan tended to Freddie by helping him raise the glass to his lips.

"What hurts?" asked Hogan.

"Everything," Freddie replied, trembling. "Everything.

My bones. Every move I make, my body hurts."

Hogan placed the glass on the carpet and touched Freddie on the shoulder.

"Hang in there," he said to his old friend.

—

As Freddie was taking a nap, Hogan took advantage of the opportunity and stepped outside to grab some fresh air. The detective's car was no longer parked on the street. Hogan only gave it a second's thought, knowing that if had given it anymore thought, then he would've never gone. He grabbed his bike from the garage and rode to Main Street. Depending on traffic, on a normal day, it was about a ten to fifteen minute ride from his house. With traffic, he was looking at around twenty minutes or so. Traffic was somewhat congested on the highway due to road work—Orson Valley was always putting up new roads due to the many potholes. The increase in the town's volume had also played an important factor in the constant construction. More residents meant more space and more space meant more lotteries.

Traffic or not, Hogan managed to hit Main Street in a record time of seven minutes. He rode his bike to the same alley where he and the rest of the gang had been confronted by Horus. The scene was more than hectic, to say the least. Police officers had the entire alley blocked off with yellow caution tape. Hogan saw two blurry-faced detectives working the scene. He couldn't quite see what they were examining—*the watch*, Hogan thought. He remembered Horus ripping the watch from his wrist and then it shattering all over the ground.

A local news crew was camped outside the alley. One of the reporters was primping her hair and rehearsing her lines for the upcoming report.

Several locals were gathered around, trying to squeeze answers from the surrounding police officers. Hogan overheard the gossip among the locals. The only words Hogan managed to catch in the wild ramblings of one elderly lady were *Mr. Ortega attacked by animal* and then *hospitalized*.

As Hogan stood on the tips of his toes for a better look, he saw that one detective, Billups, wandering throughout the crime scene.

In that glimpse of a moment when Hogan's eyes were focusing in on the scene, Billups glanced over his shoulder at Hogan and for a moment, they made eye contact.

Tempted to tell one of the detectives about Horus, about what he—or better yet—what it had done, Hogan decided to leave the scene. And he did so in quite a hurry. He rode his bike to Clay's. He walked up to the door, but the store was closed.

He peeked into the store, hoping to find movement inside.

The only movement came in the reflection of the window.

Hogan couldn't move an inch.

The blood ran from his face, leaving it as bloodless as a corpse.

He rotated around and witnessed Polly standing on the curb. She was holding a steak knife down by her side and she was picking at her dress with the tip of the knife. Hogan followed a drop of blood trailing down her leg.

"Why are you ignoring me?" she asked Hogan, but Hogan had no words.

—

Exactly at a quarter past three in the afternoon a spotless black Rolls-Royce Silver Spirit with tinted windows pulled up in front of Elisa's house. Behind the steering wheel sat a frail Killian Blanc, whose appearance had changed dramatically from the time we last saw him, which happened to be the night that he bumped into the gang at Mr. Macho's Famous Tacos and Burritos. His hand had been replaced with a prosthetic—and one that was poorly put together. Each finger was like a Popsicle stick. He had no flexibility in his knuckles and his immobility made his prosthetic hand look like a pair of thongs gripping the steering wheel. He was much thinner, too, and much uglier. The hue of his skin appeared as if he was a man suffering from jaundice or cyanosis or both. His lips were purplish-blue; yet, his eyes were like two yellow marbles lost in the red sockets of his skull. His cheeks were sunken in as well. Whatever was eating away inside Killian, it had taken away so much of a man and left very little behind to savor.

In the backseat sat The Eye.

Once the Silver Spirit had come to a complete stop, The Eye leaned forward over the driver's seat, gently touched his gloved hand on Killian's shoulder, and instructed him to keep the engine running.

Killian abided by The Eye's commands with a stern nod of his head.

The Eye stepped out of the Silver Spirit, walked up to the front door as if the pathway was his own red carpet, and rang the doorbell.

Elisa's mother, Fran, short for Francesca, was a petite lady who only stood five feet when she was wearing her off white lazy-day slippers around the house; but, on a good day, mainly Mondays and Fridays or whenever she needed that boost of energy to spring her through the remainder of the week, she stood an inch or two higher, depending on the type of shoe that she was wearing on that day—normally, on Monday mornings, which were the most hectic of all the days, she'd wear vermillion stilettos around the house. It wasn't the most ideal shoe to wear while prancing throughout the kitchen, but, to Fran, she made it work.

As Fran answered the door with a furrow of her brows and an almost naive tilt of her head, The Eye appeared like a giant to her and she found herself shrinking by the second.

"May I help you?" asked Fran as The Eye removed his sunglasses.

The Eye didn't respond to Fran, no need to; in fact, he

didn't need to do anything. As soon as he made eye contact with Fran, he owned her.

When Fran attempted to speak yet again, she suddenly fell into a state of instant paralysis. The Eye shouldered his way inside the house while Elisa's mother remained statue-like, her now bloodshot eyes carefully tracking The Eye.

Next to fall victim to The Eye's power was Elisa's father. When he went to check on his wife, he was greeted by The Eye. One simple flick of the eyes—not even a mere glance but, more or less, an indiscreet acknowledgement of presence—had turned Elisa's father paralyzed. He was left frozen in mid-stride, statue-like, his mouth dropped ever so slightly from an unfinished *what*.

The Eye didn't say a word to Elisa's father, didn't need to, nor did he want to. Instead, he kept moving forward as if Elisa's parents were nothing more than pieces of furniture to him. The Eye casually walked up the carpeted stairs and then made his way down a narrow hallway until he reached Elisa's bedroom; and when he entered her room, Elisa was sitting in front of a vanity with her back turned to the doorway. She didn't even hear The Eye creep into her room for she was so deep in thought.

When she finally saw the black figure looming behind her, she turned her shoulder and found herself face to face with The Eye.

"Stand," he commanded.

Elisa stood from her seat.

"Where is it?" asked The Eye.

Elisa didn't know what The Eye was talking about; yet, she remained too scared to speak.

"Let me see," commanded The Eye.

Elisa started to shake from The Eye's dark presence.

He removed the hat from his head, revealing the top of his skull. His entire scalp was clean bone with only several strands of thin and wiry hair glued over the very top of his skull in the most wicked comb over; and when he ran his gloved hand over his head, the hair fell over the sides of his head like dead vines.

Tears rose in Elisa's eyes, not falling, yet hanging onto the very edges of her bottom eyelids. She blinked away the tears and the tears rolled down the center of her face. She could hardly bring herself to look at The Eye's grotesque appearance. She could hardly catch a breath.

"Easy, child," The Eye said to Elisa and wiped away the tears from her cheeks. "Breathe," he whispered to her, "just breathe."

Elisa inhaled through her nose and exhaled through her mouth before she started to hyperventilate.

"There you go," The Eye said. "Better?"

Elisa could hardly bring herself to nod.

"Did you know I grew up on a tobacco farm?" The Eye asked as he kneeled down to Elisa's level.

She didn't respond. The Eye wasn't expecting one from her.

"Everyday after school," he said, "we—as in me and my brother—weren't allowed dinner until we hung the tobacco leaves out to dry." His eyes drifted in reflection and he said in a side-thought, "Even till this day, that worker's spirit is engrained in me. Anyway," The Eye faced Elisa, "one day, my father was bedridden with the flu. I watched him work through about anything. I thought he was made out of steel. It's true." He turned away, thought, and said to Elisa, "My father had never taken a sick day in his life, but he couldn't get out of bed that day. I knew it was serious. He asked me if I could stay home for the day and run the farm. We survived off the land and I knew that, even if my father missed a day's work, we would suffer severely." The Eye said proudly, "I stayed home, me and my brother both. He was probably no older than yourself. I, a couple of years older, but that day, we had to become men. If I had to do it all over again," The Eye said, eyes watering, "I would've gone to school. It happened so fast." The Eye shook his head, as if the thought of what happened had hurt every inch of his body. "While I was riding the tractor, my shoelaces somehow got caught in the tractor's blade. I couldn't pull myself free. I couldn't move. I screamed out for help. My brother rushed to my aide. As he was trying to cut me loose, he got dragged into the tractor's blade. I knew," The Eye choked up for a moment, then tightened his jaw as well as every muscle in his face, "I knew he was dead as soon as it happened. I lost consciousness. When I finally came to, I was someone else, someone unrecognizable. It was like something had taken over me. From that day forward, when I look in the mirror, I relive that day." The Eye grabbed her by the hand and leaned closer. "You must understand that sometimes we turn into the people who we're supposed to be, while other times we choose our own path."

"But *you* had a choice," Elisa said, crying.

"You're wrong, Elisa," he said, standing to his feet. In Elisa's eye, he appeared as if he was a mile-high in the air. "I didn't choose to be The Eye. The Eye, it had chose me, and now he has chosen *you*."

Elisa suddenly backed away and started shivering.

"What is happening to me?" asked Elisa.

"May I?" The Eye asked as he looked down at Elisa's abdomen.

The Eye peeled the bottom half of Elisa's shirt, revealing a badly infected cut along the side of Elisa's abdomen.

"You don't have long now," he said as he removed his glove and felt Elisa's temperature along her forehead with the backside of his hand.

Elisa trembled from The Eye's touch.

The Eye ran his hand along the front of her face, causing her eyes to close.

She suddenly fainted and he caught Elisa as soon as she fell to the floor.

The Eye carried Elisa to her bed, tucked her underneath the covers, and stood over her. He reached into his coat pocket, removed a clay flowerpot from his pocket, and then removed the plastic lid from the pot.

Next, The Eye placed the pot onto the nightstand next to

Elisa's bed and removed yet another item from his pocket. He untwisted a brown bottle and dropped a droplet of yellow liquid from a dropper into the soil.

In a matter of seconds, a tiny green bud sprouted from the soil.

"I'll see you soon, my child," The Eye said to Elisa and exited the house the same way he came in.

—

Freddie was waiting on Hogan as soon as Hogan walked through the door. Freddie asked a speechless Hogan where he had been and why he didn't tell him that he was leaving him alone. Hogan ignored his friend's nagging and eased farther into the room.

Freddie turned confused, more worried for Hogan, who still remained in a trance-like state.

"What's wrong?" asked Freddie.

Hogan finally acknowledged Freddie, the crow's feet on the far corners of his eyes, the sagging bags underneath his eyes, the pink sunspots scattered all over his forehead, and worse, his posture, which appeared more hunched over than before. There was no lying in that Freddie was aging more and more rapidly.

"I just bumped into Polly," he said, trying not to stare at Freddie.

"Who?" Freddie said owl-like. "Polly? Who's Polly?"

"The girl who's been stalking me, remember?"

Freddie was still confused. Hogan wondered if it was already starting to happen.

*Will he remember me?*

"Polly," Hogan emphasized. "You know her, Freddie! She's in our class! Brunette hair! Has a mole on the side of her chin!"

"Polly," Freddie said. "Yes. I remember. Chocolate face!"

"Yes," Hogan said with relief. "Chocolate face."

"Did you ask her out?"

"No," Hogan said in disgust. "She tried to kill me!"

"Kill you? What are you talking about?"

"She was mad at me for some reason. She was trying to ah—hurt herself."

"Hurt herself? Why would she do that?"

"She said I was ignoring her. I tried to talk to her, but she ah—she ah—"

"—She what, Hogan?"

"She tried to stab me."

"What did you do?"

"I ah—"

"—Hogan," Freddie said carefully, "*what* did you do?"

"I ran away," Hogan sputtered. "She chased after me. I thought maybe I'd lose her in the woods. So, when I was crossing Highway 60, I heard a car horn behind me. I kept running, though. And when I got to the woods, I—I looked over my shoulder and she was lying on the street. Ah—She wasn't moving—"

"—Wasn't moving? What do you mean?"

"I mean I think she was hit by a car."

"Did you help her?"

"No," Hogan said. "How could I? She was trying to kill me!"

"Hogan," Freddie said solemnly, "we have to tell somebody."

"We tell nobody! You understand! We can't!"

"Why?"

"We just can't!"

"You mean *you* can't?"

"It's not my fault she was hit by a car!"

"So, she did get hit by a car?"

"Yes," Hogan said, "I mean, I don't know." He stepped closer to Freddie. "Please, Freddie. You can't tell anyone about what happened. Okay?"

Freddie hung his head for a moment.

"Okay?" Hogan said louder.

"Okay," Freddie said. "Then, *forget* it ever happened?"

"How can I?"

"You just do," Freddie said seriously.

"How?"

Freddie smacked Hogan in the back of the head.

Hogan cringed and grabbed his head.

"What was that for?" asked Hogan.

"Forget!" he exclaimed.

"Okay," Hogan whined, backing away. "Geez Louise. You sure are grumpy."

Grimacing, Freddie retorted, "You haven't seen nothing ye—ouch!" Freddie grabbed the side of his jaw while he tongued something in his mouth, something loose. Freddie reached his finger inside his mouth and pulled out his back left molar tooth.

Hogan gasped, "Freddie—"

Freddie showed Hogan the bloody tooth.

Appalled, he stared at Hogan and said, "What's happening to me?"

—

An hour before dusk, Hogan went back to his lookout spot in front of the basement window and scoped out the neighborhood street. There was an unusual amount of activity in the neighborhood: three mothers were power-walking away calories; only four houses down a man wearing glasses was buffing his Mustang; several uppity eighth graders from the far corners of Meadow Haven were riding mountain bikes through Hogan's turf; two houses down a businessman was mowing his lawn; not too far away a girl was listening to a Walkman while walking a white Chihuahua.

Even though Hogan didn't see the detectives anywhere in sight, he decided not to take any chances.

As he did earlier, he snuck out the backdoor.

Freddie wasn't too far behind.

They ended up taking a trail through the woods.

Freddie stopped several times for he was too weak and cold. Hogan wrapped a quilt that his grandmother had knitted for him when he was a baby around his shoulders and the two headed toward the train tracks behind Chi's house.

Along the way, Freddie stopped a few moments to catch his breath. Hogan tended to Freddie, whose condition was worsening from the strain he put on his body. Hogan readjusted the quilt over Freddie's shoulders and helped him walk.

—

Elisa woke up to a bright purple flower on her nightstand. She looked over the flower, wondering how it came to be on her nightstand. She scratched her eyes, thinking maybe she was still caught in a dream. She left her bedroom and walked downstairs where her mother and father were in the kitchen; her mother was preparing dinner while her father was reading the newspaper at the kitchen table. They didn't even say a word to their daughter; in fact, they didn't even welcome her into the kitchen. Elisa sneaked out—or better yet— walked out and met up with Chi, who was waiting on Elisa. He asked her what took her so long. Apparently, he had been waiting for quite some time. She said that she had fallen asleep and had the strangest dream.

—

"Hoagie!" Freddie called out.

Hogan finally answered.

"What?" said Hogan.

"You're going the wrong way," he said. "The tracks are this way."

Freddie stopped at a fork in the trail and pointed toward the right.

"Right," Hogan said with clarity. "I wasn't thinking."

Surprised, Hogan studied Freddie and couldn't help but

think of his incredible sense of direction.

"You're still thinking about Polly, aren't you?"

"You remember?"

"Remember what?"

"You know, the accident."

"What accident?"

"The one we were talking about earlier—"

"—You know what you need to do, Ho," Freddie interrupted. "What you need is to grow a pair of testicles and ask her out." Hogan stopped and watched his friend ramble on and on. The thought alone of the possibility that Freddie didn't remember the conversation the two had not even an hour ago caused Hogan to become sick to his stomach. He didn't say anything else, didn't bother stopping or interrupting Freddie, didn't do much of anything but stand back and observe and listen. "You pretend to not like the girl or find the most ridiculous reasons not to like the girl, yet you can't stop talking about her. Polly this or Polly that. Admit it for once. You like her. And you're too chickenshit to ask her out because you're afraid somebody else will come along— somebody better than Polly—and you think you might be stuck with second-best for the rest of your life. You're going to have to accept the fact that we *all* have baggage," he widened his bloodshot eyes and pointed his crooked finger at Hogan, "including you, Hoagie. If you can't accept that reality, then you, my friend, you are going to die a lonely, lonely old man.

Hogan didn't comment on Freddie's tirade. Instead, he kept walking. Freddie didn't even follow until he saw the depression slide over Hogan's shoulders as if he was wearing a backpack full of free weights. Hogan stopped, turned around, and waited for Freddie to catch up, and the two of them together kept moving forward. Freddie only took a few steps before he stopped and spat out a thick string of blood. Hogan stopped as well; he couldn't help but notice the two teeth on the ground. This time, Hogan didn't ask if Freddie was okay or if he wanted to stop and take a break. He didn't say a word to Freddie.

When Hogan and Freddie made it to the old train tracks, Elisa and Chi were kicking around pebbles and looked as if they had been waiting for a while. Chi stepped in, gave Hogan a break, and took his place in nursing Freddie. Hogan responded with a subtle flick of his head, a nonverbal way of saying *thank you*. The gang remained relatively quiet, not happy or sad to see one another. Everybody knew that Freddie didn't have much longer before he wasn't going to be able to walk on his own, including Freddie.

—

By the time the gang arrived at Vancouver Manor, it was already dark outside. They waited outside for about five minutes or so—mostly in a tense silence—until a car burning its high beams pulled in the front of the half-mile-long driveway stretching underneath rows of blossoming cherry trees. Mike stepped out of the car, didn't even greet them with a *hey* or *hello*; yet, he went straight to the trunk where he grabbed an assault rifle from a bagful of weapons.

Chi started in awe, "Are those. . . "

"Yeah, kid," he said and pulled out a couple of magazines.

"Why do we need weapons to see the Curer?" asked Elisa.

"The Curer isn't exactly the 'friendly' type," Mike said. "Rumor has it she has traps surrounding the entire place. Better safe than sorry, that's my motto."

"What about us?"

"What about you?"

"Don't we get a weapon?"

"No way."

"That's no fair!" Chi cried out. "How come you get a weapon and we don't?"

"Because if I give you one of these, then you'll probably end up accidentally shooting one of your friends or even worse, shooting yourself in the face."

"I'll be careful."

"I said, 'No.'"

"Come on," Chi begged. "What if we see one of those things again? We have to defend ourselves."

Mike paused, thought it over, weighed the risk.

He pulled out a .45 from the trunk.

He showed the semi-automatic handgun to Chi.

"Have you fired one of these before?"

Chi hesitated. "Yeah, of course," he said, looking at the others. "All the time."

"Be honest, kid," Mike sniffed out the lie.

"I've shot one before!"

"No he hasn't," Elisa said flatly over Mike's shoulder.

"Here," Mike said and went over the basics of the gun. "Shooting 101 in only five seconds." Mike pointed to the safety. "This is your safety—"

"—I know," Chi sounded off.

"Are you finished?"

Chi didn't respond.

Mike said, "Safety is here. The gun will not fire if the safety is on. See," he aimed the gun somewhere in the distance and pulled the trigger and demonstrated to Chi one of the most vital components of the gun.

The gun did *not* fire.

Why?

Because the safety was switched *on*.

"So," he said, "always keep the safety on until you're ready to use it. Are you following?"

"Yeah," Chi said, bobbing his head.

"That goes for all of you. Understand?"

"We're listening," said Hogan.

"When you're ready to fire the weapon, turn the safety off." Mike showed the rest of the gang how to turn off the safety. "Got it?"

In near-perfect synchronization, the gang bobbed their heads.

"Now," Mike said over a sigh, "this is where the ammo goes." He pointed at the handle, showed the gang how to unload and load a magazine. "Got it?"

Again, the gang's head bounced up and down like bobble-head dolls.

"Once the magazine is loaded, then it's ready to fire. Point and squeeze." Before he handed Chi the handgun, he emphasized, "If you see one of those creatures, you make a hundred and one percent sure you're ready to squeeze the trigger. And, the number one rule: never—I mean *never*—point your gun at another person. This isn't a toy. Do you understand?"

"It's not a toy," Chi said, rolling his eyes. "Got it."

Mike switched on the safety and handed the gun to Chi, who, in return, looked it over as if he had never held a gun before.

He noticed Elisa acknowledging Chi's overt interest in the handgun, and he suddenly got all serious and carefully held it down by his side.

Mike started to hand out weapons.

A revolver to Elisa.

He went over the basics with Elisa. She handed the revolver back to Mike.

"Sorry," Elisa said, her calmness came off more strange than normal. "I don't feel comfortable with one."

Elisa backed away as if she was allergic to the steel of the revolver.

The strange reaction caused Hogan to look over Elisa.

"Fair enough," he turned the revolver to Hogan. "How about you?"

Hogan confidently grabbed the revolver.

Mike went over the basics once more with Hogan.

Then, Mike showed Freddie a smaller handgun, easy to use, light in weight.

"I can barely move my damn fingers," he said weakly. "I'll stay behind you guys."

"Here here," Elisa said as she placed Freddie's limp arm around her shoulder. "Lemme help."

"All right then," Mike looked to Chi and then Hogan.

"Don't make me regret giving y'all those."

"We'll be fine," Hogan said soberly and looked to Chi. "Right?"

"Fine," he reassured Hogan and then, most importantly, Mike, who happened to be Chi's hardest sell.

## 7. A Brief History of Vancouver

*I told myself, 'We keep moving. We can't stop now.*
*We've come too far.' And so, we did.*

THE silence only made matters worse.

Hogan desperately tried to loosen the tension within the gang by asking Freddie questions mainly about his health but each answer was short and rude and to Freddie, Hogan was starting to sound like his mother.

"How you doing over there, Freddie?" Hogan asked Freddie while he and the rest of the gang made their way down the stretch of driveway.

"I. . . feel. . . like. . . like shit. . . does that answer your question?" Freddie returned in short bursts as if each word came with the package of a deep breath.

Not even twenty yards of walking, and Elisa had worked up a colony of sweat beads along her forehead as well as the creases and crevasses of her body.

"I could use a hand over here," Elisa said, stopping to catch her breath.

Even stopping to rest, ruining the flow of moving forward and having to start back up, one step at a time, exerted more unneeded energy.

Hogan gave Chi a tap on the shoulder.

"Chi," he said, nodding at Freddie.

Chi rolled his eyes; his shoulders dropped a few inches like a stray dog. He got on the other side of Freddie, placed Freddie's arm around his shoulder, which caused Freddie to groan.

"Come on, Freddie," Chi rallied. "We're almost there."

—

Mike and the gang arrived at Vancouver Manor. From the noticeable decay of the house, it went without saying that the history was rich around here—and like all history, dark and bloody.

The manor was built by William Fitzgerald (a newspaper tycoon from London) in the late 17th century after the French Revival had spread throughout America. Fitzgerald decided to name the manor after the George Vancouver as a result of his somewhat mild obsession with the famous yet controversial navigator. Nearly a century later—1886 to be exact—the port city of Vancouver, Canada, was named after the late navigator. Around town, Fitzgerald was known as a rather eccentric man who, on an occasion, was shunned like an outcast by his grossly appearance. Throughout town, it was said that he practiced in holistic medicine—his method of using leeches to suck the toxins from his blood being his most disputable and, of course, unsavory practice among local villagers. These practices had left Fitzgerald a pale and gauntly man with ulcers along his face, as well as his body. After the many years of solitude, Fitzgerald was later discovered by his estranged sister, Alice, who was invited to stay at the manor in America. When Alice arrived at the manor, there wasn't much left of Fitzgerald's body. Only skull and bones. Alice was skeptical of William's death—tormented really. She was certain her brother's death had to do with what was buried underneath the estate. And what had possibly given Alice such ideas?

Alice, who ended up taking care of the manor after Fitzgerald's death, claimed that one night she was visited by a "girl on fire."

What William Fitzgerald didn't know was that Vancouver Manor was built on top of the buried ruins of the Castle of Cambridge, which had burned to the ground after the town of Orson Valley had accused Charles Cambridge's daughter of witchcraft—this was, of course, not long after the witchcraft trials in Salem, Massachusetts. Legend went that the wealthy statesman of Sourlack and his entire family, including his daughter, Margarine, perished in the fire; and from that day forward, very few people had step foot onto these lands—except for its following owner, William Fitzgerald, and then its next owner, who didn't discover the land until close to two hundred years later.

And in that gap of great silence, the history surrounding Vancouver Manor only grew darker, bloodier. Some even considered the lands to be cursed by evil spirits, tormented demons, lost souls—girls on fire—or worse, it was a gateway to the great Inferno. Others, especially the ones who relished in the history behind the Cambridge name, used the stories to scare bed wetters.

The country house, once pristine white, was now an off white, somewhere between a grayish-brown color; the left portion of the house was choked by a wild overgrowth of vining parthenocissus climbing in serpentine patterns up to the second floor; the bare windows as black and empty as voids, provoking the illest shadows born from neither decay or darkness; the two raised copper chimneys on top of each wing stained the roof below from the many rainstorms with the natural patina formed over time from the tarnish produced by severe oxidation.

In front of the entranceway a bicycle, as rusty as a neglected junkyard car, laid on its side. The chain, as well as the sprocket, had been stripped from the bicycle. One of the wheels was flat. The other one, like the parts, was missing as well. The bicycle was so far gone that even the slightest touch could cause the bike to crumble to pieces.

Aware of the bicycle, Hogan kneeled down to the soggy

ground; and as he was about to lay his finger upon the handlebars, his attention was suddenly pulled toward the front entrance door, which remained open and dark.

A cold, deathly draft blew from the door like the devil's breath followed by the sound of a million whispers.

Mike touched Hogan on the shoulder and said, "Don't touch anything, you hear?"

Startled, Hogan snapped his head toward Mike.

"Why," he muttered. "Why not?"

"Cause I said so," Mike said bluntly.

It was fair to say that Hogan was more than drawn to the country house—his eyes were magnetically pulled almost in its haunted appeal.

"What's in there?" he asked Mike.

Mike hesitated, wondering whether or not to tell Hogan about the horrors.

"Mike," he persisted, "does anybody still live in there?"

"Only ghosts, kid," Mike finally answered, "according to the stories."

"Stories? What stories?"

"According to all the 'stories,' the place was lost many years ago—least a decade. Now all that remains is a tomb."

"What happened?" asked Chi.

"A family once lived here," he explained. "Wife, husband, child—a girl. The husband, Jóhan Halldórsdóttir, a famous showman from New York, considered a controversial figure. Jóhan was known to exhibit—how do I say—'spooky' things."

"What kind of 'spooky' things?"

Mike thought, then answered, "The corpse of the Norwegian minotaur, the wing of Gabriel—"

"—Minotaur," said Chi. "No way!"

"Yes way," Mike said. "He displayed all of these relics throughout museums and made profits from the masses. Jóhan was also known to have delved into the art of black magic, The Eye being one of his *greatest* attractions. Many doubted Jóhan's performers, questioning their authenticity.

Simply put, kid: they thought they were conducting parlor tricks. As for the relics, people didn't know whether or not the exhibitions were real or fake, or fairy tales, the leftover remnants of ceremonial objects used by indigenous tribes to worship deities. All make believe—"

"—Deities?" Elisa said in confusion.

"Gods," he clarified as he and the rest of the gang stood waiting in front of the entranceway to the manor. "After a while Jóhan's wife—Anita was her name—was lonely and her loneliness turned her into something far worse. She desperately tried to ward off the isolation by making frequent trips into town to talk to the locals; she did everything she could to keep her mind occupied by focusing her attention on her garden. She went to the nursery everyday to buy seeds, home improvement stores for the right tools. Eventually, Jóhan's success turned locals against her. One day, they stopped talking. And when the talking stopped, the voices started."

*Voices*, Hogan thought.

"So," Mike said over a sigh, "she stopped making trips into town. By then, she was too scared to leave the house. Too ashamed. Her husband would come back home for a couple of days and then he'd hit the road again. For months on end, Jóhan left Anita here in this place. Alone. Scared."

"What about the girl?" asked Hogan. "Didn't she keep her company?"

"Maybe," Mike said. "I don't know."

Hogan drifted farther into Mike's story.

*When Jóhan returned from traveling around the world, indulging people in the bizarre while, at the same time, becoming a worldwide sensation, Anita had already started to change. Story goes that one evening Anita wanted to celebrate her husband's return as well as his success. So, she invited his merry band of circus freaks to his country house for a lavish dinner party. She prepared a feast for all of the guests. However, nobody saw Jóhan. Everybody was asking about him: 'Where's Jóhan?' Finally, Anita broke the news that her husband was not feeling well. He had come down with a bug from his travels and he said he didn't want to be disturbed—Anita's words. The guests felt awful. But, Anita continued the party without Jóhan anyway. The guests continued to fill up their bellies with alcohol and the most succulent meat. They were so full that they even had to unbuckle their belts and unbutton the top button of their pants. The party raged on. The guests waited for hours, hoping for Jóhan to join them, but not once did he muster the strength to come downstairs to join his friends. Jóhan waited behind the bedroom door of the master bedroom, nothing more than a child-like shadow flickering in the candlelight underneath the doorway. Days later, The Eye, concerned for the well being of his friend and colleague, visited the manor. The door was open. So, he walked inside, only to find Anita in the master bedroom, her nails broken off her fingers, the tips of her fingers worn down to the nub from where she had been scratching the walls. In a feverish state, she said Jóhan was trapped in the walls, speaking to her. The Eye searched the entire house for Jóhan but couldn't find him anywhere. Lastly, The Eye checked the kitchen where he came across a sink full of dirty pots, pans, and dishes, the same ones used at the party just days before. Untouched. Beside the chopping board, he found Jóhan's watch. Bloody. The Eye thought the unthinkable. He rushed back upstairs to Anita where she confessed what she had done to her husband—*

"—She didn't do what I think she did, did she?"

Mike said to Elisa, "Jóhan was never sick the night of the party. Jóhan was never upstairs in bed. Jóhan was right underneath their noses the entire time."

"Oh Dios mío!" cried Chi.

"That's gross, Mike," Hogan said to Mike.

Chi asked, "You mean they had no idea they were eating that dude—"

"—Chi! Come on!"

"That's right, kid," Mike said, ignoring Elisa. "They say you can still hear Anita scratching on the walls at night."

"What a bunch of bull!"

"So, what does the Curer have to do with Jóhan and his

crazy freaking wife?"

"She's the girl," said Mike. "She's Jóhan's daughter."

—

The courtyard behind the house, like the country house itself, was overgrown with parthenocissus, honeysuckle, an abundance of common ivy, and purple bougainvillea, the death and decay underneath making the ripest soil for vegetation to flourish.

Mike and the gang came across a bed of yellow roses, full and bright and healthy.

As twilight set in, Mike pulled out a flashlight from his jacket pocket and waved the light around the rose garden until the light landed on what looked like a cellar door covered in vines at the end of the bed.

Mike passed the flashlight to Hogan, who made sure to keep the light on the cellar door while Mike began to tug and pull away vines until the path was clear.

Meanwhile, Elisa spotted a white material buried in the soil. With her foot, she brushed aside the soil, thinking that the material might've been a piece of glass or plastic buried in the earth. She kept brushing aside the soil while Mike and Hogan continued to tug away at vines. She cleared away at least three feet in length of soil. She kneeled down and knocked on what looked like the belly of a white surfboard. The material was as hard as bone and there was so much of it. It was shaped like a skull, one really, really big skull.

She wandered away from the gang as she brushed away more soil and found more of that bone-like material.

Chi said from behind, "Elisa?"

Elisa stopped digging and turned to Chi.

"Yeah," she said.

"Let's go," he said.

Elisa joined the others even though she wasn't there—mentally, that is. She couldn't stop thinking about all of that bone.

*What is that stuff?*

Mike suddenly opened the cellar doors, giving way to a cloud of dust.

Once the dust finally dissipated, a set of stairs spiraling into darkness was revealed before their eyes.

"You mean, we have to go down there?" asked Chi.

"No time to be scared of the dark, kid."

Freddie suddenly had a coughing fit.

Elisa kneeled down and nursed Freddie. She, too, didn't appear too well either, Hogan pointed out as he started to become more suspicious of Elisa's strange behavior.

From a distance, a couple of twigs and branches popped and cracked, echoing deep in the woods behind the manor.

"We don't have much time," Mike said and grabbed the flashlight from Hogan's hand. He pointed the light at Chi. "You're either with us or not. What's it going to be, kid?"

Chi took a step back, his face long, glossy eyes swollen with terror.

"I can't," he whined, dropping the pistol to the ground.

Hogan reached out his hand.

"A horseman never abandons another," he said to Chi. "Remember?"

Chi felt a frail, papery hand slip into his left hand. He looked down at the hand and saw Freddie hunched next to him. Freddie's puppy dog eyes stared into Chi's with both confusion and wonder, as if he was trying to understand the words coming out of a mouth for the first time.

Next to place her hand over Freddie's hand was Elisa.

Lastly, Hogan placed his hand over Elisa's hand.

"Okay," Chi said and hung his head against Freddie's shoulder. "I'll do it."

"We have to go," Mike said, waiting at the cellar door.

—

As the gang battled the darkness, Detective Billups battled an agent far worse.

Detective Augustine rang Hogan's doorbell once more but received no answer. She turned to her partner, Billups.

"Got any other ideas," she said disappointedly.

By the time the detective completed the rest of her sentence, Billups had already made his way around the house.

"Billups. . . " Augustine whispered, ". . . what are you doing?"

Billups didn't answer.

"Billups?"

"I'm doing my job, Gabby," he said arrogantly and then returned with a question of his own. "What the hell are you doing?"

Augustine followed her partner to the back of the house as if she had no other choice, nonetheless, a choice that she didn't approve of.

When she caught up to Billups, he had already managed to break inside through the basement door.

"Really, Steve?" Augustine said, hesitant about entering the house. "You know how much trouble we can get into?"

"It's not breaking and entering if you have suspicion."

"Suspicion? The kid's only eleven years old, Bill—"

"—Don't tell me what I already know. Just be quiet and follow my lead."

"But Bill—"

"—The kid's hiding something."

"He's a kid for crying out loud!"

"I know," Billups said to himself.

Augustine followed Billups through the basement where they came across a sleeping bag.

Billups peeled open the sleeping bag and found a shot glass-size spill of blood that reeked like week-old trash.

They tracked a drop of blood on the floor to the bathroom where they found a bloody piece of toilet paper in the trash, as well as bloody Band-Aids.

Billups put on a latex glove, grabbed the used Band-Aid, and placed it inside a Ziploc bag.

"We got 'em," he said.

Augustine asked, "Have you lost your mind?"

Billups didn't answer as he shouldered his way through the doorway and nearly pushed his partner aside. He made his way upstairs, gun drawn.

Augustine withdrew her gun and followed her partner upstairs.

They made it to Hogan's parents' bedroom. The bed appeared as if hadn't been used in years.

Billups ran his finger across the floral comforter, which was tightly tucked into the mattress, and pulled away a fingerprint covered in a layer of dust.

Next to catch Billups' sleuth-eye was a brass urn on the dresser.

The detective stood above the urn.

On the base of the urn read: "Marilynn C. Hill."

Stunned by the discovery, Billups turned to his partner: "What in the world is going on here?"

—

*Hogan?*

Hogan heard his mother's voice: "What are you waiting on?"

The voice lost its grittiness and smoothness.

Hogan was thrust forward from his trance-like state as if a force had smacked him in the back. He suddenly gasped and turned to Elisa, who was holding out her hand.

"What is it?" she said, waving Hogan closer to the cellar door. "Let's go."

Hogan followed Elisa down the stairs while Mike led the way with the beam of the flashlight.

Chi made sure to get a good grip around Freddie's body, making sure he didn't trip or fall. Even the slightest impact against Freddie's body could've caused his brittle bones to break like glass.

It was hard to tell the difference between a cobweb and a spider web for there were so many hanging along the ceiling.

Making their presence known were all kinds of creepy crawlers from spiders hanging in their well-established spiders webs to cockroaches scurrying below their feet.

The sight of the creatures caused the gang to form closer together, nearly to the point of walking on top of one another. Hogan caught Elisa's heel with the tip of his shoe.

"Watch it, Ho!" she shouted, looking back at Hogan.

"Sorriee—"

Hogan only got through half a word before the sight of Elisa's eyes bludgeoned the base of his throat.

In that moment, he fell witness to something remarkably unusual in her eyes: a light, circular in shape, like the glow of a cat's eye in the dark. He couldn't tell if it was from the reflection of the flashlight in her eyes. Whatever it was, it wasn't natural.

When they reached the bottom of the stairwell, Hogan, out of curiosity, looked into Chi's eyes, then Freddie's, and then Mike's, but he didn't see the same light that he saw in Elisa's eyes. Hogan kept it to himself, the light, and moved ahead of the group, Elisa now making up the caboose.

Now standing next to Mike, Hogan griped, "How much farther?"

Mike shined the light down a narrow, sewage-like tunnel. The constant water drops acted like a metronome.

"We should be getting close."

"How do you know she'll help us?"

"I don't, Hogan—"

"—Who farted?" Chi blurted out as he covered his nose.

"Enough already!"

"Whoever smelt it, dealt it."

Mike didn't pay any mind to the awful smell. He asked Chi, "How's he doing?"

"I'm fine goddamn it," Freddie said snappishly. "Keep moving. . . "

"You heard him," Mike said to the others. "Let's keep moving."

—

They walked for about a quarter of a mile through the dark mugginess before they heard the *screech* of an animal behind them.

"What was that?" Chi said frantically.

A boxed specter of light suddenly darted across the tunnel and it sounded like wheels squeaking, however, moving incredibly fast.

Mike stepped forward, examined the scene, and tried to locate the source of the noise.

The noise faded, forcing Mike to stay on guard.

"Stay close," Mike said to the others.

"It sounded like Horus."

"No. *Not* Horus. Something else."

"What else could it be?"

"We have to be close."

As he scanned the tunnel with the flashlight, the walls to the right of him started to move and break apart. . .

"Get behind me," Mike urged.

Hogan, Chi, Freddie, and Elisa quickly positioned themselves behind Mike as a dark clothed figure emerged from the mud and concrete of the wall.

Two flashes of the static on an analog TV screen flickered, each flash white and translucent as a ghost.

More flashes brought out the metallic robot: lanky glistening arms, shaped like the legs of a seven foot tall spider, unfolded and extended from the very back of screen, *clinking* and *clanking* like a compactor crushing metal. The legs attached to the screen now straightened and bent underneath the screen; the robotic creature rose eight feet in height, its top inches away from grazing the ceiling. More arms and legs stretched from its metallic, beetle-like shell. A spectrum of colors deteriorated on the screen before the grainy still of a gray skull steadied over the screen, each dim flash exposing the raggedy black cloth worn over its metal frame, cables running throughout its body like a bundle of loose veins.

"Shoot it, Mike!" yelled Hogan.

Mike aimed the assault rifle at the robot. He popped off two shots, hitting the screen; the impact of the gunshots to the glass made a web-like fracture across the screen. Marble-sized pieces of glass fell from the screen and hit Hogan in the feet, causing him to take a couple of steps backward. Hogan heard a blaring *horn* over his shoulder—a car horn perhaps. The sound of the horn was intense and it sent a wave of paranoia throughout his body. He started looking around his surroundings, unable to keep focus. He concentrated on the glass on the ground, held his loose attention on the glass while several sparks shot from the screen, an eddy of smoke oozing from the bullet holes.

The skull on the TV screen scrambled like a TV picking up a bad reception.

Two metal arms slowly extended outward and once they were fully extended, they swiped at Mike; Mike, in return, dodged each blow and continued his valiant assault by un-loading on the mid-torso of the strange creature. The flash of the gunshots gave a clear image of what the robotic crea-ture looked like. Mike realized the creature was *not* a crea-ture at all but a machine, nothing more than nuts and bolts with mechanical parts jerry rigged from scraps gathered from a salvage yard; a TV for a head, a muffler for an asshole, its heart made out of what appeared to be the engine of a mo-torcycle, whereas the rest of its armor haphazardly screwed together with dull sheets of various metals, such as roofing and exterior car parts.

A bullet struck a hose, causing oil to spit all over Mike. The machine sputtered around, throwing random punches in the air but not coming close to hitting Mike, then it pooped out and crashed to the ground in a loud, whooping *hum*.

Before Mike could make sense of the poorly built robot, a spotlight suddenly switched on at the end of the tunnel.

The light highlighted Mike. Mike turned his attention to the light, his face spotted with oil stains; the rest of the gang huddled behind Mike like ducklings; then, next to the gang, the retarded mess of a creation smoking beside them.

Shadows built outside the light.

"Someone's moving," Chi whispered.

Another figure stepped into the spotlight.

Chi turned off the safety.

"Hold your fire," Mike urged.

The spotlight cast a perfect silhouette of a slouched figure, massive in size, at least ten feet in height, like a daddy of what smoked before them.

"It's another one of those robots," Hogan said.

"No," Mike said. "Too small—"

A muffle, raspy voice of a woman said from an intercom on the wall: *Who the hell are you? What are you doing here?*

The gang flinched from the sound of the voice, and yet again forced them closer to one another; all four horsemen huddled together like a tight knot, so tight they were bumping into one another.

Mike walked to the intercom and spotted a blinking red light.

"We're here to seek help from the Curer," Mike said to the wall.

The fiery woman said in her most laid-back tone, which reeked of sarcasm, "Press the button and speak into the microphone, genius."

Mike glanced around in suspicion, wondering whether or not he was currently being watched by the person on the other end of the intercom, who, by the way, might've been the Curer! *Who else would it be*, Mike asked himself. He stepped forward and pressed the button next to the red, blinking light: "We're here to see the one known as the Curer. We desperately need her help—"

"The Curer no longer treats outsiders."

"Please," Mike said into the intercom, "our friend here." Mike waved Freddie forward, then Freddie did everything he could to walk on his own power. "He needs your help. *We* need your help."

Mike heard the sound of hydraulics above him. He pinpointed the noise to a small black ball, which he believed to be a camera wedged in a crevasse where the wall met the ceiling.

He looked into the black ball and spoke into the intercom: "If you can see us, then you know that this is the work of The Eye."

"The Eye's business is no business of mine. Goodbye."

"Please, Ophelia, he's dying—"

"—Leave now," the voice said, more angrily, "or else I will be forced to take lethal force."

The dark figure in the spotlight stepped forward and let out a metal *clunking* sound, something bulky gripped in its hands.

Mike got back on the intercom: "The Eye's planning a Night of Mortals underneath the Crow's Moon tonight and you should know that those who look at the moon's light will be blinded by sickness. If we don't take action to stop The Eye, then the living will be no more."

No response.

"I know why you retreated to the shadows, Ophelia," he said. "You don't have to be down here. You still have a chance to join the living. Help us. Help you."

A tense pause before the voice returned back to the intercom: "I'm sorry, but nobody can help me."

A sleek pump-action of a shotgun reverberated throughout the tunnel!

Mike grabbed a grenade from the bag and yelled at the gang, "Get back!"

"What are you going to do?" asked Hogan.

"There must be a door on the other side of this wall," he said with a mischievous look on his face. "If this bitch isn't going to let us in, then we're just going to have to force our way in, aren't we?"

Hogan and Chi wrapped their arms around Freddie and escorted him to safety.

Mike kneeled down underneath the intercom and just as

he was about to release the pin from the grenade, a door slid open on the opposite wall of the intercom.

Standing at the doorway was the silhouette of a short, frail woman, no more than four and a half-feet tall, wearing a purple wig.

Tucked against the side of her hip rested a shotgun.

"You're a persistent son of a bitch, aren't you?" she said to Mike.

"Ophelia?"

"Just him," she said, pointing the barrel of the shotgun at Freddie, who was cowered behind a swell of pipes.

Freddie eased out from hiding.

"Yes," Mike said. "Just him."

"If I help him, will you leave?"

"Yes."

She stepped back into the lit workshop. Mike motioned to the gang. He followed Ophelia into the room. The others followed suit.

—

Ophelia's workshop consisted of two different areas: on one end of the long, narrow room sat wooden tables with various greasy automobile parts; on the other end, more tables, however, covered with various-sized jars carrying mysterious liquid, various roots and plants, mason jars of eyeballs and other appendages from animals, such as crow's feet, herbs and insects and all kinds of mysterious liquids and oils extracted from nature, holding every cure to every illness, a plethora of scents and smells.

Ophelia walked Mike and the gang toward her workstation near a sink; however, her face still remained unseen and well disguised by the inadequate lighting.

Hogan came across a raven stuffed in a stiffened and upright position; its head cocked straight upward and its beak open wide.

Intrigued by its unnatural posture, he leaned closer and

smelled a potent substance inside its throat.

The smell nearly gagged Hogan.

"Don't touch anything," Ophelia said bitterly. "Highly flammable."

"Thanks for helping us," Mike said to Ophelia.

"When did it happen?" she asked, as she started rummaging through cabinets.

"Yesterday," Mike answered.

"How long does Freddie have before you know?" asked Chi.

"You mean, before he dies?" she asked and then smartly answered her own question after a wake of silence. "Two to three days. Four day tops before his body becomes great fertilizer."

"You're scaring the kid," Mike said to Ophelia.

"I am, am I?" Ophelia finally faced Mike. "Last I recall," she said, stepping in the dim light, "you were knocking on my door for help."

The light splashed onto her face, casting heavy shadows along the wrinkles of her face. And when she cracked open her mouth to speak, she exposed what little teeth that she had left in her mouth; and the ones that she was still clinging onto were like crushed black seashells protruding from her swollen gums.

Ophelia was no longer that girl from the stories, the one who the gang had expected her to be, but only, according to the timeline, over a decade older—which would've put her around the age of sixteen or seventeen.

Now, she was nothing more than a stranger.

Hogan and the rest of the gang took a cautious step back from Ophelia.

Mike swallowed the dry lump down his throat.

"Your help is greatly appreciated, ma'am," Mike said in a slow and cautious manner to Ophelia, who stepped closer to Freddie.

"So, this here was once a young boy, now an old man, who faces the transformation of a girl once like me, all but turned to bloody shams."

"The Eye did this to you, too?" asked Elisa.

Ophelia turned away, ashamed to face her guests.

Elisa apologized for the comment.

Ophelia shouldered past Hogan and snatched a half turtle shell with a crusher tool coated with a powdery residue from the table and then stormed back to the sink where she grabbed several mysterious jars from the countertop.

With her back turned, she said, "I'll make a remedy for your friend here. The medicine will not return him to his old state—his younger state, that is—although the remedy will stop the aging process—"

"—You mean, he's going to be like this forever!"

"There is no cure for reversal," Ophelia said to Hogan. "What's done is done. The medicine will buy your friend some more time, but eventually," she turned her head over her shoulder, "he will die, like me, like you, like everybody else."

"But how much time?"

"Enough," she said as she started working on the medicine. "I assume Horus has your scent as well. Once that beast has your scent, it will *never* leave you."

"How come Horus hasn't found you?"

"I moved down here, underground, where my scent cannot be traced, masked by the scents of Mother."

*Mother*, Hogan thought.

"Why?"

Ophelia didn't answer the question.

And nobody expected her to.

—

While Ophelia put the final touches on a foul-smelling concoction of herbs and insects in a boiling pot of what Hogan thought was the most disgusting stew, Hogan couldn't take the smell any longer, so he ventured through the tunnels.

He arrived at the end of the tunnel. What once looked

like a giant robot was only an action figure. He picked up the toy robot in front of the spotlight and held it up to his face; he couldn't help but laugh at the illusion.

His laughter soon came to a slow and unsteady halt as he heard the familiar sounds of Horus stomping through a dark corridor.

Hogan turned ghostly white.

A hand suddenly grabbed Hogan by the shoulder!

Behind Hogan stood Mike, who had a look of concern on his face.

"We need to get out of here. Now!"

Hogan asked, "What happened?"

"They found us," Mike said and rushed Hogan back to Ophelia's workshop.

On the grainy monitor was a shot of four different Horuses lingering outside the cellar door.

Standing in the middle of the famished creatures was The Eye.

"How did they find us?" asked Chi.

"You led them to me, didn't you?" Ophelia asked, staring at Chi.

With a look of innocence, Chi pointed at his chest. He was completely unaware of Ophelia's accusations. Ophelia continued to glare at him.

When he looked closer at Ophelia's eyes, he realized she wasn't looking at him. She was looking at the person hunched over behind him. . .

A clamor of pots and pans crashing to the floor *rang* out behind Hogan!

Elisa started convulsing. She thrashed her arms on top of the table, knocking over flasks and other metal pots onto the ground. She fell to the ground, her body curled into a fetal position. She was grabbing her stomach in agony.

Chi went over to check on Elisa and when she acknowledged him, she was not the same girl. The bones in her facial structure were much wider and protruding from her face. Her eyes were like the eyes of a python.

"Get away from me," Elisa cried out. "Go. . . "

In her sudden attempt to shoo away Chi, Elisa's sharp, murky eyes traced the back of her hand, now twice as long as her normal hand. Her fingernails were no longer fingernails, yet the talons of a hawk.

"She's one of them!"

Chi scurried away from Elisa and hid behind Mike. The rest of the gang took cover behind Mike while Elisa began her slow and painful transformation.

"They must've traced her scent," said Ophelia.

One after another, questions were being tossed at Ophelia: "How did this happen? What do we do? Can we help her?"

"No," Ophelia said over each of the boy's feverish exclamations. "I'm afraid that it's too late. There's no stopping the transformation. She is *claimed*."

"Claimed by who?"

"The Necromancer," Ophelia said.

"Necromancer?"

"The Eye's lapdog."

*Horus*, Hogan thought.

"She was either scratched or bitten by one of its many selves. Either way, she no longer has control over her own body. She is already dead, like the Necromancer, and soon, she will be able to alter her body in ways the living cannot. Driven by only one primordial desire: hunger."

Hogan rushed to Elisa, her arms popping out of joint, bones growing in thickness and length, breaking and tearing through her flesh.

Mike grabbed Hogan by the arm.

"You heard the lady," he said.

"Lemme go!"

"Hogan!"

Hogan resisted.

Mike firmed his grip, which made Hogan squirm even more.

He tried to yank his arm from Mike.

Mike wasn't letting go.

"It's too late, kid. There's nothing we can do—"

"—I said 'lemme go!'"

Ophelia shouted out, "She's already gone, boy!"

Hogan kept fighting—and resisting—until he couldn't fight or resist any longer.

He felt powerless.

Hogan dropped to his knees and cried as he watched his friend suffer as the creature inside her clawed and chewed from her body.

Mike hooked his hand under Hogan's armpit, hoisted up his body like dead weight, and tried to drag him away.

Hogan resisted—as he should—but eventually, he could no longer watch the horror before his eyes.

"Let's go, kid! Now!"

In one final glance, Hogan shared a moment with Elisa, the very last human moment with her as her glance meet his, her reptilian-like eyes willing Hogan to leave as if she was giving Hogan a head start to run far away before she changed into Death Walking.

She mouthed the words *I'm sorry.*

As Hogan did before, Elisa suddenly resisted the creature and the two clashed inside the little left of her body. Elisa reached for a jar of "highly flammable" liquid from the countertop, the creature desperately trying to pull her away.

Elisa fought the creature, the Necromancer tainting her blood, punched and kicked her way to the jar.

She managed to grab the jar, open the jar, and dump the contents all over her body.

The creature suddenly knocked the Zippo lighter from her hand with one of its many talons; and then, it slammed Elisa, who was clinging to scraps of flesh and bone, to the ground.

She crawled to the Zippo, her fingers breaking apart as they dug into the ground, with new and more deadly fingers emerging from her last good hand. She desperately reached for the Zippo. Grabbed the Zippo. Opened the Zippo with her teeth. No longer able to use her hands, Elisa wedged the Zippo underneath her chin and then, in one last attempt to destroy the creature, Elisa drove the side of her face into the ground, the impact causing the Zippo to spark, the flint caught fire, then Elisa's body engulfed in flames.

Hogan and Mike were last to exit the workshop; Horus was closing in.

Mike grabbed the assault rifle, unloaded on Horus as it split apart into three Horuses during mid-stride, two of them scaling the rocky walls, one using its talons to dig into the ceiling.

Three Horuses, now coming at different angles, like a tidal wave of death approaching.

Hogan made a run for it. Mike backpedaled. The bullets had absolutely no effect on either three of the Horuses.

As the main Horus closed in, a flaming Elisa—or whatever remained of her—tackled the enormous creature and pinned it to the ground, which gave Mike and Hogan just enough time to catch up with Chi and Freddie and Ophelia, who led them to safety.

Ophelia guided the gang to a sewage runoff and locked the grill behind her. She said that it would buy them some time. Ahead of them were dense woods.

The only trouble was trying to find a place to hide.

## 8. Medusa's Gaze

*I don't know what to believe anymore. He betrayed me. Now, I feel like something that's ready to be torn down.*

THE whispering wouldn't stop. Voices were coming from every direction. Hogan was the only one listening to them, as in what he thought was the tormented ghosts of Vancouver Manor; each word was running into the next, a clamor of noise sending Hogan into a whirlwind.

Hogan spun in every direction, looking above the trees, then looking over his shoulder, then looking ahead at what demons awaited him. His last-ditch effort to track down the origin of the voices was making his head throb. He became lightheaded and he lost his balance.

As the remaining survivors pushed forward, Hogan began to lag behind. He braced himself against a tree as if it was the only thing keeping him from falling to the ground.

Behind him crept a dense, sly fog from the south. The fog moved like an entity through the many rows of trees.

Something was breathing in the fog. Something deadly.

"Did you hear that?" Hogan finally asked.

The others remained quiet, dismissive of Hogan's paranoia.

Mike insisted that they keep moving. So, they did. And

Hogan kept wiging out. Mike, Ophelia, and the surviving three of the Four Horsemen, including Hogan, made their way through the rugged and dangerous terrain of the damp and moonlit woods.

Hogan kept his paranoia to himself. He mainly thought about Elisa while he kept his distance from the others. He was so distant that he could've passed as a lost body wandering through the endless malaise of Purgatory; the wet logs, the thick vegetation, the hidden burrows, and a steep trek up a muddy hill made it extremely difficult for Freddie to keep up the pace as Hogan and the others kept pushing forward. It became so burdensome that they had to stop several times and wait for Freddie to catch up for his condition continued to worsen by the second. His bones started to bend like straws; his knuckles popping out of joint; most of his fingers looked like the messy design of a crap artist; and most—if not all—of his teeth had fallen out; he couldn't put any weight on his left knee for the pain was too much to bear. For each step Freddie took, the pain rushed through his body in hot waves.

They finally stopped halfway up a hill. He couldn't go any longer. He was done.

"Leave me," Freddie moaned, tugging at Chi's arm.

Chi tried to keep Freddie upright, but Chi could hardly stand. He, too, appeared as if he had withstood injury.

"We have to rest," Chi said, trying to catch his breath.

"You're hurt," Mike said, staring at Chi's leg.

Mike pulled a gun on Chi, held it close.

"I cut it on that metal."

"What metal?"

"The you know. The grate. My leg rubbed against it as we were leaving. It's nothing! I swear!"

Mike cocked the hammer.

"Mike," Hogan shouted out from behind, "he's telling the truth!"

"And what if he's not? What if Horus is now pulling his strings? He can turn any minute."

Behind Mike, Ophelia groaned, "The boy's telling the truth."

From a distance, Horus's bloodcurdling *shriek* ripped through the woods.

"They're never going to stop!" Chi cried out. "What do they want with us? The Eye has what he wants."

"Not everything," Ophelia finally confessed. "I guess he thought he killed me. Now, it appears as if he's trying to finish what he started. The fact: Your friend led him to me, and now there's nothing we can do to stop him—"

"—She didn't mean to!" Hogan retorted. "She saved us back there! We'd be dead if it wasn't for. . . "

Hogan couldn't even speak her name for the name had brought great sorrow.

"Whatever," Ophelia mumbled. She turned her back on Hogan and said clearly, "It doesn't matter now. Once The Eye's done with me, he will begin the Night of the Mortal."

"We have to stop him—"

"—You can't, boy!" she said over Hogan, now facing Hogan. "Nobody can."

"Why?"

"Why *what*?"

"Why does The Eye want to kill you so badly?"

"He's my father."

"Wait a minute, lady," Mike said. "Jóhan Halldórsdóttir is your father."

"Yes," Ophelia said. "That's right."

"But your mother killed Halldórsdóttir."

"She did, yes," she said to Mike. "But he came back—"

"Like a zombie?" asked Chi.

"No," she said. "He came back as The Eye."

"Came back? What do you mean 'came back'?"

"Reincarnated," Ophelia said.

—

The Eye and Horus stopped at the edge of the tunnel. The

Eye picked up a piece of fabric hanging on the loose wire of the grate. He picked up the piece of fabric.

"Find 'em," he said, handing the fabric to Horus.

With his dripping wet nostrils, Horus sniffed the fabric and then darted away into the woods.

—

Hogan imagined violence—and he couldn't help but laugh.

"Am I missing something, boy?" Ophelia asked Hogan. "What's so damn funny?"

Amused by the recent news, Hogan shook his head as if he was shaking away thoughts in his head.

"So, Jóhan is The Eye?" Hogan said in disbelief.

"Yes," Ophelia said shortly. "You know the story—the legend—but," she slowed down her voice in a much calmer tone, "what people don't know is that something else happened the night of this 'infamous' party—"

"—You mean the night Jóhan's crazy wife cooked her husband like he was pork chops?"

"Chi," Mike said fatherly, "enough!"

Ophelia didn't pay any mind to Chi's crude remark and said without skipping a beat, "Later on after the party was over, everyone turned violently sick, including The Eye. It wasn't until a couple of days later that I found out what she had done to my father. I made a decision to run away. I—I didn't know where to go. I hid in the only place where I felt safe." She looked around. "Here," she said, "in the woods. I thought she'd never find me. Days went by. I couldn't leave her there in *that* house. She needed help. My help." Ophelia paused and said, "She needed me. I came back home. A week passed. My mother hardly left her room. While she was upstairs, I heard a knock on the door. A man dressed in black was waiting outside. He was one of my father's friends; I remembered his face from the party. For some reason, I knew it was him, my father, the way he acted, even the way he talked. I thought my mother was insane, but this was *beyond* insane. He was aware of what my mother had done to Jóhan's body. Over the years, my mother had convinced me of my father's cruelty. Every time I looked at him, I could only see what my mother had seen. A bad man who wanted nothing to do with his family. When The Eye came into the house, he confronted my mother. He was filled with so much rage that he cast a spell on the one thing that my mother couldn't live without."

"Which was?" said Mike.

"Me," Ophelia answered and sighed heavily. "Unable to cope with what The Eye had done to me, she grabbed a piece of broken glass from the floor and ran that glass across her throat. I watcher her die. So too did my father."

"Why didn't you stop him?" asked Hogan.

"I couldn't," she replied. "Or maybe I didn't want to." She hung her head for a moment. "I remember he turned to me while I was lying helpless on the floor and he was looking down on me. He smiled at me, not like a friendly smile, but a sick smile, as if my pain had given him pleasure."

"What happened next?"

"He walked away. I never saw him again."

"But it doesn't make any sense," Hogan said, this time louder. "Why would he harm you, his own daughter? He was your father!"

"He was my father, yes, but I was *never* his daughter."

Another *shriek*, this time much closer!

"We must keep moving," Mike said to the others. Mike turned to Freddie and nodded. "Freddie," he said directly, "that includes you."

Freddie remained speechless, already determined to stay behind.

"Freddie," Hogan said, "*we* have to go."

Freddie didn't move an inch.

"Freddie, did you hear me?"

"I heard you, Hoagie," he said faintly. "Go on without me now."

"What? No! I'm not leaving you behind. . . "

"All I'll do is slow you down."

"I'm not leaving you!"

Another shriek!

"Freddie! I'm not leaving you!"

"I'll stay with him," Chi said as he puffed out his chest. He pulled out a pistol from his belt. Switched off the safety again.

"Chi? What are you doing?"

"You heard me, Hoagie Roll," he said confidently. "Me and Freddie will hold them off—"

"—What about our pact? Horsemen never abandon one another!"

"There's only one Horseman now," Freddie murmured. "You, Hoagie, you hold the power of all four Horsemen."

Suddenly, a violent, bloody image flashed through Hogan's mind: a younger Freddie, face covered with bruises, half-broken; he was painfully reaching out his hand; Hogan reached out his hand while fingering the fumy, dusty air, his fingers only inches away from touching Freddie's fingers; young Freddie slipped farther down the back of the school bus and before Hogan could grab Freddie's hand, Freddie's other hand lost grip over the slippery leather seat—

"—No, I can't!"

"You will." Freddie looked directly into Hogan's eyes. "It's time to move on."

"Why do you want to die?" Hogan whimpered.

"You can't save someone who's already dead, Hoagie."

"You're alive right now! I can save you!"

"No, Hoagie. You already did."

Mike touched Hogan on the shoulder.

"He's made his choice, kid," he said as he stepped aside and handed Freddie a pistol. "It's not yours to make."

A dark figure suddenly appeared within a distant band of fog.

Hogan turned his attention toward the top of the hill and witnessed Horus standing on the top of the hill, the palest of moonlight casting a perfect silhouette.

Mike grabbed Hogan by the arm.

"Come on, kid," he said, pulling Hogan. "Let's get out of here. . . "

Hogan finally pulled himself away from his two friends, afraid to say a final goodbye, not even an utterance of "see you around" or anything remotely feasibly as an expression to convey farewell. Hogan left without saying a word to his friends.

## 9. New Threat(s)

*Every night, I wait to die. Will they be there stand-
ing motionlessly, waiting for me to join them in the
fire? When will I ever see them again?*

HOGAN couldn't blot out the sounds. Each boom of
a gunshot ripped through the woods and doubled
over in a violent ricochet of piercing echoes. Each
shot pushed Hogan, each and every stride became longer, his
legs moved faster, his feet dug deeper. He ran and not once
did he ever look back. Three smaller *paap, paap, paap*
sounds danced like lullabies throughout the woods before the
guttural screams of Chi were crushed by a death gurgle. Hogan listening to the chaos, then imagining, then listening to
his friends' ultimate deaths, imagining how they went out, if
they were torn apart or if they were—even worse—eaten,
caused the blood to boil in his veins. A force came over Hogan, separating him from Mike and Ophelia until he no
longer remained in their range of vision. Mike chased after
Hogan. He called out to Hogan, but Hogan was already too
far to reach.

Mike ended up slowing down in order to keep Ophelia
within his reach.

She finally caught up with Mike.

But Hogan was already lost in the fog.

—

Hogan eventually reached the edge of the woods where the trees met the asphalt of a street.

Mike and Ophelia had to be at least a half of a mile behind Hogan, and Hogan knew that he had to wait for them to catch-up for there were three different directions awaiting him.

Hogan followed the lights and walked to an intersection in the road, which was covered with bright pink and green lights glistening from the puddles along the asphalt. He had only heard of such places in the stories that were told. He found the name of the road sign, King Boulevard.

"King Town," he read to himself. *A place where kids like Hogan didn't belong.*

Hogan eased back toward the woods and safely waited for Mike and Ophelia; and as he mentally went over his next plan of action, he couldn't help but remain in a state of awe from the sight of the ruined, rusted, and rancid outskirts of what used to be a thriving district of the city; now, it was nothing more than an emaciated vagabond of a city.

Each corner of King Town were now plagued with run-down strip joints covered in flashy signs of sex and enticement; a smoke shop, as well as a liquor store on every street corner; the fanciest one-star cuisine inhabiting a former post office at the end of a dirty strip mall, the pronunciation of the restaurant spoken with a foreign tongue among the local population; the buildings, once pristine and home of former local businesses, now decorated with gang symbols and comic book-style graffiti. Hogan realized where he was and where he shouldn't be.

He heard the smash of a beer bottle against one of the ruined buildings, followed by the sounds of a young man's holler.

Next to follow was the sound of a rowdy group of men speaking a language that Hogan couldn't understand.

Words, Hogan closely listened, Chi once used. Sounds

intensified. Then words had turned to numbers. Men were speaking in numbers, like a code. Hogan could only make sense of the police lingo: 187. He knew these numbers for he had heard them many times before. These numbers were associated with the one thing that Hogan could not avoid in King Town.

Screams of rage and jubilation became clearer.

To Hogan's left, the notorious gang, Knights of King Town, emerged from an alley. The Spanish name was Los Caballeros, which meant The Knights.

The Knights were a loose band of knife-wielding misfits who ran a high-valued drug ring inside the 5th District. Police didn't even bother wasting their time on The Knights' turf; yet, the way each gang member spoke was a language often spoken by law enforcement.

Hogan wondered if there was a difference between the two organizations, the street gangs and the street cops.

A Knight spotted Hogan standing on the sidewalk; and in a sort of childish delight, he pointed at Hogan, who, in return, turned toward the distant *kah-runch* of a tree branch behind him.

—

When Mike and Ophelia exited the woods, Hogan was nowhere to be found. Mike spent the next couple of minutes calling out to Hogan but received no response, except for the debris and trash skipping along the dingy streets and the rattling of the tarnished bolts of a stop sign trembling from a gust of wind.

"Hogan! Where are you?" screamed Mike.

"You're wasting your time," Ophelia said from behind.

"He can't be alone," Mike said to Ophelia.

"He'll be fine. He's just a boy."

"Hogan!" Mike screamed once more.

Suddenly, Mike heard the distant cries of what sounded like Hogan. He caught the word *help* in the cries of desperation.

"It's Hogan," Mike said and ran toward the danger.

Ophelia had no other choice than to follow Mike.

—

Both Mike and Ophelia followed the cries to an abandoned warehouse.

Mike witnessed a metal door slamming shut at the end of an alley.

"There," he said, pointing down the alley.

"We shouldn't be here," Ophelia warned as she noticed several timid locals closing the blinds and curtains of their apartment windows.

"Are you coming or not?" asked Mike.

Ophelia raised her brows.

"Do I have a choice?"

"You have two choices: go back the way you came and deal with Horus or do some good for once and help me find this kid."

Ophelia turned her sights to the sky as if she was praying to a god even though she wasn't the least bit religious—or spiritual.

The clouds broke free, revealing the full moon.

"Okay," she said clearly. "I'm right behind you."

—

Using extreme caution, Mike inched his head past the corner of the barred window; and in his speedy glance of scoping out the interior of the warehouse, he spotted Hogan being tied down to a metal pipe with cable ties.

A rickety door suddenly *squeaked* open just feet away from Mike and forced him to seek cover behind the warehouse.

Two members of Los Caballeros stepped outside for a smoke.

Mike wondered how easily he could take them out with two gunshots, but the sound of the gunfire would draw others. He searched around a dumpster and came across an empty spray paint aerosol can. He cut off the nozzle of the can with his knife. He ran his finger inside the can and the paint was dry and clumpy. He cleared out as much paint as he could and then, with the tip of his knife, he surgically cut a small hole in the base of the can.

Once the hole was made, he placed the top of the aerosol can on top of the barrel of his rifle. Screwed the homemade silencer onto the barrel until the aerosol can was snug and tight; otherwise, the aerosol can could fly off during the gunshot and that'd certainly defeat its purpose, which was to suppress the sound of gunfire.

Mike didn't waste a moment's time. He took cover behind an oil drum, aimed, and fired two shots, the first shot catching the Knight between the eyes, the next one, not too far off, the bullet grazed the side of the other Knight's cheek, causing him to drop to the ground.

Exercising great vigilance, he rushed forward and finished off the last Knight with his knife. He dragged their bodies behind a stack of broken pallets.

Ophelia emerged from hiding and rushed to Mike once the threat had been eliminated.

Mike hoisted up Ophelia to the roof access ladder.

Once she was safe, he climbed onto the stack of pallets and managed to jump onto the ladder.

They made their way up to the top of the warehouse and watched Hogan below from the murky skylight. A Knight with facial tattoos was urinating on the boy and laughing while he did so. Hogan did his very best to turn away. But gravity—as Hogan would say—was one heck of a jerk.

And Hogan happened to be a guest at the largest Jerk Convention in town.

"Forget about him, Mike," Ophelia said over Mike's shoulder. "They will kill the boy—that is, after they torture him—"

"—Not on my watch." Mike stood to his feet and faced Ophelia. "I'm going down there. Are you with me or not?"

Ophelia drifted, not in thought—more or less—a sudden dizzy spell.

"Well, are you?"

Ophelia shook away the momentary dizziness.

"Ophelia?"

"Give me a sec, will you?" Ophelia said shortly.

Ophelia thought about the one thing that they had been avoiding all night—and for her sake, the one thing that she had been avoiding every since the spell.

"Ophelia?"

"I'm thinking," she snapped.

"Think fast." Mike turned to Hogan below. One of the Knights was pouring beer on Hogan's face and everybody was now laughing around him. He pounced to his feet and prepared himself for battle. "We're running out of time."

"Okay," Ophelia said clearly. "I got a plan. It's not the most ideal way to rescue the boy, but it should work, given the circumstances—"

The abrupt *click* of the hammer of a gun sent a stir of panic through Mike's stomach.

He rotated around, first acknowledging the jerk sticking the gun in his face, and then acknowledging the utter disappointment on Ophelia's face.

—

The two Knights pushed Mike and Ophelia, both tied and gagged, into the main operational room where Hogan was being held captive.

One of them shouted out to the other Knights, "Lookie, lookie! Lookie at who I found spying on us! Two rats that would love to contribute to the slush fund!"

Another one said, "Nice to see you join the party!"

The big-eared Knight tossed Mike next to Hogan on the ground while other one groped Ophelia.

Ophelia jerked away and spat in the Knight's face.

The Knight slapped Ophelia across the face and tossed her to the ground where her wrists were bound to a pipe.

Immediately, Mike asked if Hogan was okay and Hogan returned with a stiff nod of his head. Scattered around Hogan laid other cable ties—at least a dozen of cut cable ties, now off-colored and appearing as if they had been there for quite some time. There were other bounds as well, such as pieces of duct tape and loose rope. Hogan noticed a couple of bones, which appeared human, lying behind him.

He found a nametag with the name TOMMY on it.

Hogan thought: *Surely, it's not Tommy Winters—*

"—*Impressive*, Marco Dumbo," a cavalier man said and stepped from a huddle of thugs and gangsters. He dusted off the cocaine from his nose, used the tips of his fingers, and wiped the rest of the cocaine along his gums. "So, what do we have here? A hardass," he said, studying Mike and then Ophelia, "and what looks like a recluse." The man turned to the others and giggled. "I don't think the old recluse will be of any use to us—that is, unless she has a rich relative she doesn't know about; even then, who would miss her? Really?" He directed his attention toward Ophelia. "You old bag."

"Which one shall we start with first, Loke?" asked one of the Knights.

The cavalier man who went by the name, Loke, loomed over Mike and pulled out the machete from his waistband.

"This one looks promising," he said.

"How about the old bag?"

"Forget about her," he said, waving his hand in a shooing gesture. "We'll toss her aside once we're through with her. This guy, however," Loke used the edge of the machete and placed the blade directly underneath Mike's chin, "he looks like he's got friends with money."

"Well then," Marco said, "let's give them a souvenir you know, to show them that we mean business."

"What are you going to do?" asked Mike.

Hogan was closely watching each Knight.

Loke said to Marco, "Grab him."

Marco grabbed Mike. Mike struggled. It took three other Knights to hold down Mike as he kicked and squirmed.

"Feisty one," Loke said as he handed off the machete and pulled a smaller blade, a bird's beak knife. He kneeled down to Mike's level and said in his ear, "No offense, guy. Just business."

Marco secured Mike's head with an unbreakable sleeper hold while another Knight with facial piercings pulled out Mike's tongue with a pair of vice grips.

In two sweeping cuts, Loke sliced off Mike's tongue. Strings of blood squirted from his mouth and onto Loke's arms, as well as his face, which appeared more perverse and slack-heavy in nature, as if the sight of the blood was making him hard. Some of Mike's blood shot into Loke's gaping mouth.

Mike ripped his body from the Knight's grip, fell to the ground, and spat out a mouthful of blood. He made a poor attempt to say something to the madman but all that came out were coughs and mumbles.

"What was that? Come again!" He leaned in dangerously closer to Mike and held his hand to his ear. "Looks like a cat got your tongue!"

The comment drew a few laughs throughout the warehouse.

"For the love of God, would someone pick that thing up and stick it in an envelope?"

One of the Knights delicately picked up the tongue from the ground as if it was contagious and with disgust, stuck it in an envelope.

"We'll send that off to one of his loved ones, someone he really cares about," Loke broadcasted, "we'll give them the night to cough up the money, and by dawn, we'll have enough money to move out of this hellhole! Shit! We'll take over the suburbs! Finally earn the respect we deserve! What do you say?"

The others cheered and celebrated; mainly shouting out in numbers—a *code*, Hogan thought.

One Knight, small and squirrelly, shouted out from the very back of the crowd: "Yeah! We'll start our own tennis league and bang hot bitches!"

More laughs.

Ophelia sitting back, thinking: *These fools just saved me the trouble of cutting myself.*

"Do you know what you just did?" Ophelia said amusingly.

"She speaks!"

"Sure I did, you old bag!" Loke said, brimming with a queer elation. "I just cut the man's tongue off! I mean how dark is that?"

"No," Ophelia enlightened. "You just brought it to us?"

"Oh yeah! Brought who?"

"The monster," said Ophelia.

A sudden pound on the door caused a ripple of silence!

The pounding intensified. . .

Loke ordered one of his men to answer the door.

Another *pound* caused the door to suddenly cave in!

Before the Knight could make his way to the door, the door suddenly burst open!

Horus stormed inside; the door flung open and struck the Knight in the leg.

As the injured Knight crawled away, the creature broke off into three equally sized creatures. One scaled the walls as well as the ceiling while the other jumped onto the injured Knight and treated him as if he was an appetizer before an entree. The Knight closest to the action put down the creature with a straight shot to the head before it could savor the rest of his friend; either way, very little was left of the other Knight, only limbs and a couple of toes.

The last one, the third and final one, somewhat weaker, sniffed out Mike's blood, then charged directly at Mike; the rest of the Knights brandished their weapons, then unloaded on the two creatures. The creatures dodged the bullets—one of them was struck in the arm but it kept moving as if the gunshot was a minor flesh wound—they rerouted, then stayed close to the shadows; and since most of the trigger-happy Knights were aiming their guns like they were holding their own dicks—trying to hit the rim of the toilet bowl while they pissed—the bullets were flying everywhere and hitting everything but the creatures. More bullets managed to graze the other Horus in the arms and legs but nothing severe enough to put the creature down.

As the two Horuses chewed through each Knight, Ophelia managed to cut herself free on the sharp edge of a pipe.

One Knight got a clean shot and ended up shooting one of the creatures in the chest, which dramatically slowed it down, forcing it to break off and form into two more creatures! This gave the Knights enough time to get a better shot. They took out the first creature, the one with the nub of a hand, then the other two before they could do any damage.

The last Horus still remained untouched, picking off one Knight at a time, then smartly scurrying back into the shadows. The creature's presence had already been felt, and it left behind little to none in its wake of destruction. The last two remaining members of Los Caballeros were Marco and the King himself, Loke.

Horus set its sights on the remaining two gang members—as salty as they were, it didn't eat them, didn't savor even the slightest lick; instead, it got a hold of Loke's machete, studied it in a sort of untamed animal-like curiosity, and then used it to kill Loke and his friend.

Then, once Horus was finished with Los Caballeros, it sought out Ophelia.

Horus tackled Ophelia to the ground and while it was digging its fangs into her flesh, Mike cut the binds from his wrists and used the same bird's beak knife and stabbed Horus directly in the back. Horus threw a blinding backhand, knocking Mike across the room. Slowly, the injury started to take hold and Horus scampered away.

Mike stumbled over to Hogan, cut his hands free, then rushed over to Ophelia, who had already bled out from the deep lacerations.

"What do we do now?" Hogan asked Mike.

A watery voice from behind: "*It's simple. You die.*"

They both rotated around toward the front of the warehouse. There, at the doorway, stood The Eye.

"Naawh," Mike said confidently even though he had no tongue to roll any of his vowels. He picked up the AK-47 from the ground. He marched toward The Eye, assault rifle gripped in hand.

With no other choice, he began to unload on The Eye.

The Eye, in return, moved gracefully around each and every whizzing bullet.

Once the AK-47 ran out of bullets, Mike tossed it aside and picked up another one from the cold grip of one of the dead Knights.

As Mike unloaded on The Eye, The Eye gave Mike the deathly gaze.

In his unmoving stride, Mike slowly started to age. His hair started to streak with strands of gray. His skin wrinkled and blemished. With each bullet he fired, a year was stolen from his life. Mike kept moving, kept firing; his bones went frail and brittle; his muscles weakening, hurting; even his posture was deteriorating.

By the time Mike reached The Eye, he was a cranky old man.

Mike hit The Eye square in the face with the butt of the AK-47, pinned down The Eye's arm holding the infamous Devil's Toothpick, and unloaded the rest of the magazine on The Eye's arm; the flashes of gunfire highlighted each gruesome wrinkle on Mike's face. He didn't shoot off The Eye's perforated arm but he nearly came close to doing so.

The sword slipped from The Eye's jelly-like grip, giving Hogan the smallest window of opportunity to snatch the weapon from the ground.

Horus, wounded and exhausted, made one last leap at Hogan.

With the flaming sword loosely gripped in his hands, he struck Horus in mid-air with a lightning-fast swipe diagonally across Horus's chest. The cut instantly killed Horus.

Hogan loomed over the dead creature, the power of the Devil's Toothpick giving him a godly boost of confidence as a fighter and survivor. The killing of Horus caused a strange chain reaction; and the other badly wounded, half-dead creatures scattered around the entire warehouse rapidly shriveling like a time-lapse of an annual wilting and eventually dying in the winter.

Hogan faced The Eye, who was now curled against the wall gripping his arm, which had been reduced to nothing more than these loose spaghetti-like muscles and ligaments.

"You haven't won," The Eye uttered. "You will *never* win."

The Eye gazed into Hogan's eyes but Hogan immediately turned away.

"All I have to do is *ignore* you and you will go away."

"Isn't this what you want, Mr. Hill? To prove to yourself that you are worthy of redemption?"

While Mike, stricken with dementia, crawled around in confusion on the ground, The Eye finally stood to his feet and stalked closer to Hogan.

Hogan could hear The Eye closing in on him. He back-pedaled and kept his distance.

"Come any closer and I will end you," Hogan warned as he made sure to keep his eyes away from The Eye's Lens.

As The Eye inched closer, Hogan reared back the flaming sword. He felt a sudden resistance. . .

A smoothly textured yet firmly gripped hand tightened over his wrists. A draft of fragrance came over Hogan.

Hogan spun his head around and saw a slick-haired man, suave and debonair, dressed in a suit.

The man's hand was tightening over Hogan's wrist, and the force of his powerful grip caused Hogan to release the sword from his hand.

A wave of pain rushed through Hogan's wrist, then his forearm.

Hogan could actually see the pain with his own eyes. A discoloration formed around his very own wrist, same area that the familiar man was touching. Hogan's arm started to turn green and then gray; the skin around his arm began to sag and then wrinkle, the bones started to bend with age.

Star-struck, Hogan looked over the man in the suit as if he was left in a state of powerlessness at first; then once he realized who the man was, his awareness turned to anger.

"Curtis Saeman?"

"That's correct," the man said as Hogan tried to jerk his arm away. "I reckon you've seen my face on TV, haven't you?"

The man in the suit, Curtis Saeman, finally released his grip from Hogan's wrist.

Hogan dropped to his knees and grabbed his frail arm in agony.

"What did you do to me?" asked Hogan.

Curtis held up his perfectly-shaped hand and admired it as if it was the greatest gift ever given to man.

"The question is 'What can I do to you?'"

He stepped closer to a frightened Hogan.

"I can show you a way out," he said enticingly, glancing around the warehouse in fascination. "Out of here. Out of all of this."

Hogan mulled it over.

Curtis turned to The Eye.

"You've done well, Yann. Now for your final lesson."

Curtis picked up the sword from the ground and stabbed The Eye in the chest. The Eye fell to the ground and embraced one last gaping breath before his eyes glazed over in death.

Hogan saw movement in the corner of his eye. Mike, Hogan witnessed, now an old man clinging to his nineties, blood dripping from his mouth, crawled behind one of the dead Knights. The two shared one last glance before Mike shut his eyes and passed out.

After Curtis destroyed The Eye, he faced Hogan, who, with his good hand, was aiming a gun at Curtis's head. He shot at Curtis before Curtis could utter a word or even deliver a closing line.

Curtis suddenly lifted up the flaming sword. The bullet hit the sword, didn't ricochet or pierce the blue steel, as any normal bullet would do; instead, the Devil's Toothpick absorbed the bullet!

"Cool trick, huh?" Curtis said teasingly.

Before Hogan could open fire, Curtis flipped the sword around and struck Hogan with the butt of the handle.

Lights out.

## 10. The Confidence Man

*Death comes as swiftly as the wind. It's the most unbiased thing there is in life. And it always wins.*

DROWNING in a sticky, hellish darkness, Hogan channeled every ounce of strength in his being and swam to the light.

Hogan found the light—and he nurtured it. He opened his eyes in a mechanical way, once off, now on. Both of his arms were numb and incredibly light in weight and as soon as blood flowed back into his arms, a knob of pain nestled over his head. He couldn't make any sense of the pain at the upper bridge of his nose, how it had gotten there, if he had fallen or hit his head. The last—and the only—thing Hogan could remember was The Eye and running his own sword through The Eye's chest, *destroying* him.

Doubt found a way to creep in his head like a weed; and eventually, with enough light and thought, the doubt spread throughout his entire mind.

Or was it somebody else?

Carefully, he grabbed the top of his forehead and gradually sat upright on a beige leather couch. He looked around and found himself in a luxurious penthouse suite overlooking the city of St. Square, which was the largest and most populous city west of Orson Valley.

The room, Hogan surveyed, was wide as a gymnasium; the ceilings were high enough to climb; and the walls were decorated with New York-art deco-style paintings of dark faces covered with various masks from gritty to cracked to cancerous. Very minimal furniture; the only pieces Hogan saw were made of glass and unusually shaped: a two-tiered coffee table neither round nor solid, yet triangular glass and curvature frame, a wicked design. There was a flat screen TV made of all glass mounted flush against the distant wall, the program of a train moving through a dark tunnel ran on a constant fifteen-second loop.

"How's the head?" a charming voice said from an open doorway connecting the living room to the kitchen.

Hogan turned to his right and saw the same man in the suit, Curtis Saeman, entering the living room.

"After you destroyed The Eye, you fell and bumped your head."

*I did*, he thought, *didn't I?*

"It was a good thing I was there," Curtis smirked, "otherwise you wouldn't be with us, Hogan."

"Where am I?"

Curtis held out his hands.

"Welcome to the *Last Level*."

"Last Level?" Hogan murmured.

"The name of my private suite," Curtis said, approaching Hogan. "Originally, I was going to call it the Boss's Level, you know, since I'm the boss, but it seemed to—I don't know—too literal, too—how do you say—too 'on the nose.' So, I decided on the Last Level. It's more thought-provoking, wouldn't you say, Hogan?"

"What did you do with Mike?" asked Hogan.

"Ah right," Curtis said in a more serious tone. "I'm afraid Michael didn't make it. I'm so sorry, Hogan—"

"—Why am I here?" Hogan said as he cautiously eased away from Curtis, who was now looming over him.

"There is no reason to be scared, Hogan," Curtis said charmingly. "I'm sure you're filled with all sorts of questions. And I assure you that I will answer each and every one of them. *But* first," Curtis pointed to the kitchen, "let's get something to eat. You must be starving."

"I'm not hungry," Hogan said angrily.

"A boy your age not hungry?" Curtis said, waiting for Hogan to follow. "Please. I insist."

Hogan didn't budge.

"I'm not hungry," he said.

"And I'm not asking," Curtis said over Hogan.

—

A simple act of playing possum turned into a twenty-minute nap and by the time the cleanup crew made its way onto the crime scene, Mike suddenly woke from the blaring police sirens. Fighting through the ache of old age and the weight it had brought upon his shoulders, he grabbed a motorcycle from one of the dead Knights and witnessed The Eye lying on the ground. Dead. Like the others.

Mike tracked down a knife next to Ophelia's body—or what was left of the body—and picked it up off the ground. He hurried back to The Eye and peeled open his eyelid until the Lens was exposed.

This was where things got a little messy.

—

Mike peeled away just before the cops arrived at the scene.

Several cops crept into the warehouse, guns drawn, one of the cops' jaws dropping in a gaping yawn as the cop witnessed the bloody carnage before him.

With a flashlight scanning the area, the cop came across The Eye's dead body. He noticed The Eye's face and the blood running down his left eye. He shined the flashlight on the left eye socket. The cop called out to his partner and said with confusion, "Who the hell would do such a thing?"

"A monster," his partner answered. "That's what."

—

At a highly trafficked intersection, a young man in his late twenties was caught on a traffic camera for not speeding, but zooming through a red light.

The man carried no identity, only the trademark leather jacket worn by one of the gang members of Los Caballeros, and his face was disguised by a black motorcycle helmet.

—

Only one bite was missing from the peanut butter and jelly sandwich on the plate, which was fine china.

Hogan spent most of his time staring and thinking about the sandwich and what was really in it.

"Can't be that bad," Curtis said as he sat a couple of seats away from Hogan at the bar.

"I told you 'I wasn't hungry.'"

"Well," Curtis took away the plate and placed it on the granite countertop in the kitchen, "I can't force you to eat—"

"—What do you want from me?" asked Hogan.

"Stories," Curtis said bluntly as he escorted Hogan from the kitchen, "we *all* have stories—each and every one of us, Hogan—and it is my sole duty as an entertainer to seek out those with the most unique stories and share them with the entire world. For me, it would be a crime against humanity not to share a story. In the end, stories can either bring us together or split us apart; however, there is no denying that stories keep us here, keep us going, keep us thinking, not only about others, but also ourselves. Stories have the ability to force us to peer into our souls and take a look at our own lives—show us who or what we want to be or what we what to do." Curtis placed his hand over Hogan's shoulder. "Stories have power to—dare I say—*change* the world."

Hogan glanced at the hand on his shoulder. Curtis soon acknowledged Hogan's discomfort and removed his hand.

"Over these past couple of days, I have grown particularly interested in you, Hogan—*your* story—and as I currently speak, I have a team of some of the greatest minds coming together to develop a television series called *Child of Night*, and I believe your story, Hogan, would made a great addition to a soon-to-be worldwide sensation."

Curtis walked Hogan into a massive art gallery. On the wall were many movie posters, each poster an episode from the new series, *Child of Night*. On the other side of the wall displayed older posters from movies such as *Lockjaw* and other movies based off each member of Jóhan's exclusive secret society.

Hogan turned around and noticed that the last poster on the other wall remained to be painted.

Curtis walked Hogan to the blank white poster.

"Your story, Hogan, is waiting to be told."

"*My* story?" Hogan said. "Don't you need my permission?"

"Of course we do, Hogan," Curtis said, laughing. "And that is why you are here. Your story will be showcased in one of the many stories of children like yourself, Hogan. The story, of course, '*loosely*' based off the current events that have recently transpired." Hogan furrowed his brows from the comment. He didn't exactly know what he meant by the term 'loosely.' *This whole time was The Eye really working with Curtis?* "Your gripping tale of how you met a man who would scour the earth in search of the monster who killed his little Missy; the both of you, together, man and child, abducted by a gang of ruthless killers, then faced with an epic showdown with the greatest warlock to ever roam the earth, the one who calls himself 'The Eye.'" *Is he for real?* Hogan couldn't make sense of what Curtis was saying. He was, in fact, speechless. "Tragically, though," Curtis said, "your good friend, Michael, didn't make it out alive. *But*—but if we could change the story; and instead of Michael dying, he rose from the dead where he forever rode through the night in search of vengeance." The excitement rose in Curtis's voice and Hogan no longer saw that charming debonair man; instead, he saw someone who was no older than himself. "With your permission, we have the power to bring *your story* to life, Hogan! So, what do you say?"

Curtis, smiling, waited for a response.

Hogan still remained speechless.

"I don't know," Hogan muttered, the upper part of his cheeks turning red. "It's *not* real. I mean, what about Elisa? How can you bring her back?"

"Yes," Curtis said, the excitement melted from his face. "You're right. I can't bring her back. But I can bring back the memory."

"The memory? She's dead."

"She is, isn't she? But she doesn't have to be—"

"—Why are you doing this to me?"

"I know this is a lot to take in," Curtis said as patiently as he could, "but just think about it for a moment: your story, Hogan, will be one gem among an entire collection of gems!" His excitement was rising again, in his voice, in his face. "Each night, each episode will involve new stories, like yours, Hogan, with a new villain, a new adventure. All you have to do, Hogan, is sign your signature on this sheet of paper," he pointed to a sheet of paper lying on the glass table behind him. "It's a contract saying that you agree to have your story shared with soon-to-be millions of viewers across the world. And like I said to you earlier, I already have a crew of hard working actors and special effect artists waiting for the green light—which basically means that they can go ahead with the project. All they need from you, Hogan, is your signature; and you will be guaranteed a life of success, wealth, great fame, and fortune. . . "

Hogan remained in a state of shock. He had no words. Nothing.

Once more, Curtis placed his hand over Hogan's shoulder.

"I'll tell you what," Curtis said, squinting his left eye at Hogan. He paused, which gave Hogan an opportunity to speak. He just didn't know what to say to the man. "It's a lot. I know. I'll give you the night to think it over," Curtis said to Hogan. "How does that sound?"

———

Billups was called to the crime scene. He investigated the dead bodies, each Knight, each one of the creatures, which now had all turned to a pile of decayed organic matter, unrecognizable; then, finally, he came across a white envelope covered with three bloody fingerprints. He opened the envelope, only to find a severed tongue inside.

"What do you got?" asked Augustine.

"Another breadcrumb," he said and handed his partner the envelope.

## 11. Carte Blanche

*I don't even recognize the world anymore. It feels so distant to me now, as if it's moving backwards at a million miles per hour and it's trying so hard to pull me along for the ride.*

FROM the guest room, Hogan watched the full moon cast a pale light over the cityscape; and he found himself thinking about Detective Billups. He wondered what he was up to right about now, the good detective; he wondered if he was now investigating the warehouse and the carnage inside, the monster, Horus, and what was left of it— Hogan was quite certain that Killian Blanc wasn't Killian Blanc anymore, but his body was taken over by something way more primitive; he was about ninety-nine percent certain that Killian was, in fact, the monster known as Horus.

Hogan shook away the thought of Horus and remembered what he was doing here. He tried to make sense of Curtis's proposal. *Can it be more obvious?* Hogan thought to himself. *If I sign this contract, I'm signing my soul to the devil.* Only one thing was keeping Hogan on the fence and preventing him from making any sound decisions.

Hogan seesawed back and forth with his decision: *What if he's telling the truth?*

Hogan hoped the director was someone whom he admired and not some talentless spoiled brat who had a close relative in the movie industry or even worse, a desperate hack who sucked his way into a job.

*What if Curtis and the producers and the director—whoever that may be—stay true to my story, except for a couple of minor tweaks here and there, like Mike not dying? That would be something! Instead,* he thought, *Mike could've ripped out the Lens from The Eye's eye socket and used its power on himself to revert himself back to the way he used to be. That would be some story, wouldn't it?*

Hogan turned away from the pane of glass covering the side of the guest room and walked to the lamp on the night-stand next to the bed.

Something strange happened just as he lifted his arm to switch on the light. An incredible soreness weighed down over his left bicep. His muscles locked up, nearly restricting his arm from extending over his shoulder. Hogan, being a righty, hadn't been entirely aware of the pain until now. The pain was like his friend and, at the same time, his worst enemy. He couldn't help but wonder if the pain had been there ever since he arrived at Curtis's lavish penthouse or if somehow he was injured earlier in the night but didn't know about it because of all the chaos and confusion and whatnot.

Hogan held his left arm underneath the light and noticed a tiny red dot on his arm. He touched the dot but nothing. No pain.

Then, he carefully pressed his index finger into the muscle around the red dot and the pain shot through his arm like a bolt of lightning.

Hogan suddenly hissed and pulled his hand away from his arm.

He drew his attention to other things, such as the night-stand below. A spread of reading material lay before Hogan, mostly fashion, entertainment, and special effect magazines with Curtis posing on the front cover.

He picked up one glossy magazine in particular, *Reel Magic*, from the nightstand and found an article written about Curtis Saeman.

He flipped through the article until he found a familiar

face in the centerfold. *What do you know?* Hogan thought. *It's The Eye!*

In the centerfold, The Eye was sitting at a large dining table with eleven other men and women, all unique in appearance. Hogan was more interested in The Eye than the others. The Eye was wearing a black eye patch over his left eye. At the opposite end of the table stood Curtis Saeman, villainous-like, around all of the other characters as if they were his creation.

Below the caption: *Hollywood's Next 'It' Man.*

Hogan read the opening sentence to himself: "Thought magic only happened in the movies? Meet the wizard behind the curtain. His name is Curtis Saeman and everything he touches turns to gold."

Hogan studied each face in the photograph, each person or freak who had signed a contract to make his or her story into a movie, each and every one who was a part of Jóhan's motley band of circus freaks. Hogan looked closely at the man sitting to the right of Curtis, tucked away in the shadows. It was Jóhan Halldórsdóttir himself! Hogan found the date that the photo was taken in the credits. The date was a couple of months before the date Jóhan was murdered. The only question that came to Hogan's mind: *What if Curtis is not who he says he is? What if. . .*

Intrigued, Hogan continued to read through the article. He only got about halfway through the article until his eyelids started to weigh over his eyes. He drifted several times from the lack of sleep and each time he woke up with just a little bit of energy—at least enough to get him through more sentences before he started to drift once again. Each time he woke, he read less and less until it got to the point where he was waking to only read one word at a time. On the seventh time of his reawakening, he felt an electrical jolt, like that particular feeling one gets when he finds himself falling. He suddenly woke up with a more violent flinch, both arms jerking above his body. His first reaction was to grab hold of his head.

Hogan searched his surroundings, more frightened than baffled.

For the first time in a very long time, he feared going to sleep.

—

The red sky washed over the sky. Hogan sat on the edge of the bed, wide awake and ready to face Curtis with the news.

Two men in suits knocked on Hogan's door before entering.

The two men opened the door for a slender woman who carried herself with much grace and dignity. She had sharp eyes; her chin was even sharper; in fact, each feature on her face was as sharp and deadly as a knife. She was dressed a black skirt and blazer, no shirt or bra underneath. Her brunette hair was gelled and pulled back in a bun. She was wearing black stilettos with switchblades as heels and every step she made stung Hogan's ears.

"It's time, Mr. Hill," she said expressionlessly.

Hogan exited the guest room and was escorted to the gallery where Curtis Saeman was waiting by the table with the contract.

"Did you sleep well?" asked Curtis.

"No," Hogan said.

"Well, I suppose you will tonight. So, have you made your decision?"

"No," Hogan said bluntly.

"Is that so?"

"*No*," he said again. "I'm not going to sign it."

"Hogan," Curtis said and briefly paused, "I don't think you realize what's at stake here. I'm giving you a chance to be famous. Don't you want that?"

"No," Hogan said yet again, but this time more bitterly. "I don't. I just want to go home. That's all."

Curtis let out a sigh.

"So be it," Curtis said and waved at the two men standing

behind Hogan.

———

Bodyguards escorted Hogan to an elevator.

The elevator opened as soon as Hogan stepped in front of the doors.

Wary of the bodyguards, Hogan cautiously stepped inside, so did the two unspeaking men. One man pushed the *B* button on the keypad. *Basement*, Hogan thought. He tried to think of other words that could've started with the letter *b*, but *basement* was the only word he could find.

*Why are they taking me to the basement?*

The doors closed with the tiny *thud* that sounded much louder to Hogan. He could even hear distinct bodily sounds caused by indigestion: his sour stomach making all sorts of bubbling, croaking, screeching noises, as if he had swallowed an entire swamp full of amphibians and rodents.

The elevator started its descent and before it could arrive at its destination, Hogan was already dreading stepping inside the elevator; in fact, a wave of panic caused him to sweat bullets.

They traveled at least fifty floors; but, to Hogan, it felt more than that; and the elevator made no stops whatsoever. They passed floor number one; and sure enough, the elevator stopped at the last floor, the basement.

The now rickety doors opened at a slow and wobbly rate and finally revealed a long stretch of a white marbled hallway, which gave way to this massive gray, glittery room, grandiose in nature, elegant, with Corinthian-style columns and high ceilings, much higher than the ones Hogan observed in Curtis's penthouse.

In the very center of the room were a chair and a pedestal holding what looked like a crystal ball.

Unsure whether or not to step from the elevator, Hogan was suddenly grabbed from behind.

The bodyguards made the decision for Hogan, who was

pale and shaking, and physically dragged him against his will from the elevator.

Hogan resisted, of course, but the men's strength was overpowering.

"Lemme go!" Hogan called out.

The bodyguards didn't make a sound, didn't even put up much of a fight; instead, they manually carried the lifeless boy to the chair. Hogan assumed the deader he could make his body, the harder it would be on the two men; however, that was not the case at all. The bodyguards didn't miss a step while Hogan went limp, both of his legs dragging on the floor like loose shoe strings.

They plopped Hogan in the chair and with leather straps, they secured his wrists over the armrests.

Again, Hogan resisted but his attempts to escape were merely fruitless.

A door next to a giant hearth suddenly slid open with a short *whiz* of air and Curtis stepped forward into the room. He walked directly to Hogan, who now remained speechless.

Once more, he tried to loosen the binds on his wrists. Curtis nodded at one of the guards.

"Hit him again," he said to the man in the suit, who, in return, pulled a needle from his coat pocket, then injected Hogan with a sedative in the same sore spot on his left arm.

It took a couple of seconds for the drug to set in and by the time Hogan started to feel its thorny bite, he calmed like a yoga guru.

Lastly, the other bodyguard placed a metal device over Hogan's face, which pinned open his eyes.

"What are you doing to me?" drawled Hogan.

"I gave you the opportunity to be someone, Mr. Hill, someone who everyday people could look up to for inspiration; yet, *you* chose to be one of them. Why, Mr. Hill?" he asked Hogan. "Why choose to be a nobody?"

"What. . . what makes you any better?" drawled Hogan as he began to drool from the side of his mouth. "Because you have a nice house? Because you have money? What do all of those things even mean to me? How would those things make my life any better?"

"You don't get it, do you?" said Curtis. "Without success, you're nothing."

A dark and ominous cloud suddenly billowed inside the crystal ball; and for the life of him, he couldn't look away from its magnetic pull.

"I am a somebody," Hogan said, his voice getting weak and frail. "I am a somebody," he groaned. He resisted: "I am a somebody!"

Hogan's hair slowly started to turn gray and then, eventually, it began to fall out from his head like dead autumn leaves. His face was next to rapidly age. The corners of his eyes developed crow's feet, the wincing had only made the wrinkles more distinguishable. His posture quickly weakened, so bad that he found himself falling over the armrests of the chair.

Before his transformation was complete, Hogan passed out from all of the excitement.

## 12. Not Kansas

*Do you ever get the feeling that there is something else going on beyond the surface? Something more sinister?*

**"F**OR crying out loud," a sultry voice said from the darkness, "give him some space. Will you, Bear?"

Hogan cracked open his eyes, only to be greeted by two blurry celestial-like figures looming over his body—one of whom went by the name, Barry. All Hogan could make out was that one of them was a white man and his name was Barry, and the other, a black woman. Hogan never caught her name. They were both hunched over Hogan inside a cramped space, both of their faces unrecognizable. Even when the black woman spoke to Hogan, her mouth appeared like a round, black fuzzy dot beating like the faintest pulse. The black woman's words started to slow; that tiny dot opened less and less until, finally, the blur washed over Hogan's entire range of vision.

Two high-pitch snaps of a blue-gloved hand brought Hogan back to consciousness.

"Sir," the black woman said to Hogan the same way a younger person spoke to an ailing senior citizen who was hard of hearing. "Sir," she said with an overly loud and drawn out tone, "please stay with us now. Sir. . . "

Hogan's eyes narrowed, his vision appeared as if it was let-terboxing with two black mattes on both the top and bottom of *his view. His eyes bolted farther open, then narrowed, then widened, and Hogan did this several times of narrowing and then widening his eyes until he managed to focus on a spot on the paramedic's face. The once blurry features of the black woman's face remarkably materialized: a mouth first, two voluptuous lips glossy and reflective from the hazy fluorescent light inside the ambulance; then a nose, then green eyes, which Hogan thought could've been contacts. He didn't know exactly why the idea popped in his head, but he couldn't stop looking at them, those beautiful green eyes. He moved his eyes downward and saw her powder blue paramedic outfit. More sounds came forth, a once steady drone of a cry, now a siren wailing above. Feeling was next to set in, of course, the pain hit Hogan with a quick one-two punch across the face and neck; then the vibration of tires moving below him.*

*"Whaah. . . where. . . "*

*"Sir," the paramedic said, "we're taking you to San Valley Memorial—"*

*"—Huh?"*

*"What's the last thing you remember, sir?"*

*"Dunno," Hogan murmured, "don't let 'em do it. It's my life—mine—not his to take—"*

*"—Sir, don't let him do what?"*

*Hogan's eyes flickered, the paramedics turned blurry again, celestial.*

*The other paramedic—the white man—swapped out the bloody gauze from Hogan's forehead with a brand new one and then reapplied the pressure against Hogan's head.*

*"He's going to destroy me. . . " Hogan started to trail off. "You can't. I won't. . . "*

*His eyes rolled over white.*

Hello, Darkness.

———

The smell of fresh paint was the last thing he could remember, then a WET PAINT sign made from a piece of torn cardboard roped from one side of the hallway to the next with blue painter's tape. The smell of paint was later masked by the smell of cheap, fumy cologne, then that shit-eating grin of a lawyer. The vivid details of his face were heavily exaggerated: a toucan's bill of a nose peppered with tiny black heads; each pore on his skin as deep as the Kaali craters in the island of Estonia; the iris of his eyes, rich and brown as soil stretching through the cranial nerves that bind, pupils as black and enticing as black holes; lips as sharp as scissors. Hogan couldn't quite tell if the man was wincing or smiling or both as he, in his freshly tailored suit, squatted over his body.

Hogan removed the lawyer's face from his thoughts and woke up on a painfully uncomfortable hospital bed.

Part of his gown was wedged underneath his right hip and had already left a nasty, yarn ball-like pattern tattooed on his skin.

Hogan readjusted positions and let out a series of hate-fueled grunts while doing so.

Once he was all settled—not the least comfortable but settled nonetheless—the remnants of a strange dream about being transported in an ambulance came to him in waves of warm panic; and the more Hogan thought about the dream, the nightmare really, the harder it became to grasp.

The nightmare drifted farther and farther until it started to fade into that gray haze.

He looked around the stale hospital room.

To the left, a heart monitor was chirping like a gay finch after a spring shower. His numbers looked good—at least that was what Hogan thought. His heart rate was under seventy, which seemed pretty normal to Hogan. His blood pressure was one-twenty over seventy.

On the moveable table beside the bed rested a container of water and an empty bedpan.

These minor distractions caused the past dream to become all but a forgotten dream.

And the sight of the IV on his left arm destroyed the

dream. *Not a dream*, Hogan realized. A memory. And like all memories, they never die. This, Hogan knew. Memories had a strange way of appearing whenever they felt the least amount of neglect.

A young familiar woman entered the room with a familiar walk, face, and smell.

Hogan recognized her eyes, the way they looked at him; however, he couldn't recall where he had seen them before.

"I contacted your father," the nurse said to Hogan.

"My father?"

"That's right," the nurse said to Hogan. "He was listed under your emergency contacts."

"Sorry," said Hogan. "What did you say?"

"I told him you were in the hospital—"

"—Was he upset?"

"Of course not," she said. "Why would he be upset?"

Hogan didn't answer. Instead, he turned away from the nurse. He could hardly look at her.

"How are you feeling, Mr. Hill?" asked the nurse.

Hogan ran his hand up the side of his face and felt the bandage wrapped around his forehead.

"Please," the nurse said motherly as she grabbed Hogan's right and more mobile arm, "try not to mess with the bandages."

"Sorry."

"Don't be."

She was hiding a smile from her face.

Hogan felt the need to ask the nurse if he knew her from somewhere—like if they knew each from school or work—but he didn't want it to come off as a pick-up line.

"Does it itch?"

"Yeah," Hogan groaned. "Sort of." Hogan studied the nurse's face and again, each time he tried to make sense of it, it was like trying to remember the details of a previous dream.

He pulled down his hand and realized his arm looked much different, not older, as in elderly, like before, no liver spots; and his skin wasn't as papery as an older man's skin, nor was it much younger or smoother than that of an eleven-year-old child.

Before the nurse could comment on Hogan's odd behavior, he suddenly asked, "Have I met you before?"

The nurse smiled the kind of the smile that comforted Hogan and said, "Maybe in another life." She tightened the loose cuff along Hogan's arm. "Must've loosened it when you moved." She reattached the Velcro of the cuff, which was occasionally reading his blood pressure. "There you go. Not too tight?"

"No," he said, thinking about the woman from Curtis's penthouse, his secretary with slick brunette hair, thin face, high cheekbones, and hazel eyes. *She looks so similar*, Hogan thought to himself, *if not, identical to her.* "Fine," he said vaguely.

Before the nurse exited, she showed Hogan the remote on the side of the bed.

"Just hit the button if you need anything," she said. "There's also TV. We only get like a handful of channels, but it's better than nothing, right?"

"Right," Hogan said. "Thank you."

The nurse smiled again, a forced yet cordial smile. She made yet another attempt to exit the room, and then she was struck by a sudden thought.

"By the way," she said, "I couldn't help but notice a mark on your left calf."

"Mark? What kind of mark?"

She unpeeled part of the blanket, then unpeeled the old Band-Aid from Hogan's leg, and showed him the wound.

She furrowed her brows, looked at Hogan strangely, and asked, "Were you bitten?"

"Bitten?" Hogan repeated.

"It looks like you were bitten by some kind of animal."

The nurse examined the red tooth-shaped impressions around the side of his calf and she was careful not to touch the red markings. She gently pressed her fingers around the wound, as if she was trying to release or extract something from inside it. To the nurse, the wound didn't appear infected, yet it looked rather fresh, recent—possibly a day or two old—whatever the case, the nurse had her own suspicions. Hogan thought that she was searching for a button of pain, seeing if the feel of her touch would draw any discomfort. Hogan felt nothing, neither pain nor discomfort, only the sudden rush of blood followed by a distant longing of what could've been between him and the nurse.

—

Hours passed like days.

Hogan ended up spending the majority of the afternoon flipping through one channel after another.

By the sixth or seventh pass—Hogan lost track of how many times he had cycled through the channels—all of the channels started to blend together like a wicked stream of consciousness separated by a momentary interval of a black screen: Two big city detectives on the hunt for a murdering rapist who was on the loose in the city; then Hogan flipped, a black screen; then, a wiseass game show host who had a knack for cracking one-liners, which drew a hullabaloo of phony audience laughter; flip, black screen; then a well-off mother and teenage daughter sharing fond tales about a man named Leon in a dimly lit great room; flip, black screen; an animation of a humanoid tiger with a quirky sense of humor piloting a stealthy hydrobot on a racetrack surrounded by a turbulent ocean.

Hogan pressed his thumb harder against the clicker.

On the TV: a news story about six everyday Samaritans rescuing an elderly lady in the raging floodwaters of a broken levee; then a scruff-looking backwoods man ripping an alligator from a murky river and dragging the twisting gator onto his boat; then another news story about a ruthless dictator threatening to launch nukes at the United States of America; then black screen, an award-winning science fiction novelist,

Dan Kellogg, speaking candidly about the rise of augmentation in an interview with a puffy haired journalist; a troubled strung-out young man walking along a beach, the ocean breeze running through his stringy wet hair; a giant amphibious creature terrorizing a cancerous small town in the rural South; a major league baseball player hitting the game-winning home-run; another news story about a serial killer known as "The Executioner" striking again, his latest victim was a father of two children.

Another pass of channels: a now bloody-faced detective cornering a bearded man in an abandoned factory and telling the scraggly "S.O.B." to go dork himself before putting three bullets in his chest; the audience going berserk as the contestant wins a three-day vacation to Hawaii; the melodramatic mother slapping a teary-eyed daughter across the face; the humanoid tiger swerving from a massive octopus tentacle bearing down on the track and then crashing snout-first into the side of the wall, its hydrobot bursting into a ball of flames; a family of four embracing one another in the pouring rain; the gator clamping down its jaws over the hunter's leg, the man screaming in horror; the leader of the deadly regime, Brothers Prophet, releasing a graphic propaganda video of the White House engulfed in fiery destruction; Dan Kellogg warning viewers the "end of the world is nigh" if we keep burning fossil fuels, warning people of the rise in cancer; a young man with a bookbag on his shoulder standing at the edge of a shore of the Pacific Ocean, gazing out into a red sunset; a raggedy-looking garbage man driving the "Gill-Man" look-alike into a power box, killing the monster by electrocution; a crowd at a baseball game cheering as they celebrate their team's victory; a reporter branding the name, *The Executioner*—other local news outlets calling him the "Head Thief" because he was known for decapitating his victims and stealing the heads of his victims.

Hogan zoomed through another pass—big city detective embracing his partner and then a game show host laughing himself blue in the face—before he suddenly went back to the news channel and removed his thumb from the clicker.

On the TV a reporter was talking about a boy involved in tractor accident outside Orson Valley. The boy was recovering from a minor head injury at the hospital and was expected to be okay. Then, in other news, the illegal immigrant, Julio Ortega III, who stabbed three innocent bystanders with a machete in an urgent care center on Saturday night, was expected at his first hearing in court today. Two of the victims died from their injuries. One still in stable condition. The assailant blamed the current administration for his actions.

When Hogan heard a distant *knock* on the door, a flash of anger spread like fire throughout his body.

Sweating, Hogan snapped from his trance and turned to the noise.

A short Indian doctor cautiously stepped into the room, made eye contact with Hogan; then, once he acknowledged Hogan, the doctor approached the hospital bed. He reached out his hand.

At first, Hogan was hesitant to shake the doctor's hand. Then, as the doctor introduced himself as Doctor Samir, he shook his dry, coarse hand.

"Nice to meet you," Hogan said finally.

"So, you were at the offices of Freud and Franklin when you lost consciousness and hit the side of your head on a table?"

"Are you asking or telling me?"

The doctor folded his arms across his chest and shifted his weight to one side of his body.

"According to your lawyer, you started to feel dizzy," the doctor informed Hogan.

Again, Hogan didn't know whether the doctor was asking him or telling him about the previous incident.

The doctor waited for a response.

Hogan said shortly, "I guess."

The doctor replied, "You basically blacked out. You fell and hit your head on the side of the table."

"Lawyer?" said Hogan, thinking about that one particular nightmare he had. *Or was it a memory?* Hogan wasn't so sure. "I don't remember any *lawyer*! I don't remember any of those things you mentioned!"

"What's the last thing you do remember, Mr. Hill?"

"I remember… " Hogan trailed off.

A violent image flashed through his mind: Hogan being held down as he was forced to gaze into a crystal ball-like device.

"Well," the doctor said grimly, "I'm going to be straight with you, Mr. Hill. We ran several blood tests, as well as a liver function panel, and for a thirty-eight year old man, Mr. Hill, your levels look very," Doctor Samir paused, "concerning," he said, pulling out a clipboard. "Frankly, I don't even know how you're still alive."

"What are you saying?"

"We found extremely elevated liver enzymes which, in most cases, will suggest that there has been 'significant' damage to your liver. According to the blood tests, we found traces of the drug, lysergic acid diethylamide—which you may know as LSD—as well as a cocktail of other drugs in your system, which indicate that you have might've been under the influence of a new drug on the market called, Chlorodionysus, or its street name, *Nostalgia*—that's what the kids are calling it." The doctor placed the clipboard aside; and again, he folded his arms over his chest. "Each trip can vary depending on the user's current state of mind. A user may experience hallucinations, which can range from mild to severe; periods of mania; a tendency to lose all motor functions; uncontrollable mood swings; even worse, the feeling of death."

For a moment, Hogan thought he was still dreaming.

He pulled himself from his own head and tried to focus on what the doctor was saying.

"One of the many side effects of Chlorodionysus is significant memory loss."

Immediately, Hogan's face lit up.

"Memory loss?" said Hogan. "What do you mean?"

"Well, Mr. Hill, the fact that you can't remember what happened from the past twenty-four to forty-eight hours is, in fact, concerning and we need to get down to the bottom of what's really going on in there. I'd like to order a CAT scan of your head—"

"—I don't understand what's going on."

"Of course, you don't, Mr. Hill," the doctor said. "The user may experience an incredible trip up to two to three days, but as soon as the drug starts to leave the system, the damage to the liver, as well as the brain, is irreparable. You may not remember whether or not you have taken the drug, but in *reality*, Mr. Hill, if you continue to take this dangerous drug, you will die. Maybe not tomorrow. But eventually, it will destroy you." The doctor pulled a couple of brochures from his pocket and handed them to Hogan, one of the brochures caught Hogan's eye: *Real-Start*. "I recommend a strict diet for the next couple of months. Normally, we prescribe patients trying to kick Chlorodionysus with Benzodiazepines to help with anxiety, but with you, Mr. Hill, your liver is so bad that you need to refrain from any drug use. Understood?"

Hogan zoned out for a second.

*What the hell is going on?*

The doctor leaned closer and reemphasized, "Mr. Hill, do you understand?"

"Yeah," Hogan murmured. "Yes. I understand what you're saying. No more drugs. I got it. So, what's next?"

"Get plenty of sleep," the doctor demanded. "I will be back tomorrow morning to check on your condition."

Hogan didn't have much to say to the doctor, only a simple *thanks*.

—

Hogan got up twice during the night, once to use the bathroom and another time to check the window to make sure the world was still there after he had a violent dream—more or less—a vision of what could've been. Still there. People coming and going from the hospital. Life still moved.

The nurse entered the room and checked on Hogan one last time before her shift was over and made sure that Hogan was comfortable. There was no exchange between the two, Hogan and the nurse, only a calm silence so natural and comfortable that, to Hogan, it felt as if the two had been together for years and long breaks of calm silences weren't the least uncommon, yet, every now and then, they were a necessity for a healthy, lasting relationship. While she was changing his bandage, Hogan's eyes crossed the necklace around her neck, dangling in the dark space of her cleavage. He didn't think anything of it at first; then, after a second glance, the rare ornament hanging from the end of the necklace slipped through the collar of her outfit and hung before Hogan's eyes. The pendant was shaped like a ball, iridescent, endlessly changing colors depending when the fluorescent light hit the pendant. He couldn't keep his eyes off the pendant.

The nurse looked down at Hogan, noticed his eyes attached to her necklace.

She grabbed the necklace, held up the pendant, and said, "My boyfriend gave it to me. Like it?"

Reserved, Hogan said, "It's nice."

Hogan swallowed.

Disappointment washed over him. He didn't know why he seemed so disappointed from the remark. Maybe it was because she mentioned she had a boyfriend. He made sure to remind himself that she wasn't going out of her way to be so nice to Hogan or to take care for him. He constantly reminded himself that it was part of her job to be nice and caring. He reckoned that no patient was treated differently; however, even though the somewhat steep age difference—Hogan figured she was in her early twenties, maybe even younger—he felt disappointed mainly because he was starting to like the nurse and the way she smiled at him.

"It's called a mood stone," the nurse said. "Apparently, it changes color based on my mood."

The color of the stone turned green.

"What's green mean?"

"I think it means I'm calm."

"So, what color does it turn when you're stressed out?"

"I think black."

"It's very telling, don't you think?"

The nurse bobbed her head.

"Kind of," she said, "yeah."

"I don't know if I'd want people to know how I feel."

"I think of it, more or less, as a reminder."

"Reminding you of what?"

"To not let things bother me."

"So, whenever I see the stone turn black, I should look out, huh?"

The nurse laughed and said jokingly to Hogan, "That's right. Stay out of my way." The nurse touched Hogan on the hand and said, "Everything's going to be okay."

"I hope so," Hogan said depressingly.

"Don't hope," the nurse said, gazing into Hogan's hanging eyes. "*Know.*"

They shared a glance for a moment and only a moment before the nurse walked to the other side of the room and wrote the name of the next nurse on the whiteboard. She left the room without saying goodbye.

—

Hogan drifted in and out of the monotony of late night television. The TV played a fictional courtroom drama with salary actors who were twenty years past his or her prime. Throughout the latter part of the broadcast, Hogan started to feel as if his head was putting on an extra pound after each time his eyelids crept toward closure. For a good five minutes, his eyes would close, then open suddenly, then close, then open; and this continued to happen, both eyes opening and closing, until his eyes remained closed for about twelve whole seconds. He suddenly woke up to the whispers of a child followed by the eerie *squeak* of a door. Hogan's eyes blinked open. He drew his eyes toward the TV first, three defense attorneys were making their case against three big men, then his eyes widened their way into consciousness. He followed the fading noises left of the TV and caught the tail end of a lanky man dressed in black scurrying from the room. Hogan readjusted his eyes to the darkness until other things, like minimal pieces of furniture, came forward in the reflective glow of the TV. He sat upright on the hospital bed, the blankets strangling his waist, part of the sheets tied around his shins and ankles. He kicked both legs free and ripped the damp sheets from his body and peered closer at the cracked door. He witnessed a couple of shadows moving in and out of the hallway light like specters. He heard other noises too, noises of random voices, two women chatting about their husbands. In the room next to him, a man was having a horrible coughing spell. Hogan tried to ignore the man, but the man wouldn't let up. Somehow, Hogan found himself thinking about his previous nurse, her smile. He could remember the way she smelled, too. She smelled of coconuts. He waited for a couple of minutes in a globe of haze, staring at the door, thinking, waiting. *But waiting for what?* Nobody entered. He heard a nurse talking to the man in the room next to him. He was complaining that he couldn't get it up—whatever that meant.

Hogan put aside the common late night sounds of the hospital and as he was about to change positions in the bed, he found a pale blue box sitting on the table next to the bed.

More mortified than intrigued, Hogan grabbed the box. He cautiously pulled the box close.

The front read in elegant cursive lettering: *Nostalgia*.

Inside the box was a set of contact lenses, an aluminum pack of pink pills, one for each day of the week.

He removed the literature from inside the inner pocket and using the TV glow for light, he read the booklet to himself: "Choose Your Filter."

Below were various options; Hogan only noticed one in particular, *Members Only*.

Below the filter were many other sub-filters, including genres of music—glam metal, hair metal, Italo disco, electronic, hip hop, quiet storm, adult contemporary, soft rock, and **new wave**—as well as fashion trends, like pleated acid-washed jeans, **Ray-Ban sunglasses**, shoulder pads, aviator jackets, then a sub-filter of the current technology specific to *Members Only*, including Commodore 64, **VHS**, 8-bit, Walkmans, synthesizers, boom boxes, then, finally, an ominous-looking sub-filter called "State of the Union," which allowed the individual user to choose from various categories from Reagan Bada Bing Bada Boom! to Cold War 2.0 to Bigger Brother to **The Dilly-Dally** to Velvet Deluxe to Hacker Attacker to Kill Hades to Snowball.

Hogan's face went slack, his jaw dropping into a gaping yawn.

Left in a state of mystification, Hogan started to become lightheaded. He closed his eyes for a moment, hoping the cool darkness behind his eyelids would help stop the world from spinning out of control.

*Is this some kind of sick joke?*

Hogan picked up the box, put the contents back inside the box, and made his best attempt at getting out of bed. He ended up tripping over the leg of the bed, stumping his big toe. His toe burned, but he recovered without making much racket, rolled the stand holding the IV alongside his body, and made his way to the bathroom where he slam-dunked the box in the trashcan.

After a second thought, he reached down into the trash and pulled out the booklet from the box and kept it to himself.

As Hogan made his way toward the door, the new nurse, a young man with dirty blonde hair and a face skeletal thin, stepped into the room.

"Is everything okay, Mr. Hill?" asked the young man.

"No," Hogan complained. "I'm *not* okay." He held up the *Nostalgia* booklet. "Who put this in my room?"

The nurse grabbed the booklet from Hogan's hand and looked it over.

"Where did you get this?" asked the nurse.

Hogan pointed to the table next to the bed.

"It was right there," he said frantically. "Right there on the table." The nurse didn't believe him. "Here," Hogan said and escorted the nurse to the bathroom where he showed him the Nostalgia box.

The nurse reached down and pulled out a box of Kleenexes from the trash.

"It was right there," he said, digging through the trash.

The nurse sighed.

"Try to get some rest, Mr. Hill."

The nurse exited the room with the booklet.

Hogan didn't bother chasing after the nurse.

He was too confused.

## 13. The One-Eyed Detective

*Even on the clear days when the sun is out and shin-
ing the brightest and the skies are as blue as the Pacific, the clouds are always there. And the rain will
never go away.*

THE next morning, Hogan refused the CAT scans that
the doctor had ordered the day before. The doctor
advised Hogan to visit a specialist named Doctor
Finnegan for a follow up on his condition. Hogan had already made up his mind. He was officially done with doc-
tors and whatever advice—beneficial or not—they had given
to him. And, in Hogan's mind, they were done with him.
To Hogan, it felt as if the entire world was done with him,
really, except for one man: Hogan's father—Hogan Senior—
who didn't believe in sunscreen and could've easily passed as
a light skin black man on his driver's license. While Hogan
spent the night in the hospital, Hogan Senior was vacation-
ing somewhere in the armpit of Miami with his new witty,
surgically-modified fifty-something year old weekend booty.
When the nurse reached out to inform him of his son's condition since he was the only one under Hogan's emergency
contacts, Hogan Senior couldn't catch a redeye from Miami
until early in the morning. He arrived at San Valley Memorial just as his son was being discharged on his own will. He
wasn't upset, as the nurse had told Hogan—at least he didn't
appear to be upset—however, Hogan could sense an un-

pleasant shade of a well-guided fury underneath that overly tanned, badly wrinkled face, which, Hogan thought, could've been made into a bust, left to collect dust motes in a museum. Hogan knew there wasn't such a thing as anger management—wasn't a believer of that meditation-bullshit pseudo Zen Masters taught at overpriced workshops. One either had anger or didn't have anger; however, Hogan Senior was an expert at not managing his anger but channeling it. And to Hogan Senior, there was a difference, a big one.

On the way home from the hospital, Hogan and his father didn't speak much in the car and any notion of having a relatively decent conversation was destroyed by long gaps of silence. It had always been part of the norm between the two, the silence. Short-winded rants about people committing acts of stupidity or having "senior moments" or observations of drivers doing dumb things on the road—even if it was something as incidental as a driver not using the proper turn signal while turning—were about the most they had in common. They were never really that close, Hogan and his father. They never had that infamous catch with the baseball or that birds-and-the-bees talk after Hogan turned six and had already taken an interest in other girls. After Hogan's mother passed away five years ago, Hogan built a wall between him and his father. Every now and then, he would peek his head over the wall for a couple dollars. And that was as far as their relationship had gone.

When they finally made it back home, the obvious clues of what had transpired days before Hogan was hospitalized started to come to light like the coldest of cold cases. For starters, the house wasn't in the same condition as Hogan Senior had left it before he flew to Miami. From the knocked-over trashcan outside the garage to various items of trash, which appeared as if it had been picked through by possibly a wild scavenger, scattered over the back patio—Haven's Meadow wasn't in short supply of raccoons or its slew of mischievous nocturnal creatures with well-known rap sheets, since the neighborhood was located right next to a forest, which was known to carry much wildlife, including coyotes, possums, and deer. Hogan observed other things out of place or even misplaced while doing a thorough sweep of the house, like his mother's silverware, which had somehow vanished from the kitchen drawer, to the gummy wrapper of a bean burrito crumbled up in the coffee maker—the remnants of a nuked burrito splattered over the insides of the microwave as well as several anthill-like piles of refried beans caked over the granite—to a wrinkled receipt from Oak Hill Eye and Vision found among the loose change in Hogan's pocket: these were all small clues, as fortuitous as they might've appeared, indicating the disturbing nature of a man on the verge of a mental breakdown.

Hogan spent a good hour in his bedroom trying to make sense of what happened to him. He was only given certain images and they were soaked in gray: he remembered staggering around the bathroom, searching for a contact lens as he was washing up before bed but coming up empty, then using an old pair of reading glasses with black frames to get him through the night, then going to see a laidback optometrist the next day, then, staring at his demonic eyes wrapped in blackness, in the rear view mirror.

While his father was taking out his frustration as he unpacked his luggage, Hogan managed to clean the mess in the kitchen before his father justified his claims that Hogan was unfit and lacked the responsibility to look after the house while he was gone away on vacation. Hogan headed upstairs where he came across even more clues in the media room. The room appeared as if it had been raided by a burglar. There were no signs of breaking and entering, only the sloppy actions of a confused man who was completely ignorant of his surroundings. He wondered how the house wound up so damn messy—I mean, Hogan thought, *what in the hell happened here?* While Hogan was cleaning up, he stepped on a piece of broken glass next to the window overlooking his neighbor's house. He found more broken glass from a plate in the bathroom trashcan. He did more inspecting, more thinking.  When he came across yet another Nostalgia box—this one being empty—in the trashcan, he started to question his own reality.  Hogan couldn't help but wonder: *Am I still in Nostalgia?*

Hogan soon put any notion of Nostalgia aside and found more clues around his room: a penny-sized dent in his bedroom wall; a streak of red paint next to the puncture in the wall; a chunk of drywall next to tiny chips of white paint peppered on carpet.  The alarm clock was missing from the nightstand.  It happened to be the color red, too.  Next for Hogan to discover was a paperback on the nightstand.  The book was called *Tomorrow, so far away*, and the story was about a hard-broiled private eye, John Lovell, old and damaged like a used engine, who woke up with a bottle of booze in his hand, his lungs as black and shriveled as an oily rag; he was the sour leftovers of what those close to him would call a decent man.  After many years of isolating himself from the outside world, a tragic story from Lovell's past resurfaced in the headlines, which forced Lovell out of an early retirement and sent him on an untimely quest of redemption.  Hogan was about halfway through the story; in fact, he was right at the part where Lovell was revealing his dark past to the reader during a prison visitation with a black man who was waiting trial for attempted murder and how twelve years ago—when Lovell was a young police officer in the force— he accidentally shot an innocent black girl named Chanel Rice, who, a day later, died in the hospital from his gunshot wound.  Young Chanel Rice's death made news around the country, sparking riots, protests, and unrest among urban communities.  Lovell wasn't charged; instead, he left the force, bought a secluded cabin hundreds of miles away from civilization, and he became nothing more than the man who lived in the woods.  Then, twelve years later, Rice's name appeared in the news, not Chanel Rice, but her younger brother, Devonte.  The story was riddled with one cliché after another.  Just thinking about the story, another story came to his mind, a gray story with one gray image: Mike sitting at a booth, slumped over the dinner table in a hole-in-the-wall diner, turning away, looking out the window with a *heavy* heart.

Hogan couldn't help but wonder if there was a connection between the two. The question would come up later in the heat of the night when Hogan was tossing and turning in bed. The night seemed forever plagued with graphic imagery of what he had experienced while on his Nostalgia trip. An image would come to mind, followed by another image, morphing into one another like some kind of liquid monster.

The barking of a yappy dog two houses down prevented Hogan from catching any uninterrupted sleep.

After several minutes of trying to find a more comfortable position, he decided to roll out of bed.

He checked the windows, cracked open the window to check out what the commotion was about.

Two larger dogs were howling at one another; another one soon joined in a symphony of sorrow. A domino effect happened, then yet another dog from down the street made a crescendo, then another one; and to Hogan, it sounded as if the howling was coming from another neighborhood.

Then, another neighborhood.

A whole chorus of dogs howling in unison.

Another night filled with the nightly charades.

*When will they ever stop?*

Morning came. Hogan was woken up by the sound of a phone ringing.

He rolled out of bed and checked the time, which read, "10:38."

For the life of him, Hogan couldn't remember the last time he slept in past seven o'clock—*I mean*, Hogan thought to himself, *seriously, ten-thirty!* The last time Hogan slept in to ten-thirty was during his college years and it was extremely difficult for Hogan to hold onto a decent memory of that tumultuous time period. Talk about a cloudy haze!

Hogan answered the call after the third ring. It was the same man whom the doctor had mentioned earlier—the law-

lawyer.  He only caught the name: Freud, of the law firm Freud and Franklin.  The lawyer wanted to know how Hogan was doing, but Hogan gave him no satisfaction and hung up the phone.

Later, Hogan ended up researching the lawyer on the Internet where he found a one Barney Freud.

The slogan on the website read: "The Courtesy Man." Courtesy Man?  Hogan said the name slowly, mapping out each syllable.  Cour-te-sy Man.  The *same man from a TV commercial*, Hogan thought, *not* a celebrity or famous TV producer.  One of those slimy ambulance-chasing lawyers.

He clicked on a better picture of Barney Freud.  Hogan knew the face, he just did; he had seen that face before—Curtis Saeman?  That was his name.  Not Barney Freud.

Right after breakfast, Hogan and his father used a courtesy car service, *Go-There*, to Earl's Towing and Automotive to pick up Hogan's vehicle, which had been impounded after Hogan spent a night in jail.  The man in charge of the place, Earl, charged Hogan an extra eighty dollars for keeping the car on a Sunday.  Hogan's father paid a hundred and eight dollars for the tow—that was only the first of many payments to come.  Soon, there would be more payments, Hogan realized, including hospital bills.  Hogan didn't even want to think about how much—or better yet—how little insurance was going to pay for it.  He skipped the doctor's advise of resting and spent the rest of the day doing house chores, starting with the lawn.  If the day couldn't get any weirder than it actually was, he ran over a pink animal leash while mowing the lawn.  A metallic object bounced off the blade of the mower and forced Hogan to suddenly stop the mower.  He searched the grass but couldn't find anything.  It wasn't until much later in the day when he was grabbing the mail that he came across a piece of pink leash.  He found the other remains of the leash, as well as the chewed up remains of a bell.  First, Hogan thought it was a floater in his eye, but then after massaging his eyes, the glint was still there.  He noticed the light coming from an object in the grass.  He kneeled down. Grabbed two more pieces of the leash, one half with the letters 'miss' and the other half with the letter 'y.' He put the two pieces together, the name reading "Missy" in jewels. He didn't think much of the name, Missy, not at first. Then, when he went back inside and threw the mail on top of a stack of old mail, he drew his eyes toward one particular envelope. As he was flipping through mail—mostly junk mail—he came across a letter from a luxurious retirement community outside Lake Augustine called *The Villas*. The retirement homes weren't like your ordinary retirement homes. They were, more or less, a part of a community with its own frivolous amenities, like a pool, a spa, and a workout room. Like an elder's paradise. The letter happened to be from a man who went by the name, Stephen Billups, who was in charge of financing. In the letter, he stated that he received Mr. Hill's inquiry and he left Mr. Hill a number to schedule an appointment. Hogan couldn't help but look twice at the seven digits of Mr. Billups' telephone number: 1211867. Strangely enough, these numbers were important to Hogan. He didn't know exactly why. But they were.

The next clue to come to Hogan's attention happened as he and his father were heading toward the grocery store to restock the pantry. On the post of a stop sign were the words MISSING CAT.

Below the words was a professionally done photograph of a white feline named *Missy* positioned in a regal pose in front of a gray backdrop.

Hogan found himself laughing at the photograph, not by the professional nature of the photo of the cat acting like a fashion model, but Hogan laughed at the name of the cat, Missy.

Hogan read the name of the owner of the cat below the photo.

Michael Morrow?

When Hogan returned from grocery shopping, it hit him when he was placing a box of Moon Pies into the pantry. He was suddenly caught off guard by a more than obvious plot hole in his story.

He raced to the computer where he googled the 1990's movie, *Total Recall*.

The movie was released in theatres in June. A full moon in June was known as Strawberry Moon or the Rose Moon, recognized for its red hue, whereas the Crow's Moon—also Worm's Moon—happened in March. Hogan realized that it just didn't add up, the story, his story.

*But it was real*, he thought, *wasn't it?*

Real or not, the story didn't make the least amount of sense to Hogan.

## 14. The Neighbor

*I want to meet the Wizard behind the curtains, and
I want to tell him how disappointed I am in him.*

THE rest of the afternoon turned out to be a wash.

Hogan didn't do much of anything but just lounge around the house, occasionally stretching his legs by wandering into various rooms of the house, thinking of something to do to pass the time—even pulled out a dusty jigsaw puzzle of pirates called *Black Skull* from the closet, only put together a couple of pieces on a poker table before moving onto something else, such as rummaging through manila folders from his desk drawer of old headshots of himself, wondering where things went so wrong for him, kicking back on a couch, staring at the flickering images on a TV screen, which seemed like an impossible task for Hogan. He flipped from one channel to the next but couldn't find anything to hold his attention, so he decided to play video games on his PS4. Then he wandered around the house some more, thinking about the authenticity of his story until his father returned home.

Around seven thirty, Hogan's father stepped out of the house yet again, this time for one of his weekly social gatherings at a local watering hole. Once a week, he'd meet up with a single woman around his age through a dating app called Lure on his smartphone—most of them were either divorced or desperate or both, but every now and then, he'd get a younger cougar who preferred much older and dapper men. This week happened to be more personal for Hogan's father, especially after his son came clean about his night in jail and the soon-to-be expenses swiftly coming his way.

Not even a minute after Hogan Senior left, Hogan was pulled from his train of thought by the sound of a doorbell.

Hogan thought maybe his father had forgotten his keys or wallet and he was too much in a hurry to go through the garage. He checked the front where his next-door neighbor, whom Hogan had never met, only observed, was standing on the porch. Strangely, Hogan knew why the neighbor was standing there outside the house.

Hogan embraced a deep breath before opening the door, a deep inhale through the nose, then an exhale through the mouth.

The neighbor first introduced himself by telling Hogan his name: "Yann Blanc." The neighbor pointed toward the house right of Hogan and said, "I live in the house next to you."

Hogan zoned out for a moment. He had heard the name before—*Yann*. What kind of parents would name their kid, Yann? And that last name, *Blanc*, sounded more familiar; and the more Hogan put thought to the name, the sicker he became. His heart rate increased, his throat tightened, and for a moment, he felt as if he couldn't breathe; the words came out half-complete, spoken without the least shred of confidence; even Yann ended up finishing his sentences for him.

Hogan's neighbor, Yann, looked at Hogan foolishly and asked, "Do you need some water?"

*Water?*

"To be frank—" Yann started.

Hogan snapped from his trance.

"Frankie?" Hogan said rudely.

Yann tilted his head to the side.

"Are you okay?" he said again.

"Why wouldn't I be?" asked Hogan.

"I don't mean to disturb you," Yann said as he held out his hand, "Mr. Ah—I'm afraid I never got your name."

"Hogan Hill," Hogan said and shook the man's hand.

Yann pointed at the driveway. Twice Yann pointed at something, which made Hogan realize that he was a man who liked to point at things.

"And the man who just left, is he your father?"

"Yes."

He touched the top of his forehead as if he was placing a thought inside his head. He queerly ran his fingers through his hair like a comb, which made Hogan question the man's sexuality.

"Two years I've been living beside you and we've been complete strangers. It's nice to finally meet you."

"Likewise."

"Mr. King was telling me that you were hospitalized. Is that correct?"

"Mr. King?"

"Your neighbor who lives behind you."

Hogan paused.

"You don't get out much, do you?"

Hogan turned red around the face.

"Yeah," he said, tightening his jaw, "well, Mr. King has a big mouth."

"I apologize," Yann said, his face reddening as well. "I didn't mean to intrude."

"It's all right," said Hogan, shrugging his shoulders. "I had an accident." He pointed at the stitches on the top of his scalp. "Bumped my head."

"I'm so sorry to hear about that," Yann said and found himself pausing over the tense silence. "Is there anything I can do—"

Hogan thought about calling Yann's bluff and taking advantage of the comment, like making him cook dinner for him or paying off all the hospital bills.

"—No," Hogan said vacantly. "I'm fine."

"Thought I ask. *Anyway*," Yann said over a sigh, "I'm also here to ask you if you've seen my dog."

"Your dog?"

"That's right," he said. "Horus. My dog, Horus."

The sound of the dog's name smacked Hogan across the face with a violent image racing through his mind: Hogan jumping over Yann's fence, then, Yann's now missing dog, taking a chomp out of his leg—his calf muscle to be exact. *The bite mark*, Hogan thought about the nurse and sudden depression slid over him and the nerves were like a bundle of tangled thorns underneath his skin. He snapped from his trance yet again. Embraced yet another deep breathe.

"As you may already know," Yann said as he carefully studied Hogan's odd behavior, "he's been missing for a couple of days."

Now careful in everything he did or said, Yann pulled out a wallet-sized picture of stout English bulldog from his wallet. He showed the picture to Hogan to refresh Hogan's memory. Hogan looked over the picture with carelessness.

"Maybe he and Missy ran off together," Hogan teased.

"Missy?"

"The missing cat," he said.

"Right," Yann said, "Mikey's cat. I doubt they ran off together. Horus and Missy don't exactly get along, if you know what I mean." Shaking his head, Yann said from the corner of his mouth, "Mikey, I swear that kid hates Horus."

"Who's Mikey?"

"He's the little goth kid who cuts my lawn every week. I wouldn't be surprised if he kidnapped Horus to get back at me."

"Get back at you?"

"Mikey has this wild theory that Horus may have killed his cat."

"Doesn't seem so wild to me," Hogan said seriously. "They're animals."

Hogan paused, then Yann paused.

"So," Hogan said before Yann could retort, "you're here because you want to know if I had anything to do with your *little* dog's disappearance? Is that what you're getting at?"

"Not at all, Mr. Hill," Yann said sincerely. "I just want to find my dog—"

"—You know what," Hogan said over Yann's voice and thought about whether or not to take up on Yann's previous offer. He stopped, rethought, and said in one breath, "Good luck in finding Horus."

Hogan nodded goodbye and shut the door behind him. Yann remained on the front porch for a couple of seconds with his shoulders hunched over in dismay before plodding back to his house. Hogan wished to never see the man ever again; in fact, he wished for a lot of things to happen right then and there but none of them seemed the least plausible.

## 15. A Place on the Hill

*Nothing is what it seems anymore. Nothing is real.*

EVERYTHING didn't quite set in until Hogan started to go over all of the paperwork that was given to him by the arresting officer, as well as the magistrate on the night of his arrest. The paperwork included the details of Hogan's incarceration, why he was arrested, the results of the "on sight" drug test, and, of course, a precursory of *all* of the fines that Hogan was going to have to fork out to the court, including the five hundred dollar bond Hogan owed his boss and friend, Tommy Winters, who ended up picking up Hogan from jail the following morning after being arrested for driving under the influence and public intoxication in the retail store, Ciel Fleur. Hogan sought legal services elsewhere and found a more reasonable, more professional, more genuine lawyer named Damon Sears, who was asking for a retainer of fifteen hundred dollars, opposed to the other more "commercial" lawyer, Barney Freud, who was asking for five thousand dollars to represent him. Now, Hogan wasn't entirely sure why or how he fainted in Barney's office, but he figured it had to do with either money or coming down from his Nostalgia trip.

He was leaning toward money.

Hogan Senior, being a former literary agent from New York who once dealt with lawyers on a daily basis, came prepared with a list of questions for Mr. Sears and did most of the talking while Hogan sat next to his lawyer and acted as if he was sincere in wanting to put all of this mess behind him by accepting the plea bargain and facing punishment.

Mr. Sears had thrown around the words *possible prison time*, but in Hogan's case, since it was his first offense, he was more than likely looking at a choice of either twenty-four hours of community service or twenty-four hours in jail, the punishment falling under a Level 5, Level 1 being the most severe; *but*, according to Mr. Sears—he couldn't make it more clear that this happened to be Big-Apple-sized but—anything could happen in a court of law. *Anything.* Hogan poked and then prodded at Mr. Sears, as he tried to gain more clarity and crystal-clear answers as to what he meant by his recent remarks. What it really boiled down to at the end of the day: Hogan's fate rested in the hands of a man or woman who harnessed the power to lock up Hogan for good—throw the book at Hogan, so they said—and it all depended on what "mood" the judge was in that day. And that was when Hogan felt like fleeing far away, at that very moment when Mr. Sears broadly painted a grim, yet unpredictable reality that Hogan could possibly see the inside of a prison cell, even though seeing a prison cell was less likely going to be the outcome—but still, there was that doubt in the back of Hogan's mind: *who knows?*

Physically, of course, Hogan was present, but mentally, he was traveling to somewhere else, somewhere far away. While Hogan tuned out Mr. Sears, he had lucid visions of crossing the border and never coming back, putting America in his rear view once and for all and starting a new life in a new country. In his mind, he was done with America, done with the system which routinely kept its citizens in check, done with all the malarkey, the noise—Hogan constantly complained about all of the noise as of lately—most of all, Hogan was done with what he called the dumbed down bullshit. Like many, he was done with technology; he was done with smartphones, apps, done with it all. He saw—or at least thought he saw—the detrimental effects technology was having on people; he saw the change in them; saw the ultimate savagery, saw the inhuman nature of technology—greater technology, lesser humanity—instead of helping out a fellow man in need, it was considered more acceptable to record and document even though, at times, it seemed more reasonable that Hogan only saw what he wanted to see; he saw these things—acts of human betrayal—as the outsider who distanced himself from the horde and he decided to run away from what was now known as the new world. Hogan didn't know exactly where it all stemmed from, his decline, but he suspected it possibly had something to do with the suicide of his all-time favorite actress who went by the name Sidney Davenport. Sidney's manager found the actress in the bottom of an overflowing bathtub; empty bottles of Percocet and other pain pills scattered over the tile floor. In a suicide letter that she left behind, she addressed the reasons why she decided to take a short cut and end her life or simply put, drift away in a sea of medication—one of the most common themes happened to be her outrage for the current state of the country, the divisiveness and the exclusion of certain races and backgrounds; her deep-seated hatred for the wealthy leaders in charge failing to acknowledge the threat of climate change; she addressed the lack of equal rights, the slow deterioration of civil rights; addressed corporate greed, politicians sticking his or her hand in the hands of dirty pockets; monster retailers owning the markets; Wall Street; addressed the rise in political corruption; social injustice; and last but not least, intolerance. Her untimely death was heard around the country as well as the entire world and, for a day—but *only* a day—everybody, especially her fans and those who praised her or talked about her in the highest regard or paid money to watch her on the silver screen, mourned for her. People from all corners of the globe came together in unification and shared stories of the talented and ever-so inspiring Sidney Davenport, and reacted lines from her movies; reminisced in the roles, such as her role in *Hurt*, where she played Vinca Rumsfield, the witty, snaggletoothed recovering drug addict, or the charming, graceful housewife, Ethel Deschain battling cancer in the Academy-awarding winning *Last Day in Paradise* or the crafty yet incredibly deceptive scientist Sidney played in the suspense-thriller, *Hard Copy*, which ended up being a launching point to a prolific acting career. For a day, there was peace in the world. Then, a day later, Hogan remembered, people were back at it once again, at each other's throats, mad and bloodthirsty. Somehow, the letter leaked onto the Internet, which started a brutal backlash and it was the first of many, like Sidney Davenport, to extend the divide of an already divided country, instead of bridging the increasing gap. Hogan saw people whom he once admired change—like Sidney Davenport, ones who easily stole the limelight, habitually appearing in tabloids or gossip magazines inside the checkout lines of grocery stores, the celebrities, athletes, musicians. *Hate* was the new trend.

And it felt as if it was never going out of style; however, it wasn't uncommon for people, like Sidney Davenport, to voice opinions about certain issues going on in the world—in fact, for decades, both celebrities and artists alike had been jumping on the bandwagon of change while others played a significant part by simply giving that bandwagon a gentle push. Hogan felt as if modern day artists could no longer carry the depth he or she once embodied through the expression of art; instead, they were pedestrian, less than pedestrian, two-dimensional cardboard signs behind bookstore windows. He often wondered if the divisive climate had uprooted the foundation of self, turned the individual against the indidivual, resulting only in two ever-changing groups, *good/bad, right/wrong, black/white*, which left very little room for gray.

Hogan's feelings about Sidney Davenport aside, except for the typical mischief of a typical American adolescent—smoking pot, drinking alcohol stolen from the parents' liquor cabinet, smashing mailboxes, egging houses, rolling trees—Hogan had been what one would call a law-abiding

citizen for most of his adult life. He followed orders. He
had a job. He wasn't a violent individual by any means—
wasn't in his genes—but he was well aware of what prison
could do to even an ordinary person like himself. When he
spent the night in jail, he felt something ugly; yet, at the
same time, something beautiful came alive inside him, ugly
in all its form yet beautiful in its nature. Hogan thought it
might've been like a survival mechanism or something, an
instinctual switch buried deep down within the marrow of
his bones—and that night in jail, that ugly, beautiful beast
somehow found a way to claw its way through the muck and
flip on that switch. He was more than terrified of that individual, that thing; in fact, Hogan was so terrified that he
locked him away the day after his arrest and hoped to never
see him again.

But *what if* the beast returned? What then?

Hogan felt as if it would never come for him if he surrounded himself with smiling faces. Mexico was too hot,
only criminals ran to Mexico—like the ruggedly handsome
ones in the movies—and Hogan never, not once, saw himself as a criminal even though Hogan was guilty of breaking
the law. He wondered when all of the thoughts would turn
to actions. Over the past couple of years, that was all Hogan
heard from distraught people who were more than upset by
the direction of the country, "moving to Canada," as if it was
going to be a modern day mass exodus; but really, the talk
was mostly concentrated around former celebrities so desperate to chop off the *ir* from that awful yet burdensome adjec-
tive, *irrelevant*; then, all of the talk spread like a Black Plague
across the Internet and anybody who threatened to move to
Canada wasn't to be taken seriously. Hogan knew it was all
talk, people shooting the breeze, or simply airing grievances
to destructive contingencies.

But at that very moment, while Mr. Sears was informing
Hogan Senior that his son, Hogan, would save a lot more
time, as well as money accepting the plea bargain instead of
hiring an investigator and taking the trial to court in front of
a jury of his peers, Hogan fled far away to a strange land

where the air was clean and pure and he hiked the Snowcap Mountains and he so desperately wanted to stay there on the mountain, in the bitter cold, but only for a short while—at least until he could get his mind right.

## 16. Happier Days

*How can I find a way to pull myself from this hole?*
*I wish someone would just throw me a rope.  Throw*
*me anything.*

OGAN Senior wrote a check for fifteen hundred dollars and Hogan didn't mention a single word about the money on the way home from the lawyer's office.  After Hogan muddled along by giving an ambiguous explanation about everything he remembered the day of his arrest—which wasn't much, really, only that he was bitten by an animal, which he now believed was his neighbor's lost dog, Horus, then everything that transpired after that hung on the balance of light and darkness—Mr. Sears informed him of the basic procedure as well as what he could expect in the next couple of months.  Since Hogan's timeline was pretty hazy, the lawyer would need Hogan to show up for the first hearing.  He would not have to do or say anything but make himself present and, of course, presentable.  During that time, the lawyer would meet with the arresting officer where he would gain a clear picture of what occurred on the day of Hogan's arrest—watch the dash cam video, listen to any audio recordings—and decide whether or not the arresting officer was "credible," if the arrest was unlawful; basically, looking at any angle to approach the case and see whether or not Hogan *had* a fighting chance.  The lawyer also went into more detail about the punishment, which included twelve to sixteen hours of mandatory classes at Wellness Center and Support. Mr. Sears couldn't stress enough that Hogan attending the classes before the hearing would look better on Hogan. Not only that, he was looking at fees on top of fees, fines on top of fines, mainly court fines, which could range up to three hundred dollars—even more. Since Hogan was being charged with a DUI, he would also lose his driver's license for a year since he was driving while under the influence of Nostalgia. If Hogan chose to drive after forty-five days of suspension, he would be able to obtain a limited driver's license, which would allow him to drive during a window of time; however, whatever vehicle he would be driving required a blood test machine to be installed into the ignition. The law was passed two years ago that any driver convicted of a DUI of Nostalgia was required to have the device hooked up to his or her vehicle. It was similar to the interlock device but instead of blowing into a Breathalyzer, the driver was required to put his or her finger into a device that drew a sample of blood; and if one's blood showed any traces of the drug, Chlorodionysus, then the vehicle would not start. It was as simple as that.

—

After Hogan and his father left the lawyer's office, Hogan's father drove Hogan to the closest One United Bank where Hogan scrapped the bottom of the savings account to pay back his father. While Hogan handed over the money, Hogan's father didn't say a word to his son, not even a thank you or an acknowledgment of any sorts.

—

*You're on your own with this*: those happened to be the only words Hogan Senior mustered during the entire drive home from the bank and yet, he acted as if he had an entire world of animosity on his mind from the way he paced around the kitchen.

"I know," Hogan said mindlessly as he was playing his PS4 while, at the same time, sneaking glances at *The Last Crusade*, which was blaring in the next room.

The movie had aired twice in only one week and Hogan caught the movie each time.

Hogan's father waited for further acknowledgment but Hogan was too wrapped up in fighting goblins in a mountainous landscape. Hogan Senior made his way to the edge of the kitchen, his hands sinking deeper into the sides of his hips. Hogan spotted his father in the corner of his eye. He pressed the pause button on the control; and finally, he acknowledged his father.

"I just need you to pay for these classes," said Hogan.

"I'm not paying for your goddamn mess," Hogan Senior replied.

"But I'll pay you back—"

"—Oh yeah?" A jovial madness suddenly rose in Hogan Senior's voice. "With what money?"

"I have money."

"From what you make at the video store?" Hogan Senior chortled. "You can't work there for the rest of your life, Hogan. You need a job with stability."

"I'll get another job then."

"Where? Retail? You hate retail!"

Hogan thought more about retail. If there was a word stronger than hate, then that would be how Hogan truly felt about retail. Even the pettiest act of rudeness from one of his customers would ruin his entire day.

"It's money, isn't it?" Hogan said over the tense pause. He stood up from the couch and waited for a response from his father. "I could be living on the streets somewhere. Is that what you want—"

"—Stop this! You need to get your act together!" Hogan Senior shook his head in disappointment. "You can do so much better, Hogan. You have the talent. You *had* the talent. Why do you do this to yourself, Hogan?" asked his father. "This isn't life!" Hogan had no response. He had nothing. His father persisted, "Why choose to live a life like this, wasting it away on video games and movies all day?" Hogan Senior waited for a response but received nothing. "For God's sake, Hogan, you're still hung up on what happened years ago. So, what happened to you? Huh? *What* the hell happened to my son?"

Again, Hogan didn't know what to say to his father. He didn't even know how many years had passed since the time spent in Los Angeles until he pulled himself from his body and saw himself from the outside looking in—a mere observer from a different point of view—so many opportunities had slipped through his fingertips, so many distractions, so many wrongs.

Hogan Senior shouted, "If you want to throw your life away, then so be it!" This was the first time in a long time that Hogan had seen his father so upset. For a while, Hogan wondered if his father still had any anger left inside him—he always knew that he had the anger, the rage, saw it withering away in the back of his eyes, but it was always there, only resting. Hogan's father turned away, almost ashamed to look his own flesh and blood in the eyes. He said over his shoulder, "It's your choice, Hogan. But don't you dare bring me down with you—"

"—What should I do then?"

"Hogan," he said, walking to the doorway, "as long as I'm alive, I'll always give you a place to stay. You know I would *never* toss you out on the streets, but it's time for you to start living on your own. You will never have a life as long as you live here."

"But I don't know where to go."

"That's up to you, Hogan, to figure it out."

Hogan became silent again.

"What do you want, Hogan?" asked his father.

"I don't know."

"You were angry in Jersey and now, you're angry here,"

Hogan Senior said, the anger returning. "What's it going to take for you to be happy, Hogan? Huh? Tell me!"

Hogan mumbled, "I don't deserve happiness."

"Stop it, you hear me?" Hogan Senior said.

Hogan kept to himself while his father left the room.

He could no longer listen to his son.

## 17. Patient Zero

*I think I found a way out and you're not going to like it.*

OGAN completely lost his appetite and whatever lunch he managed to hold down made him sicker to his stomach. He told himself that he would only take a twenty-minute catnap—to recharge the engines—but he ended up eating up the rest of the afternoon in bed. He was napping more, getting tired earlier in the day. Hogan wondered if he had mono or if his body was fighting off some other disease. When he woke, he made himself a cup of mint tea and killed some time by rummaging through old headshots again. Wondering again. He thought about what his father was saying earlier about Los Angeles, how he *had* the talent, had the look of an actor—or at least, his father thought he did; he used to have that eye of a tiger, the sharp face, high cheekbones, hollow cheeks, strong jawline, smooth skin, penetrating eyes, long and dark hair, which was slicked back, not with a comb but with both of his hands, not messy either, but right enough to look important but not too perfect and tight to look like an avaricious broker on Wall Street from the nineteen-eighties. Hogan used to often change his look. People often said he looked like Christian Bale— Hogan even gave a fanboy at a bar his autograph because he thought he was that psychopath from *American Psycho*. People even said that Hogan looked identical to one of the Baldwin brothers—the skinnier one who doesn't appear in that many movies. When he cut his hair short into a crew cut, people—mostly customers at the store or people who frequently saw him—said Hogan could pass as Luke Wilson's twin. He'd often thank them for the compliments—if that was what they really were, he didn't think so. Truth be told, he hated the compliments so much that he thought they were insults, thus creating more hostility for anybody who talked about his looks. Through his eyes, especially when he returned home from Los Angeles, he started to feel as if everybody was looking at him. They wouldn't stop looking while shopping at the grocery store or pumping gas at the gas station or sitting at the cocktail bar of a seedy lounge. He often wondered what these people were thinking, if they were wondering if he was someone famous. He enjoyed the spotlight and yet, at the same time, he hated it. He didn't want to be another copy of a copy. Most importantly, he didn't want to look like another guy.

Hogan thought more about his father's comments. Once when his father was doing his nightly finger-workout by flipping through channels on TV, he came across his son as an extra on a rerun of one of those hospital drama shows. Hogan Senior rushed from the bedroom and woke up Hogan in the middle of the night and together, the two of them watched the TV show, Hogan spending the duration of the time talking about each character and the actors who played them and what they were like to be around in real life. For four years, Hogan pursued a career in acting, slept in a car for months, stayed in motels whenever he could afford a room; he couldn't find much work in LA, only jobs as an "extra"; he did that for a while, dogging roles for one audition after another while working two jobs, one as a boom mic operator for a low budget production company, and the other one, cleaning dishes at an upscale five-star restaurant called *The Wave*. When he dreamed, he lived another life:

the small-town actor who *finally* made it as an A-list actor; constantly reliving the moment when he won his Academy Award, each dream he'd come up with a new winning speech depending on the current state of the country, his words mattered, they carried the weight to change the world; then he'd wake up, disappointed, wondering if his dreams were a glimpse or even a window into another realm, parallel dimensions with alternate timelines. It was fair to say that Hogan paid his dues but he never went anywhere with acting, never "made it," as one would say. By the time Hogan fell into acting, Hollywood was searching for "other" faces; and by then, he just wanted to go home. He starred in a film, *Saturday Night Slit*, that wasn't even considered low budget but more like gutter budget. The director, an overly pretentious hack artist whose father was a famous producer on the "outs" of Hollywood, spent the entire shoot trying to provoke fear into Hogan and the other actors with scare tactics and empty threats. Most of the sets on the film were thrown together with scraps found in the director's storage unit. It was a film that Hogan never talked about; in fact, he tried to distance himself from the film. However, whenever he met people, he would never shy away from the time he used to live in California—his California Days almost always came up in a conversation—and he'd almost always brag to everyone how he was in the action movie, *Cut From Darkness*. If you blinked, you'd miss his moment of fame as the snarky valet attendant who *quickly* appeared in the frame once the hunk-on-the-run, Scott Burns, played by the B-List heartthrob Bryan Somersby, pulled up in a shot-up Mercedes in front of a swanky hotel in Malibu. He tossed the car keys to the valet attendant; the valet attendant snatched the keys from mid-air, and said, "Rough night?"

At times, he'd end up saying that line to the locals at bars or an establishment wherever alcoholic drinks were being consumed.

He'd often dig up old pictures of himself before the days he left for Hollywood to pursue a career in acting.

Hogan looked so different back then.  He looked important.

Now, he could hardly recognize himself whenever he
looked in the mirror.

Through his eyes, he looked like something that could've
been easily tossed in the trash.

He looked used.

## 18. Minor Details

*After living a third of a lifetime asking questions,
I'm ready for answers.*

HOGAN had less than sixty days until his first hearing and as his newly hired lawyer, Mr. Sears, recommended, it would be in Hogan's best interest to finish the rest of the recovery classes before the day of his hearing. Mr. Sears couldn't stress enough about the importance of taking a "pro-active" approach in his admission of guilt and following through with whatever the courts demanded. The sooner Hogan showed remorse for his actions, the easier it would be to convince the judge that Hogan was ready to learn from his mistakes and be a contributor to society.

Before Hogan called Gregory Khan of Wellness Center and Support to set up a time for an assessment, which was going to cost Hogan a hundred dollars, he stopped by the county jail where he was held overnight and from there, he worked his way backwards.

According to the arrest report by Officer Mario Abascal, Hogan was spotted outside One United Bank making an erratic driving move. Officer Abascal never flipped on his siren; instead, he tailed Hogan to a floral shop called Ciel Fleur.

Hogan read through the details—the breadcrumbs—and as he was leaving the county jail, a brief yet jarring flash of what seemed like a distant memory sparked in his mind.

The sudden flash of a camera snapped his photo in front of a gray backdrop.

While Hogan both mentally and physically retraced his footsteps, a memory came to him in the image of a face and then from there, his eyes panned downward, revealing this short, stocky man who didn't bat an eyelash. The man was instructing him to remove the keys from his pockets, then his belt, phone, and he told him to empty all of the contents from his pockets. According to the Prisoner Property and Custody Control report, Hogan was carrying thirty-three cents, a billfold, one credit card, a watch (which turned out to be one broken watch), a belt, one set of keys. The unsmiling man handed him a pair of dirty slippers, which, to Hogan, appeared as if they were contaminated with every disease known to man. Hogan was then escorted to a gloomy office filled with all sorts of incoherent chatter where the man took Hogan's picture.

Say salami!

He kept the self-investigation moving along and headed toward Main Street where he came across a used bookstore called A to Z Reads. He spotted a familiar book in the corner of his eye as he was passing the storefront window. He stopped and took a double take at the book, *The Vancouver Murders*. On the book cover was a spooky-looking mansion.

Hogan stepped inside the bookstore and walked to the front of the store where the books were displayed. Another book caught his eye: *Woman From Manor*. He skimmed through the flap of the hardback. The town in the book was called Manor. He went back to the other one, *The Vancouver Murders* and read through the summary. The story was about a ragtag band of circus freaks involved in a string of murders. Evidence pointed at the circus freaks; however, there was a killer hiding among the circus freaks and he or she turned out to be worse than a freak.

He skimmed through the book and found out the names of the freaks: *Fingers*, a man who had fingers as long as swords; *Lockjaw* had a jaw as wide as an alligator; *Rabbit*, a little person who had super hearing—Rabbit had the ability to listen through walls and overhear distant conversations.

Hogan put the books aside and couldn't help but think if there was a connection.

Next for Hogan to discover was an ATM a couple of shops from the bookstore.

He read the sign above: One United Bank.

Nothing too suspicious about the ATM. The machine was like any other machine; however, what grabbed his eye were the tiny pieces of glass nestled inside a crack separating the wall from the sidewalk.

Hogan kneeled down and picked up a shard of glass and held it close to his face.

The glasses, he remembered, belonged to me.

*My glasses.*

Eventually, after several minutes of searching the vicinity, he found one half of the frame, which had been stepped on and kicked aside like a pebble.

Hogan carefully examined the frame and concluded that the frame *did* belong to him. He went back to the ATM and thought: *I must've been getting money out.*

But how did Hogan's glasses fall from his face?

He thought back but couldn't find a single thought as to how his glasses ended up as street debris.

Only one thought: Hogan squaring off with Ophelia's robot-creature. Mike unloading his gun on the thing, striking it in its TV for a head. *That was what really happened,* Hogan thought. The glass rained onto the ground. Pieces nearly hit him in the feet.

He snapped from his trance and turned toward the ATM machine. He stared at the screen and he found himself almost willing it to flicker with life, move, or give him a sign or whatever. Hogan figured if he stared long enough, then maybe something would happen. It just had to, he thought.

Suddenly, the still image came to life!

A young woman's face appeared on the screen.

Intrigued, he stepped forward and listened closely to the woman but realized she was only an actor promoting a new rewards card in an advertisement.

He studied the woman's face and realized she was not an actor. She was Jóhan's wife, Anita.

—

The very moment Hogan stepped foot inside Ciel Fleur and heard the flat *clunk* of a cowbell, he was struck by a momentary case of déjà vu. An intense feeling of both bafflement and blissfulness washed over his body and he felt as if he had been here before; in fact, he felt as if he had visited this place often and every time he did he always felt a calm ambience about being among all of the foliage. Was it from being surrounded by the many plants? He wondered if the various colors released some kind of natural response in his brain, one of great serenity, or if the aroma of certain flowers triggered something inside him—a memory? Whatever the case, he knew he was on the right track of the investigation.

He made his way toward the front counter, which remained absent of any life. He looked around but didn't see any employees or customers. The place was, indeed, dead.

Hogan made his way toward a rack full of magnolias.

A petite woman rounded the corner and stopped directly in front of Hogan.

The blood suddenly rushed from her face and she found herself lost in a pale, lifeless stare.

Hogan remained speechless as he studied her face. He recognized her face, Ophelia's much more youthful face, without wrinkles, a slight sag in her face, a head full of fried hair climbing down her shoulder like vines.

"Please," the woman said, her voice trembling, "I don't want any trouble. . . "

Hogan held out his hands.

"You have the wrong idea," he said timidly. "I didn't come here for trouble. I swear—"

"—Then, why are you here, Mr. Hill?"

"How do you know my name—"

"—*Why* are you here?"

"The truth," Hogan said over a tense pause. "I just want to know the truth."

Ophelia gazed into Hogan's eyes and as he did with her, she studied them carefully as if she was reading a book.

Squinting her eyes, she said, "You *don't* remember, do you?"

He opened his mouth in an attempt to answer the question but nothing came out. Even the words that somehow slipped from his lips sounded like the incoherent rumblings of a madman.

"My lawyer," she started, "he advised me to file a restraining order on you, but over the years you've been a loyal customer. He even said that I shouldn't be talking to you; he said specifically, if you came back here, then I should contact him immediately."

"I. . ." Hogan stuttered, ". . . I think you have me mistaken for the wrong person."

"Are you for real?" asked the familiar lady. "You don't remember anything?"

"No," Hogan said sincerely.

"Nothing?"

"No," he repeated.

She looked over Hogan once more, but this time showing more concern. She noticed the wicked-looking scar at the base of Hogan's scalp.

"Follow me," she said coldly. "You want the truth. I'll show you the truth."

Hogan followed the look-alike to an office directly behind the front counter. She took him to a small boxed television, inserted a DVD into the player, and pressed play.

"I made a copy just in case."

"Just in case of what?"

"Just in case you decide to sue my husband—or shall I say—my soon-to-be ex husband because a liability issue."

"Why would I sue your—your ex husband?"

"The store belongs to him," she said to Hogan, more at ease. "Well, not entirely. He owns the place, but me, I run it."

"I see."

"Let's just say it was his last pardoning gift to me," she said loosely. "He got the house. I got his store. You know, I'm surprised you haven't met the man already, you know, since you live right next door to him and all."

The sudden thought of the owner of the dog, his neighbor, Yann, came to Hogan's mind.

"Blanc's your last name? Yann Blanc is your husband? You're Ophelia?"

"Yes, yes, and. . . yes," she answered each one of Hogan's questions; then she corrected herself, "well, technically, *no* to the second one. We're currently separated."

Another image swiftly came to Hogan's mind and that image was of Ophelia sitting on Yann's back porch, sipping on a glass of iced tea, enriched in thought. He remembered Yann coming outside to check on his wife—or soon-to-be ex-wife—Ophelia, but she acted as if she wanted nothing to do with him; in fact, she acted no different than how an unruly daughter would act in front of a nagging estranged father. Hogan didn't know if it was her height or the way she was acting or what. She surely didn't look like his wife—at the time, that was. Except for several random pop-ins, that was the last time Hogan truly saw—as in Hogan trying to make sense as to what was going on with her life. He *saw* Ophelia on the porch, drinking iced tea, trapped in deep contemplation, then when Yann showed up, acting as if she didn't want to be there.

"Who is the older man living with him?" asked Hogan.

"That's Yann's ornery father, Killian."

"Killian?"

"That's right."

Another image came at Hogan like a straight jab to the face: Yann bossing around his old man and treating him as if he was an infant who was always making a damn mess all the time. The more Hogan thought about the father and son relationship, more images came to mind, more arguing between the two, more yelling, more fighting—the two were *always* fighting with one another.

"I don't know where things went wrong with us," Ophelia said. "I'd like to say that things went south whenever he moved in with us—"

"—You mean Yann's father?"

"Yes." Ophelia paused and cleared her throat. "Maybe it all started when Yann and I moved from St. Square." She shook her head, not with disgust, but, more or less, self-pity. "I really shouldn't be telling you this."

Hogan remained quiet and ready to listen.

"Yann would have my head." Ophelia paused yet again and looked over Hogan, studied his face, the emptiness running deep into it like a gaping hole, and she nearly teared-up from the sight of his face. "The truth, right?" she said to herself as she paced her words. "We were so—what's the word? So *naive*," she said in reflection. "I guess I thought that we could never turn into our parents. When we moved from the city to Orson Valley, all of those distractions we had bubbling up in the city started to lift like a curtain; and Yann and I started. . . we. . . we started to hate each other."

"Really?" said Hogan.

"Really," Ophelia returned. "I'm talking about the very antithesis of love. You can say we grew apart—*way* apart. You can also say we had already been apart and it was the small town that showed us who we really were." Ophelia let out a sigh. "After a couple of months of living in the suburbs, Yann's parents got a divorce and his father, Killian, moved in with us. He said it would only be temporary. Temporary turned into indefinitely. It only drove us farther apart. For a while, I thought family only brought families together." Ophelia rolled her eyes and shifted her weight against one side of her body. "Boy, was I wrong!"

Hogan zoned out for a moment and found himself walking down an alleyway in the middle of night. Hogan passed a possum, *not* a cat, eating a dead cat. The possum showed its fangs to Hogan before darting away. He kept walking until he came across a couple hiding in the shadows of the alley. A man and a woman. *The man*, Hogan remembered, was Yann. He only caught the side of his face, the other side, the side holding his cryptic Eye was lost in the shadows. The woman was his lover. Again, truth came at Hogan like two fists of fury. Hogan kept going backward on the timeline. Two more right hooks across the face: Yann's black BMW pulling into the driveway; the car parked, then two doors open, the driver's side, then the passenger's side. Two dark figures emerged from the car; then the two stood outside Yann's garage in the late hours of night; Yann then revealed part of his face in the floodlight, his mistress entwined in his arms, the two elusive lovers making out as if it was the last day on earth.

"I'm sorry," Ophelia said, reeling Hogan away from his thoughts.

"No," Hogan replied. "It's okay. It sounds like you are better off without him."

"Maybe."

Ophelia faced Hogan before she pressed the play button.

She sighed, again.

"Are you ready?" asked Ophelia.

"Yes," Hogan said clearly.

Ophelia pressed play.

The surveillance footage of Hogan walking into the floral shop, his eyes bloodshot, played on the screen.

He noticed that the timestamp on the bottom of the footage read the same date of his arrest.

Intrigued, Hogan watched the drama unfold: it started with Hogan mindlessly stumbling around like a drunk without a cause. Certain flowers lured him in. Hogan stopped three times, once in front of a hibiscus to smell its bright orange flowers, another time he ran his fingers along purple spiky flowers of a salvia plant, then became mesmerized by a colorful row of impatiens. Hogan stumbled to the cacti. Pricked one of his fingers while touching it. He wagged his hand. Then, for some reason, something came over Hogan. He accidentally—or deliberately, he couldn't tell which—knocked over the table of cacti. The cacti spilled on the floor. Then Ophelia rushed from the back and checked on the commotion. She found herself face to face with Hogan, who was acting belligerent. Hogan was rambling on about a cure. He needed Ophelia's help. Hogan said that she was the only one who could save him from the end of the world. Ophelia cautiously backpedaled to the telephone and called the police. Not even a minute passed before a police officer, Officer Mario Abascal, was on the scene; in fact, his cruiser was already outside when Hogan arrived. When Officer Abascal approached Hogan, Hogan was sitting on his knees next to the overturn cacti. Crying hysterically. Even customers who entered the store were keeping a safe distance from him. Hogan became aware of the officer's presence and started pointing his finger like it was a gun. He pointed his finger at the customers, then at Officer Abascal, who inched toward Hogan with his hands nestled over his belt, his right hand closest to his holster, ready to draw his weapon if necessary. He asked Hogan to take it easy—Hogan didn't—then the officer grabbed him by the arm; Hogan shrugged away and it appeared as if he resisted. As the police officer firmed his grip over Hogan's arm, Hogan complied; then Officer Abascal escorted Hogan out of the store. The End.

Ophelia happened to pause the video at the exact moment the officer glanced up at the surveillance camera.

"That's enough," she said.

Hogan leaned in closer to the TV for a closer look. The officer was the same man from his Nostalgia trip, the leader of the Los Caballeros—*How could this be?*

Ophelia removed the DVD from the player.

"You see, Mr. Hill," Ophelia said, "when you came to my

store the other day, you were in a very—how do I say—fragile state."

Hogan pointed at the TV.

"I can hardly remember *any* of that. I swear."

"Mr. Hill, do you know that you've been coming to my store on the same exact date for the past seven years. I was surprised to see you because normally you stop by around September. Every year, you buy the same exact toppers."

"Toppers?"

"Of course," she said. "They're called toppers because people normally put them on the top of headstones."

Hogan's face went pale and slack. He looked at Ophelia the same way she had looked at him just minutes ago.

"Is everything all right, Mr. Hill?" asked Ophelia.

"I need to. . . " he mumbled, ". . . I need to go. I'm—I'm so sorry for what happened here."

He rushed out of the store before Ophelia could make sense of his mumblings.

He never looked back.

## 19. The Day The Earth Stopped Rotating

*I just wanted to save them from death, but I wasn't
strong enough. And that makes me a guilty man.*

HOGAN ran.

He ran until his lungs burned. Then, he stopped to catch his breath and he ran some more. He made it to the edge of downtown where urban decay came in an unpleasant form of abandoned businesses, graffiti, barred windows, haunted houses, and the empty stares among what was known as its leftovers. Hogan didn't know where he was going—at least not until he passed the wrought iron gate to Orson Valley Cemetery. He wandered through the old cemetery, wondering when things went so bad for him, wondering why this town had so much of a grip on him, wondering why he was drawn to this very place, the cemetery and its skeletal residents. He just wanted to go back to a time when everything made sense—or at least didn't have to make sense. He noticed a purple topper on a headstone, which was unlike any of the other flowers. To Hogan, they stood out the most. He didn't know why he was drawn to that particular color. At this point in time, Hogan didn't know a lot of things, only that he was in deep, *deep* trouble. He put aside the previous interaction with Ophelia and walked to the gravesite of his childhood friend,

Fredrick Swan.

The headstone read:

JUNE 8, 1979 - SEPTEMBER 29, 1990

"*Freddie. . .* " Hogan murmured.

He kept wandering through the cemetery, kept searching for the same purple toppers. He found more purple toppers, more faded and not as together as the others. He walked to a headstone which read: "Chi 'Ching' Aguilera."

The date of his death read the same as Freddie's: "September 29, 1990."

He kept wandering, kept wondering about that particular date, September 29, 1990. He kept walking until he stopped at the last headstone, Elisa Fields. The death date was the same as his other two childhood friends. That was when he knew what had really happened to his friends.

The thought alone of what happened, that horrific accident, was so heavy that it forced Hogan to his knees. He couldn't hide the emotion any longer. Hogan started to cry, unlike his breakdown in the surveillance footage, slow and slightly restrained at first, as if he was doing all he could to keep the tears at bay; and whatever emotion that seeped out sounded like hiccups. Eventually, the memory of the accident came over Hogan like a tidal wave, a memory, nonetheless, attached to so much pain and misery. He couldn't hold in the tears any longer. He finally let go.

## 20. Her Name is Apolline Walker

*Sometimes, I wish somebody would try to physically harm me so I could release this thing I got locked inside me.*

O N the slow walk home, Hogan received a phone call from his boss, Tommy Winters, who owned the video store, *Hit Box* Rentals. Tommy was checking in to see how Hogan was doing. He was close to the area—actually, since Orson Valley was such a small town, which only shared two counties, Orson and Gibbonsville, the counties combine holding a population of about twelve thousand, Hogan was not even a mile away. He told Tommy that he'd stop by and grab a schedule from him. When he arrived at Hit Box, the place was empty—as always. Tommy's parents, who, like Hogan's parents, were from New Jersey; and they happened to fall ass backwards into money. Tommy's father was in the home improvement business for twenty-plus years. He was kind of a fixer-upper kind of guy who specialized in various trades from painting to carpentry. Tommy's mother, a former English teacher, independently published a children's book called *Little Wolf*, which ended up making her three times of what she received from a yearly salary from teaching after she sold the book's rights to a famous producer in Hollywood. Tommy's parents' substantial contribution to the store was the only reason Hit Box kept its doors open to the public. After Tommy's father was forced to retire from the home improvement business due to a bad back, he won the lottery—literally. Everyday for eleven years, he'd stop by the 24/7 and play scratch offs until one day he scratched off a winning number. The winnings made Tommy's father fifty thousand dollars richer. Mr. Winters took half of his winnings and hired a stockbroker who strategically invested his money in the stock market. Twenty-five thousand dollars turned into a million dollars in a matter of weeks. Mr. Winters wanted to give his son of a piece of the cut. Tommy declined. Instead, Tommy asked his father to keep the store alive. And that he did.

Hogan looked for Tommy; he checked the cash register, then the aisles, thinking maybe Tommy was putting away returns, but he couldn't find Tommy anywhere in the store. Hogan called out to Tommy; then, moments later, Tommy arched his head from the back of the store like a curious cat once he heard his name. He fully revealed himself, as well as the unrestrained excitement, to see his friend in one piece.

Tommy mentioned to Hogan that he spoke with his old man on the phone and apparently, Hogan's father informed Tommy about what went down inside Barney Freud's office—one second the lawyer was going over expenses, then the next, Hogan's world turned into two worlds, then three, then four, then lights out.

"How you feeling, man?" asked Tommy.

"Better."

"You sure?"

"Yeah," said Hogan. "I'm good."

"Man," Tommy said, "I ain't never seen you so 'out of it.'"

"Me either."

Tommy's eyes drifted in thought.

"You know," he said with a hint of laughter in his voice, "when I picked your ass up from jail, it was like you were acting like you hadn't seen me in years."

"I did?"

"Shit yeah," he said ecstatically. "Must've been some trip, huh?"

"Yeah," Hogan said quietly. "Guess so."

"You kept rambling on about some dude named Mike."

"I don't remember that?"

"Hey, I'm sure you don't remember anything about that night. I think it's probably best you put it behind you."

"Tell me about it."

"Curious," Tommy said, tilting his head to the side as if the question was better told at an angle. "So what was your old man's reaction when you broke the news to him?"

"You mean about what happened at the flower store?"

"That's right. He must've been pissed, huh?"

"Not as much as I thought he was, but I think he's more pissed about all the costs and what's it going to do to my car insurance, like jack up the cost. I heard it might be even double than what it is right now."

"I bet," Tommy mumbled. "That's the system for you. Given it to us little people, right?"

Hogan glared at Tommy.

"Little people, right?"

Tommy slapped Hogan on the shoulder.

"Hey, they could at least offer you some lube, right—"

"—I've learned my lesson," Hogan said seriously. "It's not like it's going to happen ever again."

"Maybe so, but somebody's gotta get paid."

The only word Hogan could spit out was not a word at all but more or less an airy *pfft*.

Tommy wanted to know when Hogan was available for work and Hogan said he could work whenever—in fact, the sooner the better. Tommy asked Hogan if he could come to work tomorrow. Hogan agreed.

Right before he excused himself, he asked how things were going with "What's Her Name?"

Hogan furrowed his brows.

"What's Her Name?" said Hogan. "Who's that?"

"You know, ah, Apolline, right?"

As he had been known to do these past couple of days, Hogan found himself in a trance-state. The name, Apolline, caused his stomach to churn and he became almost nauseous from the sudden punch of panic. *Apolline Walker*, he thought, *the crazy bitch*. He had completely forgotten about her. He mentally took himself back to the night of his Nostalgia trip, checking the dating app on his smartphone as the drug was coursing its way through his system. She texted Hogan over thirteen times that night—Apolline did—which he thought was unusual for only having gone out with the woman a handful of times. The last time he saw Apolline he realized the chemistry wasn't there. Not even a spark.

"I'm done with her," Hogan said finally.

"Another one bites the dust, huh? Seems like you're not having much luck with the whole Internet thing." He said louder, "Seems like your old man's having better luck with that dating site than you."

"I know," said Hogan, depressed. "I have a lot of catching up. Sometimes, I think he treats being a widower as if it's a privilege—an easy one liner to pick up women."

"Don't sweat it," said Tommy. "It's not about the number of women you've been with. It's about being with the right one."

"Oh yeah? Where'd you hear that?"

"Doesn't matter," he said. "Hell, if I were a woman, I'd date you. I mean, come on! You were in *Cut From Darkness*, one of the greatest movies ever! A guy like you, Hogan, you don't need a one-liner."

Hogan didn't respond to the compliment. Didn't know how to respond. So, he gave Tommy a smirk.

A customer entered the video store. Hogan and Tommy parted ways, Hogan going one way while Tommy going the other as if they got caught doing something illegal.

Hogan moseyed the aisles, browsed each bay, skimmed through DVDs on the shelves. Stopped at one bay in particular called *Hogan's Picks*.

Underneath were shelves of VHS tapes, mostly movies from the 1980's, including movies such as (all in alphabetic order) *A Nightmare on Elm Street, Altered States, Big Trouble in Little China, Body Double, Brazil, Critters, Dark Crystal, Dead Ringers, Enemy Mine, Evil Dead 2, Firestarter, Fright Night, Hardware, Legend, Lifeforce, Near Dark, Night Breed, Poltergeist, Pumpkinhead, Risky Business, Red Dawn, Scanners, Silver Bullet, Stand by Me, The Breakfast Club, The Evil Dead, The Fog, The Howling, The Hunger, The Labyrinth, The Lost Boys, The NeverEnding Story, The Outsiders, The Shining, The Thing, They Live, Top Gun, Troll,* and *Weird Science.*

Usually, he set aside a movie marking a particular day and placed it under his *Hit Pick Of The Week*—for example, he usually picked *Die Hard* during the week of Christmas, John Carpenter's *Halloween* during Halloween; while other days, Hogan picked a movie that related or corresponded to a particular event or tragedy, which gained media coverage around the entire country—in essence, opened a "dialogue." Last week, there were multiple deadly shootings throughout the country, all of which involved police officers gunning down innocent civilians due to the lack of training.

Hogan picked up the movie, *Robocop,* from his Hit Pick of the week, flipped it over, and skimmed through the back of the VHS tape.

"Give the man a hand, will you?" Tommy said from the back.

Hogan drifted into a trance. Looked over his hand.

"Hogan?"

Hogan turned his shoulder. Tommy was pointing at a customer waiting by the checkout.

"Hey, Hoe!" shouted Tommy. "Can you give the gentleman a hand?" he asked while rocking back and forth, his body curled forward as if his stomach was making a fist.

"What's wrong?" asked Hogan.

Tommy said, "I'm going to be a while. Bean burrito is running right through me—"

"—Yeah. Sure," Hogan said as Tommy rushed to the

restroom located in the back of the store.

Hogan walked to the cash register and rang up the customer.

—

Later that day, Officer Abascal paid a visit to Hogan Senior's house. Hogan's father happened to be in the shower when the police officer knocked on the front door. Hogan would be lying if he thought about not answering the door. Why should he? Why even deal with the officer after all he had put him through? Hogan had an idea of why the officer was standing outside the house.

Hogan took in a deep belly breath and opened the door for the officer. He eased himself outside while the officer stood at the bottom of the staircase. Hogan made sure to close the door behind hi. If his father got out of the shower while the officer was still at his house, then he wouldn't notice Hogan standing outside.

Hogan acted incredibly subdued in front of the officer, almost submissive in his reserved behavior. He made sure to keep the greeting short and to the point.

The officer first stated his reason for his visit. Like Hogan, he was short and to the point.

"Stay away from Ms. Blanc," he said robotically. "Do I make myself clear?"

Hogan completely understood what the officer was not asking, but demanding; yet he didn't know why it was coming from him and not Ophelia.

"Why?" he said, his heart beating faster. "Did something happen to her?"

"Ms. Blanc informed me that you stopped by her store this afternoon." The officer said bluntly, "She doesn't want you coming around her store anymore. You make her feel uncomfortable."

Hogan zoned out from the sight of the neighbors walking their dogs. No more than a couple of seconds passed in the conversation when Hogan witnessed three couples walking their dogs along the sidewalk. He didn't know why he was so captivated by the dogs. He felt as if it had something to do with his Nostalgia trip. Hogan could only squeeze out a word before Officer Abascal interrupted, "This is your *final* warning. Stay away from Ophelia Blanc or there will be consequences. Clear?"

The officer waited for Hogan to answer before leaving the property. Hogan was well aware of the consequences. If Hogan kept coming back, Ophelia would be left with no other choice than to file a restraining order on him and the last thing he wanted was to be "that" guy, even though he had every reason to visit her business establishment. After all, Hogan had rights; however, he just couldn't be that guy. He wasn't.

"Clear," Hogan said, his voice trembling.

He watched the police officer strut back to his cruiser and drive away. He turned his attention to his neighbor's house, Yann's house, and saw a younger woman, not Ophelia, but his lover, unloading a bag of mulch from the back of Yann's BMW; Hogan remembered seeing the same young woman in Yann's driveway during the night of his Nostalgia trip. That neighborhood kid, Michael—or Mikey, as Yann called him—entered the frame. The kid was cutting the lawn. Hogan thought more about the kid—*that name, Mikey. Mike*, he thought, *couldn't be a coincidence.*

Later that evening, while Hogan was nearing the end of *Tomorrow, so far away*, he had a moment of clarity. Hogan couldn't help but notice the similarities between the two of them, Mike—or Mikey—and the anti-hero, John Lovell, the heavy-hearted private eye who Hogan had, over time, come to fall in love with. He admired his resiliency, as well as his tenacity. John Lovell was incredibly flawed in every way, yet it was those flaws that made him an exceptional character. Hogan thought about Mikey earlier that day in Yann's lawn. The kid was looking around in suspicion, as if he was making sure nobody was spying on him; then he moved the push mower directly toward Horus's doghouse. The kid wrapped a piece of duct tape around the handlebar of the mower to keep it from shutting off; and while the mower was running, he discreetly searched in and around the doghouse, then inspected the ground.

Was he looking for clues?

*Clue to what, though*, Hogan wondered.

## 21. Best Kind Of

*I don't understand this place.*

FRUSTRATION boiled over into the following day.
Hogan spent the better half of the day fantasizing about what should've gone down between him and Officer Abascal. They'd burn him at the stake, he knew. He wondered if he could get arrested for even thinking of such horrible things filled with carnage. Hogan wasn't a murderer, wasn't close to one, but Hogan knew that he could've been one, if it wasn't for his mother and how she had raised him. The night in jail aside, that killer wasn't in him; it wasn't in his blood or his bones; but something was simmering deep inside Hogan, something much worse than a killer, something unpredictable. He felt as if he could've been more honest with the officer, told him how he truly felt about him, about the system, about Man. *But what would that even accomplish?* Hogan thought. A particular quote came to his mind while he was pacing around his bedroom: "People fear what they don't understand." He didn't know which movie the line had come from for he had heard it in several movies or TV shows and the line became nothing more than a cliché—and that went with many other lines, half-thought, the hand-me-downs from one movie or televi-

sion show to another; nonetheless, he couldn't help but think about how the screenwriters—the ones dictating the outcomes of stories—had gotten it *all* wrong; and if one heard these lines enough, one could only start to actually believe them, thus steering the masses in a unified direction, being politically and socially motivated. He concluded that people *didn't* fear what they didn't understand. People feared change. Hogan, being a creature of habit, knew all of the ins and outs of fear; he knew how to take fear by the reins and wield it to serve a greater purpose. Hogan was—in his eye—a master of fear; however, the only thing that Hogan feared the most was his own self and what he was capable of doing.

Hogan didn't sleep that night, not a wink, then the night after that, nothing. He could taste the ulcer forming inside him from the whole ordeal. He wondered when it was going to end and if it would *ever* end. The following night, he rolled out of the bed in the dead of night since lying in bed, wide-awake, wasn't accomplishing a damn thing but only making matters much worse. He checked the neighborhood from the vantage point of his bedroom window.

In the backyard, he witnessed the ghostly face of a possum hanging out on the branch of a tree.

The possum could've been the possible murder suspect involved in Missy's case; in fact, he witnessed a possum on the night that he heard that horrible wail of a cat.

What if the possum had murdered Missy, not Horus?

The plot continued to thicken!

—

The pain carried over into the early morning.

Hogan couldn't sleep a wink, which meant he couldn't think. He turned on the TV and hoped that the sound of the TV would help guide him to sleep, but it didn't work. He was left tossing and turning from the early chirps of songbirds, constantly trying to piece together the past events and replay a scenario where he saved his friends from their untimely death. The fact was his friends were gone and there was no other way of bringing them back, except maybe for one way. It was the *only* way.

—

Before noon rolled around, Hogan woke to a Barney Freud commercial. Hogan grabbed the TV remote wedged underneath his leg and flung it at the TV screen. Wasn't the best way to start off the day, that was if the day was even going to get started.

—

Twenty-four days later after Hogan's trip, he reclaimed his driver's license from Orson Valley County Clerk of Court. Another charge of a hundred dollars to stack onto his massive pile of debt; and then, later, he met with a trained counselor, Gregory Khan, who conducted an assessment at Wellness Center and Support, which ended up costing him yet another hundred dollars. Since Hogan was driving under the influence of the street drug, Nostalgia, Hogan fell under the required sixteen group counseling sessions, with each session lasting around two and a half hours, which, altogether, was forty hours of sessions, including one on one counseling, not twelve sessions as his lawyer had previously mentioned. The four-session difference only made him angrier. Not only that, each session was held in an intimate setting, not in a classroom, as he first imagined. Hogan feared sharing his story to a bunch of strangers; he feared what they'd think of him. He told himself that he wasn't going to be an open book. Instead, he'd rather stay vague and elusive like a good mystery novel.

Despite his story—at least this was what Hogan had told himself over and over, constantly practicing in front of the mirror that he did not have a drug problem and that the incident at Ciel Fleur was only a one-time thing—Mr. Khan made Hogan sign a memo stating that he would attend the required counseling classes within ninety days of the first session. The classes would cost Hogan over three hundred and thirty dollars. Expenses kept piling on and on and it wasn't just raining over Hogan. It was pouring. Now, Hogan was up to his neck in debt. To make matters worse, he would be required, by law, to have one of the blood devices installed in his vehicle after forty-five days of his license being suspended. Otherwise, Hogan couldn't drive for one year, which meant he would soon be out of a job. Soon, he would have no money, which meant he would be left to beg the streets for money and live off the discards of food that society threw away. He knew his father wouldn't let that happen, but he was sick and tired of being given everything.

## 22. Down the Road

*Feeling is starting to fade. When it finally fades,
what will happen to me? How can I get it back?*

A NOTHER news report broke about a major video store chain, *Video Mania*, filing for bankruptcy and closing the rest of its stores due to the rise of streaming. That was three major video store chains in the past two years to file for bankruptcy. First, it started with laying-off employees, then closing stores that brought the least revenue. Stores were vanishing one at a time. Finally, the coffin's nail came in the form of a closed sign. It was soon to be followed with a new coffee or yogurt shop. Skeptics said that movie theatres were next on the list to feel the swift decapitation of the modern day consumer. The report only made Hogan hate the entire world. He feared change, and the world had become too strange for him. His nerves calmed after Hogan and his father went to the gym. When Hogan got back from working out, he reached deep down inside himself and wondered if this was the reason why he chose to work at a video store, knowing it would inevitably change; and somehow, he knew that he couldn't fight that change and yet, he chose to stay the course anyway despite its soon-to-be demise. By the rate stores were closing, Hit Box would soon be the last store left standing. The notion alone made him angry; however, underneath all of that rage, he felt a sense of great pride. Alas, he would truly be unique.  And that uniqueness was worth fighting for.

—

The dream always started the same, with Hogan staring at his own reflection in the window of the bus.  He was sitting in the same seat in the second to last row.  Fingernail-like pieces of cracked leather cut the sides of his leg whenever he shifted positions.  In the seat behind him was Chi, who was hogging an entire seat.  Across sat Freddie and Elisa.  In the most verbose language, Freddie was going on and on about one of his "what if" scenarios, as in "what if two directors did a movie together."  Freddie was adamant about Team Verhoeven and Cronenberg, suggesting that their two powers combined would be the holy grail of cinema.  Then, Chi argued that Spielberg and De Palma would make one heck of an unlikely pair; however, with both of their creative forces, they'd make the greatest flick ever!  Freddie and Chi continued to go back and forth, arguing which team would make the better movie—Elisa would occasionally chime in to make a suggestion of her own.  All of a sudden the activity bus swerved to the right, causing all of the children sitting on the left side of the bus to catapult toward the right.  In the blink of an eye, Hogan was launched through a crack in the window.  He landed on the side of an embankment while the bus toppled over and started rolling down a steep mountain. That was when the dream ended the same, with Hogan bolting upright in a cold sweat.  He rolled out of bed and went to the attic where he climbed over dusty cardboard boxes, which were leaking childhood toys and action figures.  Most, if not all of the boxes, were badly torn and coming apart around the edges.  He came across a particular box labeled "childhood photographs"; he peeled away the loose packing tape, which no longer had any adhesive, and flipped through the photos.  One photograph in particular caught his eye: his

childhood friends, Freddie, Chi, and Elisa, were leaving the
infamous comic book store, *Heroes Inc.* Hogan, being the
photographer of the bunch, happened to snap the photo. He
caught the three by surprise, especially Elisa, who had a slack,
gaping expression on her face as she was glancing over her
shoulder where only a couple of feet away from Freddie, a
raggedy homeless man was standing on the street corner. He
was wearing this frayed eye patch over his left eye and was
staring at the three while rummaging through a shopping
cart full of used soda cans. The resemblance was uncanny;
however, the homeless man was *not* The Eye, nor was he related to The Eye. He knew it was a moment captured in
time; a moment that he wished could last forever. Hogan
kept flipping through the photos. He found a photo of Halloween '89. Hogan was around ten years old. He was
dressed as a traditional ghost: an old bed sheet with two slits
for eyes. Freddie was going as Frankenstein's monster; Chi
was Dracula or at least supposed to be Dracula—he looked
more like Eddie Munster from the TV show, *The Munsters*;
Elisa was dressed as The Wicked Witch of the West from
*The Wizard of Oz*; and lastly, there was a light-skinned kid
named Henry, who was a few years older than Hogan, going
as a werewolf. Hogan even found the same bed sheet that he
used on that same Halloween in '89—now, the bed sheet
was no longer white but more off-white, and the seams were
tattered and frayed. He used to find so much comfort in the
bed sheet, so much safety. At night, he used to hide underneath the bed sheet and read any book he could get his hands
on. He placed the sheet aside in a more useable, more stable
box; and then he kept flipping through more photos until he
came across the very last photograph taken of his three childhood friends. Their teacher, Mrs. Watkins, who also died in
the bus accident, had taken the photo of Hogan, Freddie,
Chi, and Elisa standing at the summit of Grandfather Mountain. If only he knew that—hours later after the photograph
was taken—his life would change forever. The sight of the
friendly faces brought him to tears. He kept flipping

through photos, the weight of the memory bearing down on his shoulders.

Hogan placed the photos aside and dug out an old brown newspaper clipping from the very bottom of the box.

The headline read: "Deadly Bus Crash in the Mountains, 13 Dead."

## 23. A Tear in the Sky

*I don't want to leave. I can't. I just want to live in there forever.*

THE following week, Hogan showed up at his first recovery class with a check made out to Wellness Center and Support for a hundred and ten dollars (Hogan chose to pay the three hundred and thirty dollars in three increments instead of paying all at once).

As he pointed out before the assessment in Mr. Khan's office, Hogan immediately noticed the circular arrangement of chairs in the center of the room. The setting was very intimate—maybe too intimate. A short, stocky man, who appeared as if he just crawled out of the woods, sat down in the seat next to Hogan. He was wearing frayed clothes that looked as if they were fished from a dumpster. The size of his pants was three sizes too big. Even his skin looked cancerous. Over a dozen open seats remained available; yet the smelly man sat right next to Hogan. Hogan was immediately hit by a wave of pungent odor, a one-two combo of burnt cigarettes and indigestion; and every time the smelly man coughed, he didn't even cover his mouth, and tiny bullets of phlegm shot from his mouth. Hogan did his best to think positive—*these are real people*, he thought, *people who have real problems*. The last thing Hogan wanted to do was to make a scene. Not only that, he decided that he was not going to share any stories about himself—even promised himself countless times before attending the recovery class that he wouldn't be an open book, yet he'd remain—as promised—elusive; but it all depended on what kind of crowd showed up. Only thirteen people ended up attending the class, from junkies to an older lush in his sixties to a dark moppy-haired man around Hogan's age who appeared as if it was his only intention to become friends with Hogan. The smelly man who was sitting next to Hogan broke the ice with questions that were restricted to answers that would only reassure the man like "Is this your first time offense?" or "You get one of 'dem lawyers, too?" or "How many classes you gotta to take?" or, since Hogan answered the second question with a yes, "Did your lawyer say it was required to take them classes before your hearing date?" He made sure to keep his answers as short as possible and never let the man know anymore about Hogan than someone could find on the Internet.

Mr. Khan eventually joined the group and took a seat at the front of the circle while everyone signed their names on a piece of paper.

Before the session began, he made everyone in the class sign a confidentiality form stating that whatever happened during the sessions would not be openly discussed beyond these doors.

Hogan signed the form. Then, Mr. Khan went around in a round robin-like introduction. Hogan found himself getting sweaty palms and extremely dizzy after the first three introductions. He zoned out for moment—but only a moment—and heard the whispering again.

When the time came for Hogan to introduce himself, the whispering stopped and he shared a little about himself—a little, as in his name, how long he had lived in Orson Valley, what he was doing here. Hogan stayed true to what he set out to do and remained elusive.

—

After the first session was over, Hogan waited for his father to pick him up outside the recovery center.

While standing on the sidewalk, he was hit by a cloud of cigarette smoke. He distanced himself from the two junkies, who were smoking next to the entrance. Even the people who worked in the unmarked suites above the recovery center were greeted by clouds of cigarette smoke as they exited the building. Hogan couldn't help but think how inconsiderate these two were, polluting the very air he breathed, slowly killing him. He wasn't even a smoker and yet, he knew he risked secondhand smoke like those poor victims from those anti-cigarette commercials, struggling to breathe, waiting to take that final breath. He didn't want to be hooked up to an oxygen tank by the time he turned forty or suffer from asthma or lung infections. He found himself taking in deep panic breaths from the thought alone of dying from lung cancer. He tried to block out words like *suffocating, choking, hyperventilating.* Each time he breathed, he smelled cigarette smoke. He could no longer stand by and watch these two junkies slowly kill, not only himself, but also each person who walked through their cloud of smoke. So, Hogan did what came natural to him: he distanced himself some more.

As he began to inch his way farther down the sidewalk, he overheard the junkies talking about "post," which was another street name for Nostalgia—one was calling it "lo-ro," a much shorter version of Chlorodionysus.

Hogan fought through the secondhand smoke and held in his breath; and whenever he needed some air, he'd take a baby inhale through the corner of his mouth. He crept his way back toward the junkies, stood above a sewage drain, which helped mask the smell of cigarettes; and he eavesdropped on their conversation. Apparently, one of the junkies was sent on a court order to the Wellness Center for his chronic Nostalgia usage. One of them was cracking jokes about a rumor that the drug was manufactured from strands of Spielberg's DNA. Another rumor: there was this brand new black and white filter, which allowed its user to experience a black and white trip, which, immediately, grabbed Hogan's interest. The junkie also mentioned another filter making serious waves on the streets. The filter was called "Night Dream," a filter heavily influenced by cyberpunk. Being an avid fan of the subgenre, Hogan was overwhelmingly intrigued. Another rumor: the pharmacists and scientists working around the clock at a place called Dynocorp—previously named Aerodyne before our valiant antihero burned it to the ground—were coming up with a more advanced, more potent Nostalgia pill. Rumor had it that they were ushering in users to this secluded Institute; users were paid boatloads of cash by staffers who were known as "architects." The architects' main objective was to extract childhood memories from the user and then create unique filters based on each memory; the user was said to undergo extensive tests, mentally and physically, before he or she could be prescribed the drug. The junkie said it was illegal, of course, not yet approved by the FDA. The sound alone of the two junkies talking about Nostalgia had Hogan thinking about *Tomorrow, so far away* and the urge to use again had nearly stolen his breath away. The anxiety became unbearable; so much that Hogan couldn't stop thinking about it for the rest of the day.

—

Late in the night, Hogan snuck downstairs while his father was sleeping and rummaged through all of the junk, including wooden sleds, rockers, and plastic crates of high school textbooks, stacked in the corner of the garage, until he came across his old bike from his childhood. He hadn't been on the bike in years—in fact, the last time he rode the bike he was around the age of twelve. The back tire was flat but nothing he couldn't fix with a manual air pump. He ended up having to reattach the chain as well.

Once the bike was good to go, Hogan snuck out from the house and used the rest of his money to buy Nostalgia on the street corner of Main Street from a kid half his age. He took the box of Nostalgia back home with him and spent the remainder of the night staring at the Nostalgia pill in his bedroom, contemplating.

—

"September 29, 1990," the counselor said to Hogan, "what does this date mean to you—"

"—Don't," Hogan started as he became more fidgety on the couch.

"Don't what?"

"I don't want to talk about it."

"I understand," Mr. Khan said quietly as he crossed his legs. "Then, we don't have to. So, what would like to talk about?"

"I don't know."

"We can talk about anything," Mr. Khan inquisitively tilted his head to the side and narrowed his eyes as if he was casting a line into a pond full of thoughts, waiting for Hogan to take the lure. "I mean *anything*."

The counselor waited for a bite—even a nibble.

"So, how's the treatment going so far?" asked the counselor. "Have you thought about using?"

"Sometimes," Hogan finally said.

"When these thoughts of using come about, how do they make you feel?"

"Anxious."

"Did you try exercising more, especially when you have these urges?"

"Yes," Hogan said. "Exercising helps—I mean, sometimes."

"How about reading? Does that—"

"—It wasn't my fault, you know."

"Your fault?"

"September 29, 1990," Hogan paused.

"Continue. . . "

"Our class was on the way home from a field trip in the North Carolina Mountains—Grandfather Mountain," Hogan said. "I didn't know how it happened, but the investigators said the driver took his eyes off the road for a second. They said he had a record. Speeding tickets. Once, he was caught driving recklessly. He shouldn't have been driving in the first place. I knew the guy. I think I might've liked him. I remember the kids called him Beast because he had a hairy back; and sometimes, you could see the hair coming out of the back of his shirt whenever he'd wear tee shirts. Only a few of us survived, you know."

The counselor didn't respond; in fact, he didn't make a sound. Yet, he gave Hogan a nod as if, by displaying tenderness and the willingness to listen to Hogan's every word, he was allowing Hogan to rightfully unburden himself from the horrible grief he had been carrying for so many years.

"I think there were eight of us or something like that."

"Have you spoken with any of the survivors?" asked the counselor.

"No," Hogan said.

"How about your father?" he said. "Have you spoken to him about the accident?"

"I can't talk to him anymore."

"How so?"

"He doesn't listen," said Hogan. "He hears me, but he's not listening. He never listens. It's almost like he shut off after my mother died. His room is the same as it was when she died. He hasn't even thrown away her clothes. Sometimes, I'll walk in on him and I'll catch him crying in front of her urn. I'm nothing like the man, yet I'm just like him. If that makes any sense."

"And that makes you upset, being like your father?"

"No," Hogan corrected. "I mean, I don't know. Sometimes, it feels as if I died in that bus crash and now, I float around day in and day out, undetected, scouring the waste-lands left behind by men. I feel like a ghost."

"And why do you feel that way, Hogan? You feel as if nobody sees you?"

"I don't know," Hogan mumbled.

Hogan's comment drew a sigh from Mr. Khan.

"You were close to your mother, weren't you?"

"Yes," said Hogan, voice trembling. "I think so. After her death, I started drinking again. Then, it just got worse from there. It felt like I was trapped—I am trapped—and I know the only person who can save me is myself. My father, he'll do anything for me. He doesn't want me to fail, yet, at times, it feels like he does."

"Do you think your father allowing you to live with him is only making your condition worse and preventing you from becoming a man on your own?"

"Yes."

"Why stay?"

"I don't know. Maybe I like feeling this way."

"I don't believe that, Hogan. I believe that you felt this way for so long that it has become customary to you when, in fact, it's not a healthy way of living." Mr. Khan adjusted position in his seat, leaned closer to Hogan. "Tell me more about your trip. How do you feel when you take Chlorodionysus?"

"It'll be like a momentary glitch," Hogan said, thinking. "I'll wake up in this strange place, not knowing how I got there."

"Tell me, Hogan, have you ever found yourself drifting deeply in thought, so deep that it almost feels as if everything around you suddenly pauses?"

"Pauses? You mean like zoning out?"

"Yes. Of course," the counselor said. "You see, Hogan, when you're feeling the effects of Nostalgia, an alternate world is being pulled over your eyes and you only see what *you*—the user—want to see."

"I see them," Hogan said clearly. "I see my friends."

"And what do they tell you?"

He struggled to say the words. He even made an attempt to force them out from his mouth, but they wouldn't come out, the words.

"It's become hard to even concentrate anymore," Hogan said, sniffling while fighting back tears. "I feel like a child who loves being a child, yet, at the same time, a child who hates being *just* a child."

Mr. Khan said to Hogan, "All of us deal with tragedies different from one another. Some of us run from the singular thought of what happened to certain loved ones while others, like you, Hogan, embrace tragedy."

"Embrace tragedy?" Hogan said resentfully. "What the hell does that mean?"

"It means you must learn how to accept what happened, then from there, you simply move on with your live."

"It's *not* that simple," said Hogan.

"Nothing ever is." Mr. Khan paused, waited for Hogan to gather himself. "In order to move on, Hogan, you need to confront what's holding you back. You need to face the skeleton in your closet once and for all—"

"—What if I can't?"

"Then, it will destroy you. In the long run."

Hogan hung his head in sorrow, thinking about the unavoidable task of finally facing his skeleton, his demon per se.

"What's on your mind, Hogan?" asked Mr. Khan.

Hogan fell into a state of silence.

"Every night," he said in deep reflection, "I see myself dying."

Hogan paused yet again, gathered his thoughts.

"Continue," urged Mr. Khan.

Hogan said, "I often wonder what it would feel like if I actually died in my dreams, if I stayed in long enough to commit my soul to the void. If I died in my dreams, would I die in real life?"

"And what do you think Hogan?"

"What do I think?" asked Hogan.

"Do you think you can die in your dreams?"

"Of course not," he said, "but *what if* I could?"

—

After the each session, Hogan would come home disgruntled and often times, he'd go on tirades of the moral decay of society. He often spoke about running away from it all, starting over in a new country, as if a new country had new people. During the fifth session, he was dissed by a young, attractive, twenty-something who, to Hogan, came off as an uppity brat who didn't want to waste time on him. He came home, pissed off, slamming things and rambling on and on to his father about how he couldn't take it anymore. After a while, it felt as if his back was against the wall.

And he constantly thought about only two things: either fighting until he couldn't fight any longer or saving not only himself the trouble, but also his greatest supporter the trouble and press the delete button.

He so wanted to press delete.

## 24. A Glimpse

*I am free.*

THE next few weeks seemed like a gray blur to Hogan.
Hogan ended up finishing the rest of his sessions
just in time for the first hearing. He arrived early at
his hearing, as his lawyer had advised. The very first thing
he did before he entered the courtroom was glance over the
docket. Over two hundred people were listed on the docket,
which Hogan thought was an extremely high number. He
thought there'd only be a handful of people in the courtroom.

The thought of being in a room full of that many people
made him even more anxious. He didn't have to do much
during roll call, except for sit there among the citizens.

The smell was the worse for Hogan who was sitting just
inches away from people who reeked from all kinds of aw-
fulness. Only this smell would come from an individual
who hadn't showered in weeks—maybe even months.

Some of the people sitting in the courtroom, Hogan
knew, were okay in his book—maybe good, even decent—
however, there were just so much of the bad that he couldn't
help but overlook the good or, in Hogan's case, the misfor-
tunate. After roll call was finished—the whole process took

twice as long as it should have due to the constant interruptions and misbehavior—the lawyer gave Hogan a court date of sixty days from the hearing. Hogan's lawyer had to meet with the arresting officer, Mario Abascal. A couple of weeks later, Hogan met with his lawyer to discuss their plan of action, how they wanted to approach the case. Hogan decided to go with a plea bargain; he'd take the punishment on the chin. After all, it wouldn't be much of a fight—if Hogan went to trial—since he was caught on the cruiser's dash cam driving incapacitated. The officer conducted a sobriety, as well as a drug test, which Hogan failed; and this resulted in Hogan spending a night in jail. The lawyer put together a timeline, which was more consistent with Hogan's story: he drove to the eye doctor; he withdrew money from the bank; as Hogan was leaving the bank, Officer Abascal witnessed Hogan driving erratically; then, the officer followed Hogan to the floral shop where Hogan was arrested. When the next court date arrived, Hogan and his father came to a mutual decision the night before to get a continuance, which meant forking out more money to help cover the lawyer's expenses; however, deciding to go with a continuance would help minimize costs in the long run, especially when it came to car insurance. Since his son was still on his car insurance and a DUI conviction would only jack up the rates, Hogan Senior wanted to drop his son from his plan. And when the time came, Hogan would have to buy his own car insurance. Hogan just wanted it to be over.

He dreaded standing before a judge.

He just couldn't stand a lot of things anymore.

—

That afternoon, after having spent the morning in court with his son, Hogan Senior stepped out of the house to run some errands while Hogan anxiously paced around his bedroom, looking for something to do. It was when he pulled out the box of old photographs that he finally knew what had to be done. He dug out the old, holey bed sheet from his

closet—the homemade Ghost costume that he used for Halloween—and rode his bike to the shopping mall, Orson
Valley Plaza. He mindlessly slipped on the Ghost costume
and stormed the food court of the shopping mall. Not once
did he ever receive any strange looks and pensive stares. He
felt almost invisible. He dizzily weaved through the tables
in the center of the food court. People were too busy eating
to look up at him. Hogan was, more or less, confused by
the people's reaction—or lack of reaction. He kept moving,
faster, louder. Never had he ever felt so alive, gliding
around the food court, zigzagging around each shopper as he
waved his arms around and made *boo* sounds. After a few
minutes of running around, Hogan stopped and paid closer
attention to the people. Nobody was acknowledging him.
Not a single person. He noticed a haunting trend. Everybody was staring down at a smartphone or tablet in his or
her palms. He kept wandering throughout the shopping
mall; he shouldered through another crowd of people. A
couple of people bumped into him, nearly knocking him to
the floor. Only one of them, Hogan noticed, finally acknowledged him and it happened to be a boy who was no
older than twelve years old. The boy smiled at him, then
pulled out a smartphone from his back pocket and started
recording Hogan with his smartphone.

—

The next day, Hogan woke up on the floor of his bedroom,
the rays of sun spearing through the cracked blinds. He felt
refreshed, certain. Even the sun shone much brighter than
usual. The air even smelled crisper. All of Hogan's senses
felt enhanced, back to they way he once remembered when
he was younger.

He stood up and found the Ghost costume lying on the
other side of the room. He walked over to the bed sheet and
found a red smear of blood below the two eyeholes of the
sheet. He picked up the bed sheet and noticed more streaks
of blood, fingerprints of blood. He spread out the sheet and

found a much darker circular stain of blood covering the bottom half of the sheet. He checked his hands and the rest of his body for any injuries but couldn't find any. He didn't know where the blood came from, but it didn't belong to him. That, he was certain of. He tried to think of how he ended up back in his bedroom. He had absolutely no memory of the day before, only one of dressing up as Ghost and running through a wheat field; however, not being able to remember what happened the day before didn't bother him the least. He balled up the Ghost costume, took it downstairs, and before he threw it away in the trashcan in the garage, he looked it over once more and smiled.

Not thinking much about how he wound up with blood on the Ghost costume, Hogan decided to take breakfast with him. He rode his bike to Main Street and stopped at the post office first where an elderly man wheeling an oxygen tank got in line behind him. The two shared a standoff before Hogan gladly let the sickly man step ahead of him in line. He waited patiently until it was his turn and picked up a box of envelopes. He was planning on writing again. He wanted to start sending letters to agents. The other night he was watching a TV show on a famous Polish photographer who went by the name Notalp. He learned that he too had dyslexia. Notalp was born with the disorder and knew that he was special ever since he was a child; he embraced the disorder as if it was his and his alone. Hogan knew if Notalp could be widely successful, then he too could be successful.

Hogan was leaving the post office when all of a sudden he witnessed Mike smoking a cigarette and standing next to a mailbox. He was wearing The Eye's Lens in one eye.

Mike winked at Hogan with the other eye.

In return, Hogan stopped in mid-stride and looked over Mike yet again and he appeared much younger, around the age of fifteen or sixteen. The kid was Mikey. He was staring at Hogan with a chewed-up toothpick hanging from one corner of his mouth.

The kid threw his bandaged hand up in a wave.

Hogan waved back.

Mikey strutted to his bike and peddled away.

Somehow, though, Hogan got a feeling that this wasn't the last time he would see Mikey.

In the corner of Hogan's eye, he witnessed a flicker of light coming from a TV set. He turned to his right and saw a display case of TVs behind the front window of an electronic store.

One of the TVs, Hogan noticed, pulsated with TV snow, then shut off and filled with TV blackness.

A strange man rose from his kneeled positioned behind the display case with a power cord in his hand. He slovenly dropped the power cord onto the floor, then wiped both of his hands clean, squared his body until he was looking directly at Hogan; then he lowered his head in a nod of reverence.

Hogan ignored the strange man, ignored the televisions altogether, ignored reason, as well as any creeping shadows of doubt, and walked back home.

Happy, carefree, and optimistic, Hogan looked forward to the future.

## 25. The Loop

*I can't help but laugh at myself. Life is all but a joke.*
*And death is its greatest punch line.*

HOGAN once questioned if the stories that he read paved the way to what a possible future in his lifetime could very well look like—a mere glimpse at that grandiose "what if"—or if they painted a much broader picture as to what was inevitably going to transpire; and it was up to us, the members of the human race, to choose our own fate.

For years, whenever Hogan wasn't writing, he contemplated these very things while spending the bulk of his days glued to any kind of screen, whether it be TV or computer, watching one breaking news report after another: the terrorist attacks—after Crisis, it was Brothers Prophet, and then, after Brothers Prophet, the terrorists no longer came in the form of an organization, yet a faceless global network spreading havoc throughout the entire Internet—daily suicide bombings; knife-wielding slaughters; workplace massacres; shootings; stabbings; plane crashes; a spike in automobile accidents caused by self-driving cars; train accidents caused by human error; increasing wildfires; building fires; cannibalism—which caught Hogan by surprise (after doing more investigating, he came to the conclusion that a counterfeit drug on the market was turning people suffering from arthritis into zombies. Everyday, reports doubled from the previous day, the fatalities rose. New weapons were introduced. New diseases. Words like *biological*, *chemical*, and *cyber* warfare had become daily practices. America was on the verge of yet another Cold War—"Cold War 2.0" was what people called it—same scenario, different pawns involved. More radical demonstrations were popping up like zits on the face of a greasy-faced teenager. More chaos.

Not only to Hogan, but also to the ones watching from the safety of their own homes, it felt as if one had a front row seat to Hell Freezing Over. A never-ending domino effect of horror. Scientists in London turned the Doomsday Clock to one minute before midnight. Provocative talks of World War III were part of daily discussions. Paranoia was left hovering in the air like the putrid stench of a rotten piece of fruit. The usage of Nostalgia increased dramatically—even yuppies and baby boomers were using. The drug was officially legalized by four states so far, California being one of the first states to legalize Nostalgia for recreational use; however, dosage was significantly less; in fact, it was nothing more than a watered down version of Chlorodionysus. It allowed users to experience a three to four hour high, a somewhat soft crash accompanied by a mild headache. Those who were prone to seizures were warned not to use the drug. Several kids died. There were many lawsuits against several leading distributors on the West Coast; however, after the distributors hired a monster public relations firm that supplied them with new advertisements, which were no different than beer commercials during football games, even a new clothing line with 3D graphics, it was as if all those kids' deaths never happened. Nobody—especially the recreational users—wanted to believe that Nostalgia was bad for his or her health.

It wasn't until the dawn of artificial intelligence that the members of the human race woke up from their trips. Most felt as if the fate of the human race was sealed to extinction. But for some, it was the party of the century. Either way, it was fair to say that "whatever progress was gained in technology was equally lost in humanity."

What was once fiction was now reality: Augmentation; brain processor implants; access to the Internet via contact lens; robotics; animatronics; barcode imprints; even artificial infusion. Historians said everything went wrong when man first stepped foot on the planet, Mars. It wasn't what the astronauts found on Mars that changed the course of the human race. It was what they brought back to Earth. The Mars Plague, a new disease resistant to any antibiotics, was introduced to Earth. The Mars Plague ended up wiping out nearly a fourth of Europe's population. The plague could only survive in Earth's atmosphere for no longer than four to five days before it died; and it only had an incubation period of two days, but the damage that was done was catastrophic. After the Mars Scare, the rise in printed organs increased, and new ways of eating such as recycled food, became the norm. Nothing went to waste. In addition, another new threat was upon the human race: mind hacking. The enhanced hacking was the new telekinesis.

Then, the inevitable happened, the Internet became so complex and volatile that even its users were at risk of being destroyed with the click of a button or the swipe of the mouse. People had become products.

And nothing was safe.

Even the grocery stores were being emptied out left and right, restocked, then emptied out. First, it started with livestock. Super bugs spread among the entire chicken population like the common cold. Chickens were the first ones to go. The cows were next to become extinct, then the fish, then, last but not least, the pigs. Extreme weather had left a shortage in the food supply. Crops were destroyed. Fruits and vegetables were extremely rare like hummingbirds. Resources were running short.

And Hogan eventually caved into the mass hysteria. He ended up clearing out his upstairs office and turning it into an extended pantry which was already packed to the brim. He had enough food to last him for years, decades if he rationed carefully. He even bought hundreds of packets of seeds in case the canned food ran out, as well as bags of fresh soil in fear of radiation contaminating the earth.

Nonetheless, life continued to rage on.

So much unrest and hate.

The violence overflowed into the streets until the sewers ran red with rivers of blood.

After a while, silence prevailed.

And the rain, a steady rain that never stopped.

Small towns flooded.

Homes and businesses washed away.

For Hogan, it felt like a calm before a much more devastating storm.

A precursor of what was to come.

—

When news broke during the five o'clock broadcast on the local news channel, WCBC11, Hogan was in the middle of cooking his famous marinara sauce made from garden-fresh tomatoes. He stopped everything he was doing and rushed to the TV where he listened to the reporter give a breaking news report on a man identified as Barney Freud, who was found dead on the sidewalk of 5th Street.

According to the report, Mr. Freud was discovered with glass scattered around his body. The window on the third floor of the Freud and Franklin suite had been shattered; and investigators believe Barney was either pushed through the window or jumped or even possibly fell from the window. The investigation was on going.

Hogan couldn't help but wonder about the strangeness of the dream last night.

Was it a dream inspired by reality?

Or was it a premonition?

While talk of war lingered, another one was upon Hogan.

In other news: Multi-billionaire Marlin Hanky, owner of SpaceU, confirmed in an official statement that his ambitious

Mars Exploration, *Red Horizon*, was only three years away from blast off.

—

Every single day consisted of the same routine for Hogan, only shuffled around in a disorderly fashion. Hogan didn't realize where the time had gone until he met a young man named Edward Flick, an outsider who, one day, showed up at Hogan's residence.

For any outsider searching through into Hogan's home, it was no different than watching the time lapse of the cycle of a flower. Second by second, minute by minute, hour by hour, day by day, month by month, year by year, watching that flower grow, then bloom, then blossom, then wilt, and then, eventually, die.

But Hogan didn't die.

Yet, he remained in a state of absence, neither living nor dying, somewhere in between.

Clinging to near death, Hogan never step foot from his property, never ventured into the real world. Yet, he stayed trapped inside that house, glued to his holoset.

When Edward found himself face to face with the reclusive man, he witnessed regret in his eyes. Edward happened to be passing through the countryside searching for food, when all of a sudden he crept inside a dusty, cobweb infested house, only to be greeted by the pump action cock of a shotgun. Edward rotated around, so slow that even Death himself was starting to grow impatient.

In the shadowy corner of the room rose a hunched-over man as old as the house itself; and it was as if he had somehow manifested from the wall.

Edward didn't recognize the old man—at least not until he took a step forward for a closer look.

Awestruck, Edward's eyes filled with wonder.

Years of searching had finally come to an end.

He found the legend.

On the holoset beside Hogan aired the same broadcast

that had been running on a constant loop for the past seven years after the freeze.

Edward held out his hands and asked the old man if he was, in fact, *the* Hogan Hill.

Even the name sounded foreign to Hogan.

Eventually, it took some convincing that Edward was not a scavenger; in fact, Edward told the legend that he had been searching for him for a long time; and when the legend asked why, Edward said, "Let's just say 'I'm a fan.'"

He was baffled by Edward's comment—but, in a sickly way, he was more or less intrigued to find out more about the young stranger.

Edward told Hogan that he once saw an interview that Hogan did many years ago, a couple of years after the First Campaign; however, Hogan didn't remember a thing about the interview nor did he recall doing such an interview.

The fact still remained: Hogan didn't remember a lot of things.

Edward went on to tell Hogan about how Hogan found a way to channel all of his frustration into energy and he used that special energy to write over dozens of screenplays, four of which landed Hogan great success and fortune—but, of course, Hogan knew nothing of these accomplishments.

After the First Campaign, there was a great fallout along the West Coast, Hogan playing a pivotal role in what was known as "The Revival of Cinema," which consisted of a small group of actors, producers, and directors who joined forces. This uncanny pair started making films again after the first writer's strike, which forced production for major projects to be put on hold; filmmakers dropped the use of digital cameras and went back to vintage cameras. Streaming turned into a thing of the past, since the Internet was no longer secure to use and plagued with viruses and malware and malicious websites and monitored by watchdogs and attacked by hackers. The group had a drawing from sub-missions, Hogan's script called *Man of Dawn* was a runner up but ended up getting a green light a year later after sub-mission. The story was roughly based around this *Rambo-*

style action hero who saved a spit of a town from destruction; his name, Doug Stake, a man of true grit, had become a tagline over the years. Stake: kids used that name as slang whenever another kid threw one helluva tantrum. "You know, Dee went all Stake on Mr. Smith" or "That kid, Dee, he's all talk and no Stake." The movie became a cult classic and many years after its initial release, gradually gained worldwide success. Producers had also grown interested in reading more of Hogan's work. Edward said Hogan liked the name, Doug. Sounded close to dog. Not only that, it rhymed with rug. And, according to Hogan's interview Edward kept referring to, that was exactly what Doug reminded Hogan of, a man who had been stepped on and beaten; and then, finally, once Doug started to tear and fray at the seams, he was tossed into the trash, only to be spat out the other side as clean as a housecat. Hogan kept submitting; eventually, producers wanted to meet with Hogan face to face; Hogan did; signed a contract and all, went on to have great success and all; gave people a way to escape after dealing with such tragedy; he gave them Doug Stake. All of Edward's accounts came as a shock to Hogan and he thought that Edward had him mistaken for the wrong person.

With no other option, Edward pulled out a photograph of Hogan and his family.

Hogan immediately snatched the photo from Edward's hand.

"Where did you get this?" asked Hogan.

"The Archives—before they were all destroyed."

Hogan turned away from the young man.

"I had a dream once," he said, his voice trailed off into a mumble. "*They* were in my dream."

"You may have dreamt of them, Mr. Hill," said Edward. "But they were real."

"Wha—what happened to them?"

"You don't remember?"

"I don't."

Edward took another more cautious step toward Hogan and closely studied his face.

"What happened to you?"

"Nostalgia," he said clearly. "That's what happened."

"Mr. Hill," Edward said, "your entire family was murdered. They weren't imaginary. They *were* as real as me standing here. Do you understand?"

Hogan thought back to that one dream. He remembered a man burning all of their possessions and everything that were attached to them in a rusty oil drum. He desperately wanted to erase these people from his mind and forget they ever existed because maybe—he thought—just maybe this man would be spared of any pain.

That man was Hogan.

And that pain was still there, lingering, waiting to step forward whenever it was called to rise.

"Mr. Hill," Edward said directly to Hogan, "I know the man who killed your family."

Hogan's face slackened.

"You do?"

"I know him all right—"

"—Where can I find this man?"

"I'll show you."

—

Edward walked Hogan through the wilderness of what was once a small town known as Clifford.

Edward nodded at a red eCar, which was parked behind the old Laundromat covered in vines.

"I'm parked over there—"

"—What the hell happened to this place?" said Hogan as he glanced at the overgrowth on the streets as well as the abandoned buildings.

"Nostalgia," Edward said, mimicking Hogan. "What else? Nostalgia is what happened to the world." Edward stopped in front of his eCar. "After the First Campaign, everybody had become so addicted to Nostalgia that people lost interest in their environment. People wanted to escape reality, but reality wouldn't let them."

"Why you?" said Hogan. "Why do you want to help me avenge my family?"

"You seriously don't know who I am, do you?"

Hogan didn't answer. Couldn't.

"After the Fourth Campaign—I stopped keeping track after the Fourth—the bombings had gotten out of hand. Everyday, an attack, either chemical weapons or cyberattacks. It was like we were stuck in one helluva vicious cycle. After a while, nobody could tell the difference what was real and what was not. Former President Mark Cannon—"

"—Cannon," said Hogan. "That name rings a bell."

"It should," Edward said. "Mark Cannon, the wealthy businessman who had opened up the door for future businessmen to run for office, lost reelection to an up and coming software developer who went by the name Damon Roth, a globalist who stuck his hands in the wrong pockets—"

"—Politics doesn't interest me."

"Is that so?" Edward said arrogantly.

"You didn't answer my question," Hogan said and waited outside the eCar as he waited for Edward to answer. "Who are you really?"

"I was a friend of Darwin."

"Darwin? Who is Darwin?"

Hogan found himself drifting in thought.

"Was, you mean. Darwin was your son."

Hogan thought about a young man named Darwin; however, two images of two different faces came to mind and none of them were alike.

"You, Mr. Hill, you wrote a novella called *The Party Crasher*, which was adapted into a screenplay called *Kill For Light*, which ended up becoming one of the most controversial movies of all time. The story was a satire based around President Cannon. The protagonist was a young man named after your son in real life, Darwin Jennings. He was what people once called social justice warriors, fighters of injustices. After his grandmother was turned down for treatment at a hospital, he had enough of the broken promises laid out by politicians. So, he founded the movement,

'One Stand,' and he took his fight directly to the White House. People thought he was out of his mind. Others, a con man. Eventually, Darwin started to gain followers. People were paying attention and reading what he had to say. Everything he wrote had a ripple effect. Even his words started to hold weight. The things he ended up writing about came to fruition. People thought he was some kind of celestial being sent by God—How could anybody predict the future? But Darwin did. And many thought that his fanatics were committing these acts of violence, but there was no proof. The police tried to assassinate him—came close, once—but they failed every single time. Darwin took his fight all the way to the top and met with senators and other politicians and congressmen. The only problem: they couldn't read sign."

"Sign?"

"Sign language," said Edward. "So, Darwin taught all of them. One word at a time."

"He was deaf," Hogan said, thinking. "I had a dream once—"

"—It wasn't a dream, Mr. Hill," Edward said over Hogan's thoughts. "It happened. You wrote it. Say what you want, but ideas can change the world. Your idea changed the world. People started to stand up and fight for what was right."

"I don't believe you."

Edward smirked and said, "I knew you'd say that."

—

During the drive throughout the countryside, a vacuum of silence filled the car.

Edward finally broke the silence: "I can see why you decided to move away from the city. It was to start a family, wasn't it?"

"No," Hogan said. "I mean, I don't know. I didn't want to be a part of the circus anymore. I wanted to be the guy on the outside looking in."

"The observer, huh?"

"Yes."

"So, you wanted to be the guy who watched from a distance as the whole world went insane?"

Another wave of silence sucked the air out of the car. Hogan found himself taking in a deep breath.

"Is it really true?" asked Edward. "Did you really destroy The Eye?"

Somehow, Hogan remembered The Eye. Of all the characters he had written about, The Eye was the one character who had stayed with him the most.

"Fiction, Edward," Hogan said finally. "It was fictional."

"Yeah, but aren't stories based off reality? There is some truth to fiction."

"Not in my world," Hogan said; and when Edward kept prodding for more answers, Hogan rested his head along the headrest and told him to keep quiet.

—

It was a good five-hour drive to Detroit.

Edward stopped twice during the trip, once to recharge the super alkaline battery of the car and another time for Hogan to stretch his legs. When they arrived in Detroit, the city was overwhelmed by bright lights and massive holograms the size of skyscrapers. Edward drove Hogan to a gritty nightclub called Razor's Edge. Most of the clubbers had augmented limbs. One of the clubbers, Hogan witnessed, had artificial lungs and he was hooked up to a portable breathing device attached to his jaw, which had been replaced with a sheet of metal. Hogan had only read articles about all the new technology, the augmentation especially, but he had never seen it with his own eyes. Edward told him that tonight was just a recon mission. "Tomorrow," he said, "you kill."

—

While waiting in the hotel room, Hogan spent most of the night thinking about whether or not go through with Edward's proposal—mainly since the vague memory of his family was still remarkably hazy. He wasn't completely sure if what happened to them really happened in real life or if he was still somehow trapped in a nightmare that he couldn't wake up from. He had certain memories—false or not—of his family. Blurry fragments of their faces. Smells and scents. He remembered the feel of his wife's frizzy hair in between his fingertips. Making love to a beautiful light-skin woman—his "Queen," he called her—who was neither white nor black but somewhere in the middle. He remembered cutting wood with a small boy and showing him the proper way to hold an axe. So much had happened since then. Time had happened.

As Hogan was about to catch some shuteye, he stumbled across Edward's backpack while Edward was washing up inside the bathroom. The inside of the flap happened to be open. He found a metal plate attached to the inner pocket. The plate read, "Dynocorp."

—

The next night, Edward drove Hogan to Razor's Edge where they waited outside in the parked eCar. Edward specially went over the murderer's description. A white male. Six foot two inches. Long brown hair gelled back like one of them actors from the old days. Edward even went into detail what the murderer was wearing. The whole time while Edward was going over the minor details with Hogan, Hogan was thinking about Dynocorp. He reached around the back of his right ear and felt a tiny slit in his skin. He kept picking at the cut until he pulled away a two-inch layer of skin.

"The man in the book, *The Party Crasher*, Darwin," Hogan said flatly as he reached his finger into the hole behind his ear and pulled out the artificial eardrum from the right side of his skull. He faced to Edward in the driver's seat. The bottom of Edward's jaw started to tremble; yet his mouth remained tightly shut. "He wasn't named after my son," he said to Edward.

Hogan suddenly grabbed the zinger next to Edward's seat. The two wrestled around for the zinger until Hogan elbowed Edward in the face. He gained control over the zinger and fired a highly controlled electromagnetic pulse at Edward's facial region. A blue, fiery ball of light hit Edward directly in the face, causing his face to peel clean off and reveal all of the wires and circuitry underneath. Sparks shot up from Edward's face, smoking up the car. The android convulsed in its seat, jerked and flailed before it finally powered off in a staticky hum.

"Fucking robots," Hogan said and opened the driver's side door and kicked Edward from the eCar.

He reached into Edward's bag and pulled out the photograph of his family. He held the photo to the neon light suspended above the nightclub. The faces in the photograph faded, except for Hogan's. Hogan was the only real thing in the photo. Everything else, his son, his wife, they were all but fabricated memory implants.

He thought about driving away, leaving Detroit, putting the city in his rearview; but, then, once more, he thought of his family. They weren't real and yet, they were.

Curious, shocked, and confused, Hogan decided to go inside the club. He recalled Edward's description of the murderer. He found a man—a white male, around six feet, but Hogan couldn't quite get a good look at him for he was sitting in a booth surrounded by cyborg ravers. He kept the zinger concealed inside his trench coat and remembered what Edward had told him last night, that there was nothing to worry about. "There is no law here," Edward emphasized. "Only justice."

Hogan grabbed a shot of black ice from the bartender and stalked through the crowd until he found himself face to face with the murderer seated at the booth.

As Hogan raised the zinger to shoot the murderer, he

realized the man sitting in the booth was himself, a younger and much more handsome version of himself. Even Hogan found himself smitten from the young man's glowing appearance. He was in his late thirties, around the same age when he first woke up from his Nostalgia trip; and from the looks of the gorgeous women hanging around the booth, he had quite the fan club. Hogan ignored all of the commotion around him, ignored the beautiful synthetic women, the ravers, ignored the sex, ignored each and every doubt in his mind; and he aimed the zinger at the strange man's face, pulled the trigger, and the world as he once knew washed over with gray.

—

The gray world brightened with an array of colors.

Hogan cracked open his eyes and he found himself face to face with Freddie, who was shaking him on the shoulder.

"Yo, Hoagie," Freddie said, "time to split. . . "

Freddie was pointing toward the front of the theatre.

"Dude, Hogan, I can't believe you fell asleep to possibly one of the greatest movies of all time," Chi said, laughing.

The ending credits to the movie, *Terminator*, were rolling on the screen, and half of the audience had already gotten out of their seats and left the theatre.

"You okay, Hogan?" asked Elisa.

Hogan leaned forward and saw Elisa sitting next to Chi. He could only see one half of her face. The other half was lost in the shadows; however, the little Hogan could see of her face appeared as if it was covered in old burn marks.

Elisa finally turned toward Hogan. She didn't have a single mark on her face.

Hogan stood from his seat and wrapped his arms around Elisa.

"You're alive!" he shouted out and gave Elisa a great big bear hug.

"Yeah," Elisa said in a drawn out tone. "Why wouldn't I be?"

"I'm glad to see you."

Elisa remained stiff and uncomfortable.

"What are you doing, Hogan?" Elisa asked, displaying disgust on her face. "Get off me already!"

"Sup, Hoagie," Freddie said from behind. "Why you actin' so weird, dude?"

"Sorry."

Hogan backed away and placed his hand over Freddie's shoulder.

"You sure you're okay?" asked Freddie. "You're totally actin' like you haven't seen us in years."

"Yeah," Hogan said. "I'm better. I mean, I'm good. Just a little tired. That's all."

"Sure?"

"Yeah," he said. "I'm sure."

"Let's get outta here."

"Good idea."

—

Hogan and the gang left the theatre and spent most of the night talking about certain scenes in the movie, especially that one truck-explosion scene where the *Terminator* emerged from the flames, skin missing and all.

Suddenly, Hogan's ears started to ring. A feeling of nausea came over him, forcing Hogan to stop and regain his composure.

While the others continued to walk ahead of Hogan, Hogan turned his shoulder and studied the desolate street behind him. A gust of wind kicked up a piece of old newspaper and sent it skipping down the sidewalk.

Hogan asked his friends, "Did you hear something?"

Freddie stopped as well and acknowledged Hogan.

"I think it's just the wind," he said.

"It sounded like..."

"Sound like what?"

"I don't know," Hogan whispered.

He shrugged off the noise and walked away with the rest

of the gang.

Chi was complaining about how hungry he was and if he didn't eat something fast then he was going to die—in fact, Chi was so hungry he could eat a horse.

Elisa teased Chi by impersonating the slow and lifeless slog of a zombie; and to sell the effect, she added in a moan when she told Chi that she was so hungry that she could eat human flesh!

Chi suddenly recoiled his shoulder as Elisa attempted to bite his neck. She never did, though. She was only pretending.

Nonetheless, the comment drew laughs from the rest of the gang, including Chi.

And it was in these very moments Hogan felt alive.

www.ingramcontent.com/pod-product-compliance
Lightning Source LLC
Chambersburg PA
CBHW030251200626
46816CB00002BA/598